I0700712

A Match MADE IN Autumn

BY JESSICA BOOTH

No part of this book may be reproduced or transmitted in any form or by any means, electronic or mechanical, including photocopying, recording or by any information storage and retrieval system, without written permission from the author.

This is a work of fiction. Any names or characters, businesses or places, events or incidents, are fictitious. Any resemblance to actual persons, living or dead, or actual events is purely coincidental.

First edition: October 2022

Identifiers: ISBN 979-8-9870116-0-7 (trade paperback), 979-8-9870116-1-4 (ebook)

*For my husband, Mark, who always shows
me that love is often communicated better
through actions than words.*

Chapter 1

AMELIA

Everything comes so easily to some people. Money, careers, relationships. And then there's me.

I glance down and take in my worn slippers, dog hair clinging to their fuzzy toes. My knee peeks through worn pajama pants that I refuse to let go of because they remind me of the time I spent living in Aunt Margie's country home. Despite the comfort they offer, I can't help but think about how ragged I look and how worn down everything in life seems to be.

There's a whole wide world full of things for me to fumble. Nothing ever comes easy. Not money, not my career, and definitely not my romantic relationships. Okay, maybe I shouldn't say "nothing." I am a natural at rescuing animals, hoarding books and eating cheese...

My thoughts spin around my head like a cow-toting tornado as I watch the family across the street. I went to high school with Fran, the thin Lululemon-clad mother pushing her adorable, laughing toddler in the tree swing. Her hair is in a perfect ponytail and her leggings hug her fit, muscled legs. As I watch, her equally perfect husband parks in the driveway and walks over to press a kiss on her cheek.

Nestled in the chair next to my kitchen table, I gaze at them out my bay window as my foot taps a rhythm on the floor. It's my favorite spot in my small, old house. I fold my hands around my freshly brewed pumpkin spice coffee, allowing my fingers to trace the raised autumn leaf adorning my mug.

It's a trick my psychologist taught me to stop fretting so much about the future, to be more present. Focus on points of touch. My legs against the chair, my fingers on the mug, my foot tapping the floor.

Closing my eyes, I inhale the coffee's spicy scent and try to calm the anxious insecurity bubbling inside of me. I imagine the tree outside my window alight with autumn colors. The occasional leaf breaks free and makes its slow, meandering glide to the ground. I can see it now: Tucker, my one-eyed dog of a questionable breed, rolling in the leaves, the sound of their crunching beneath his wiggly bottom. Woodsmoke meanders through the air as neighbors burn piles of leaves.

I slide my hand over the worn copy of *Anne of Green Gables* sitting on my lap, focusing on the feel of its wrinkled cover. I've read it a million times, and Anne's scrapes never fail to make me smile. I recite my favorite quote from the book: "I'm so glad I live in a world where there are Octobers."

There. I've found it. My happy place.

The sound of a car horn tapped in quick succession jolts me from my thoughts. Groaning, I place my mug down on the worn wooden table. I stretch and study the coffee stain on my t-shirt. Briefly wonder if I should wrestle my wavy chocolate locks into a bun before I decide it's not worth the time and make my way to the front door. When I open it, the suffocating humid heat of a Louisiana autumn smacks me in the face, giving me a solid reality check. Maybe I should add ice to my coffee and some whipped cream to make the disappointment of a sweltering October more palatable.

"I've got peach jam!" Aunt Margie shouts over the rumbling of her worn—or as she liked to call it, "vintage"—Ford truck idling in my driveway. "Give it a try! I've added bourbon to give it a little *zing*. It will be the talk of the Fall Fest this year!"

I smile as I stroll up to the driver's side window, where she sits proudly holding up the jam jar. A piece of twine is wrapped around the lid and a tag declaring "Margie's Machinations" hangs from the side.

"Aunt Margie. Don't you think a fall festival should sell pumpkin products? I thought peaches were more of a summer thing," I tease.

"Nonsense! These are our famous Ruston peaches. People will travel from miles around and fight each other to get their hands on these in October," she declares with pride.

I have to admit my aunt has a point. I pause for a beat and then decide to seek her wisdom, even if it comes with a healthy dollop of sass.

"Why don't you come inside for a bit? I just put on the coffee. There's more than enough for both of us."

Aunt Margie eyes me closely, running her hands through her soft, wild, gray-tinged auburn curls. "Is it *hot* coffee?" she queries. "None of that iced stuff? That's not even real coffee."

I laugh. "It's hot. And I've even got cinnamon to sprinkle on top," I coax.

Aunt Margie cuts the engine as she swings the truck door open. "Well, in that case, don't mind if I do."

Tucker greets us at the front door, his hoarse bark welcoming Margie with all the enthusiasm his small, wagging body can offer. Hinges screech when I swing open the screen door. I shoo Tucker back into the house. I make my way over to the coffee pot and reach for my largest mug, the perfect size to suit Aunt Margie's insatiable thirst for coffee. I pour her a cup and add an extra helping of milk before sprinkling it with cinnamon – just the way she likes it.

"So, speaking of, how's the festival planning coming?" Aunt Margie asks, accepting her coffee with an indulgent smile and patting Tucker's head as he settles next to her. With those words, a garbage disposal switches on in my stomach—all rumbles and chaos. After years of petitioning my boss to assist with the marketing plan of the Fall Festival, I've somehow been put in charge of the entire event. Just the thought of all I have to do pushes my frantic feelings of inadequacy back to the surface.

"Umm, well, um, you see…" I start.

"That bad, huh?"

"It's not that. It's just…"

"It's not Matt again is it?" she asks, sitting up at full attention, ready to grab the nearest piece of furniture and go after my ex like some rogue vigilante. Or Batman, gravelly voice included. "If that man is harassing you again… Lia, the police won't have anything left to arrest after I'm done with him."

I wince. "No, no, it's not that," *though it would be if I hadn't blocked his number*, I add silently and shudder. I have to fight the feelings that rise in my gut and threaten to make me sick at the mention of his name.

Aunt Margie stares at me, eyes knowing, piercing me to my very soul. "Well, spit it out already, Lia. I know you didn't ask me inside just for the company."

I scoff, "Aunt Margie! You know I love it when you visit!"

She stares in silence, continuing to quietly pat Tucker's head. My dog, traitor that he is, turns his one-eyed gaze on me, too.

I roll my eyes. "Fine. How in the world am I supposed to promote a fall festival when it's 85 degrees outside? Even the pumpkins are sweating in this humidity!"

A beat of silence passes.

"Well, is that all, darling?" Aunt Margie croons. "Honey, everyone south of the Mason-Dixon line knows that October is gonna be hot, and then cool, and then hot again. The trick is to make them *feel* like they are experiencing autumn even though they are swatting mosquitoes and wearing matching, monogrammed pumpkin tank tops. In fact, maybe I should sell some of those at my vendor booth this year…"

Closing my eyes, I slide my forehead into my palms and sigh.

"There's more," I mumble.

"Of course, there is, honey." Aunt Margie settles in and sips her coffee.

I look at Aunt Margie between my fingers, wondering how much

I should share. Taking a deep breath and exhaling slowly, I lean back against the counter, leaning my head against the worn, wooden cabinets.

"Janet, my boss, says they need this year's festival to bring in double last year's profit to keep going… and she expects me to pull off this miracle single-handedly. Me! The person who somehow manages to corrupt everything she touches, like some real-life Rogue from X-Men. Remember that time I helped co-host a baby shower and fell butt-first into the cake? I still don't think Paige will ever forgive me for that one. And that was just a baby shower. Then there was the time I volunteered at the library book sale and knocked all the shelves over like a set of the world's largest dominoes." I pause, wincing at the memory of how long it took to clean up the mess. "The festival is a million times bigger and its success will make or break my career. And you know how small this town is. If I let this thing sink, the entire community will pin me with a scarlet letter."

"First," declared Aunt Margie in a matter-of-fact tone. "Look at me. In the eyes. That's right. Now, first. This festival won't fail. But—and this is the important part, my dear—if this festival fails, it's because *the people of this city* didn't come out to support it. So they can take that misplaced anger and sit on it."

Aunt Margie sets her cup down on the table, squaring her shoulders, preparing for one of her infamous diatribes.

"Next," she continues, "This festival has slowly been dying over the past several years because people have taken for granted that it exists. There's nothing new. Nothing exciting. The Junior League hocks their cookbooks, and the Methodist Church rolls in a few pumpkins. Hell, anyone can drive thirty minutes away and go to a *real* pumpkin patch with photo ops, goats, and live owls."

"Owls?"

"Yes, I said owls, and I meant owls."

I raise my eyebrows, imagining a rogue owl swooping down on some unsuspecting child and launching a lawsuit against the city.

She continues, "And this is the first year the Chamber of Commerce was smart enough to put you in charge of the festival. And they did it because you are innovative and brilliant. You don't give yourself enough credit. Lia, you've been pitching ideas to Janet for years. She's ignored them, and that's part of what got them into this mess. You've got resources and friends who will help you. One text to Beth, and she'll rally the entire Junior League and make sure the inside of the vendor barn looks like it belongs in *Magnolia Magazine*. And you know I'm a deft hand at giving out marching orders. I'll be your general. It's time to pull up your big girl britches, pour up another cup of that coffee, add a little bourbon, and get to work!"

Satisfied with her speech, Aunt Margie leans back in her chair, picks up her coffee, and stares at me in a challenge. Her eyes laser into my soul, and I feel her little speech spark something to life in my heart. Hope? Possibility?

"Oh, alright," I sigh.

I look down at my fuzzy slippers, tracing the linoleum pattern with my toe, then glance back up at her again.

"I do have a few ideas. Want to hear them?" I ask with a cautious smile.

"That's my girl. Pull up a chair. Oh, and be a dear and grab the bourbon while you're up."

Chapter 2

RHETT

The cursor blinks accusingly on the blank document screen. It has been months since I've written a good story for *The Ruston Daily Leader*. Even longer since I felt the surge of adrenaline that comes with being an investigative reporter. Actually, it's been months since I've felt much of anything besides numbness and the occasional bout of sadness. *I'm well and truly pathetic.*

I close my eyes, driving my knuckles deep into my eyelids, trying to push the memories of my broken marriage out of my mind. I will the pain to drive away the images of how Chels looked at me when I begged her to understand that I would be ten minutes late getting home. The lecture she inevitably hammered down on me and then the silent treatment that followed for days…

"Wake up, man!" Jacob says as he slides into the seat across from my desk, startling me. He pushes back the chair and kicks his obnoxiously large feet up on my desk, shiny new sneakers knocking carefully stacked papers to the ground.

I stare at the fluttering papers, then slowly look up at my best friend and coworker. I'm already arming myself for whatever he's about to throw my way. He flashes his signature grin, his white teeth contrasting with his dark brown skin. It's the same smile he uses with everyone to charm his way into getting what he wants—including really good interviews for the paper. His dark eyes flash with mischief as he rubs his hand over his close-cropped hair.

"You look like Casper, the not-so-friendly ghost, man. You have got to snap out of this," he demands. *Today it's the "tough love" talk, apparently.*

Jacob slams his feet down on the ground as if the sound will be enough to wrench me out of my never-ending numbness. He looks around, then leans across my desk conspiratorially as if he's about to unveil the secrets of the universe.

He whispers, "The Boss has been patient with you for a long time. You've got to at least try to write a decent article. Go on an easy feature story. Write about volunteers helping children or Girl Scouts or rescuing animals. Do *something. Anything.* I know those old ladies at the art gallery would jump at the chance for Rhett Hebert to visit," he confides, lifting his eyebrows knowingly.

I sigh, clasping my hands behind my head and leaning back to stare at the ceiling. "Jay. I've lost my fire. Maybe it's time to step away from reporting. I could work at the hardware store or something. Some place I could coast for a while. Get my life together. Maybe figure out a way to get Chels back."

"I say this to you with the utmost brotherly love," Jacob says, tone serious. "But please, for the love of all things holy, get your head out of your ass."

I look down sharply, embarrassment tunneling through my insides. Jacob rarely speaks to me this way.

He leans into his speech. "I'm serious. Chels was not good for you. I know it. Your parents knew it. Hell, even The Boss knew it. Sure, all that angst helped you pound out some good stories for a while, but that's the only good thing that girl ever did for you. You need to find someone else to help get you out of this funk. Hell, even a one-night stand would do you some good. You are a free agent now. Jump back in the game. Live a little. I'll even help you. We can hit the bars and find a girl. Then, we'll find a story. I'll help you research… Just promise me you won't tell anyone else that I can be nice," Jacob says with a smirk.

"Chels wasn't *that* bad," I mumble, looking down at my button-up shirt, neatly tucked into my slacks. It's easier to visually retreat from this conversation than tackle it head-on, even with Jacob.

"Wasn't that bad?! Wasn't that bad?! Rhett, my man, Chels refused to talk to you for four days because you complimented The Boss' editorial prowess. She thought you should never compliment another woman, even if it's on her perfect use of a red pen." Jacob takes a deep breath and runs his hands over his face in exasperation. Then says slowly and deliberately, "That. Is. Not. Healthy."

I finally look at him, really studying my friend. My reporter's instincts kick in as I read his emotions and note the earnestness and worry on his face. Resigned, I give in. "Fine. I'll work on a story." I glance at that irritating cursor on the blank screen and close my laptop. "I'll start tomorrow."

"You'll start today," says Jacob. "Otherwise, you're just going to be moping around here again tomorrow morning, and I have already given you the only pep talk I have the energy for this week. Let's hit the archives for some inspiration. See what the late greats did. What stories won awards. Shit like that. Now pick your sad ass up and follow me."

With a pained sigh, I slide out of my chair. We head to the dimly lit and vaguely musty-scented newspaper archives in search of inspiration. The yellow lights that illuminate the dimly lit room help preserve the old paper and always make me feel like I'm stepping into another universe. I try to remain optimistic, but after thirty minutes of sifting through old bound copies of newspapers, I've only succeeded in learning who the local Peach Festival queens were over the last decade.

Finally, acknowledging our mission is a "failure for now," Jacob calls an end to our research in order to make it to an interview at the old fall festival site for a prep piece on the event. As we shuffle back into the newsroom though, he looks at me and shakes his head.

"Come on. Ride with me," he says as if it were some sort of

foregone conclusion.

I glare at him. "I don't need a pity story," I bite out.

"Who said anything about giving you *my* story?" Jacob said with mock indignation. "And if you don't want pity, don't look pitiful. Plus, I'm hungry. We'll stop by Dean's on the way and grab some bbq burgers."

Chapter 3

AMELIA

Sweat trickles down my brow as I shade my eyes from the oppressive Louisiana sun. Any hope I still held that the temperatures would drop before we start work on festival setup is running far, far away and likely planting itself in front of an air conditioning unit and pouring up a margarita.

Tucker is wandering the pasture around me, taking in the scents of freshly mown grass and rolling around in what is likely a dead armadillo. He's going to be a joy to bathe later. My eyes follow his path as he takes off running after a flock of sparrows that immediately take flight when he gets near. I take stock of the land around me. In the distance, I can see the entrance to the corn maze, one of the biggest draws to the Fall Fest. At least the heat doesn't seem to be deterring corn growth. However, that maze entrance sign is hanging by a single, rusty nail and is liable to turn into a lawsuit or tetanus.

I turn to my right, squinting at the empty field bordering the woods. I start imagining how to fill the space. I can see it now: a platform stage with twinkle lights hanging above and speakers at its sides. It could be an area where families gather, singing and dancing as they sip their apple ciders. Maybe we could even offer s'more stations. I suppose I'll need to find a band, too.

Just add that to my ever-growing list of things to do in a very short amount of time. That nagging feeling of not being up to the task threatens to crawl into my brain and take charge of my body again. I picture my insecurity as a squirrel, giving it an anxious bushy tail and twitchy eyes. I can feel it clawing its way up my body with its persistent, jagged little toenails. I mentally put that fuzzy rodent in a catapult and launch it high over the corn maze, admiring how its legs scramble for purchase in the air.

Laughing at the mental image I've created, I purposefully turn my ideas back to overhauling and updating the festival. There will be laughter, good music, pumpkins, hay rides, and, yes, maybe even owls. There are already horses in the barn that bordered the festival site, but Aunt Margie told me that Fred's horses are "old and crotchety." Yet another accident waiting to happen.

And then there is the matter of the aging old house that borders the property. The one that local lore says belongs to the town witch. I stare at the house from a distance, noticing the plants bleached by the sun and rusted birdhouses that litter the front porch. Cats lurk outside, darting in and out of the woods that grow around its property line.

I wonder what its occupant looks like. My imagination conjures up images from some of my favorite books – an old crone with a hunched back, stringy hair, warty nose, large cauldrons, and an ear-piercing cackle. Maybe the old house and its air of foreboding could add to the festival's aesthetic... or be yet another liability.

"LIA!"

I turn to see Aunt Margie dragging, well, *something*, into the old barn that will house the festival vendors.

"Give me a hand, will ya?" she shouts.

I hustle over, dust clouding up around my boots. I reach Aunt Margie just as she is about to drop what appears to be an enormous hunk of old wood.

"And what are you going to do with this… exactly?" I ask, skepticism lacing my voice.

"Putting my peach jams on it. What else?" Margie responds.

I roll my eyes, but I know she won't be deterred. I inspect it briefly, then give it a quick kick and hop back to make sure a nest of red wasps isn't about to erupt out of the thing. Finally I lean down and hoist it up. Together we drag what turns out to be a beat-up, ancient picnic table into the barn. Tucker has abandoned his bird-chasing pursuits and is now curiously sniffing the table. I note that even though the barn was supposed to be locked up since last year's festival, it still reeks of manure, hay, and horse… or maybe multiple horses? And— is that a dead possum? My stomach lurches at the smell. Tucker will be pleased, at least. We'll have to do something about that soon… very soon.

"I thought this place had been locked up since last year," I say.

"Wouldn't surprise me one iota if Fred had been bringing his horses over here when no one was looking," Aunt Margie huffed. Always the cynic, my aunt.

We continue dragging the table into the barn in stops and starts. We finally get good forward momentum going. I'm at the front end of the table, tugging at it like a field horse with a plow, when my foot snags on something. I instantly go down, barely managing to get my hands in front of me before the rest of my body hits the ground. The dirt swirls around me like an angry desert storm as the wind is knocked from my lungs. I struggle to catch my breath as pain from the hit my jaw took when it made contact with the dirt floor radiates up my face. The table lands behind me with a crunch, splinters flying out like stray bullets. Tucker, my ever-ready rescue agent, runs to me and shoves his snout in my face, sniffing and licking to ensure I'm still alive.

Finally catching my breath, I yell, "Shit!"

"Amelia, are you okay? What in the world?" Aunt Margie is still idly holding one side of the table and looking at me in horror. She takes in the dirt covering me in patches from the top of my ponytail to the tips of my new boots. "Honey, is your leg broken or something?" She finally ducks down to help me up.

"No," I half whimper in indignation. "Literal shit. I tripped over a *pile of poop*."

And sure enough, my entire right boot is covered in horse dung. Ugh, and it smells foul.

"Well, shit," Aunt Margie agrees, stepping back to take me in. She places her hands on her hips and presses her lips together, sucking them in to stifle the booming laugh I know is itching to erupt from the depths of her soul. I glare at her and hate-whisper, "Don't you dare!"

"Is everything okay in here?" A male voice echoes across the barn from the doorway.

"You have got to be kidding me," I whisper, pushing myself up off the ground. I tentatively put weight on my ankle to make sure I could walk on it. And when I look down, I see two round brown spots on my white button-up shirt–right over my boobs. I start frantically trying to dust off the mess as two men, silhouetted by the outside light, walk toward us. Tucker issues a few soft woofs at their appearance.

Stepping between the men and me, Aunt Margie assumes her best defensive position: hands on hips, ample chest pushed forward, chin held high. "And how may I help you, gentlemen?" she asks with an air of authority. Tucker sits by her leg in solidarity.

"Um, I'm here to meet with Amelia for the pre-press story on the festival," said the deep, confused voice. "My name is Jacob. I'm a reporter with *The Ruston Daily Leader*," he clarifies.

Aunt Margie looks over her shoulder at me, and I instantly duck behind her, arms folding tightly over my boobs. I awkwardly try to cover myself and scrape horse poop off my boot simultaneously. I'm going to kill Fred.

"Are you now?" she deadpans. "Well, thank you for coming to our rescue, gentlemen, but I think we've got it under control. Why don't you give us a few minutes, and we'll meet you over by the corn maze."

I take that moment to peer over Aunt Margie's shoulder at the two men standing awkwardly in the barn. I can practically feel the elephant in the room squatting on my chest. The first man, Jacob, I've spoken with on the phone. I recognize him from my publicity work with the Chamber of Commerce. Our spokesperson has always had a good working relationship with him and speaks highly of his reporting integrity. It certainly doesn't hurt that his mahogany skin, strong jawline, and confidence are a natural draw to those around him.

Then I shift my gaze to the other man standing next to him. He's staring at his shoes as they sift through the dirt on the barn floor. Dark, close-cropped, auburn curls, straight Roman nose, nicely built. Even though he's looking down, I can tell he's handsome. Definitely, the kind of guy my best friend Beth and I would take turns staring at and reporting on to one another if we saw him at a bar or restaurant. But just as quickly as those thoughts enter my mind, I shake them off. If my last boyfriend taught me anything, it's that I do not need to be eyeing any man with interest beyond polite conversation.

But then he glances up and looks me right in the eyes. I'm frozen, locked in place like I've stepped in wet cement. The emerald green of his eyes completely transfixes me. But as my gaze widens to take in his whole face, a buzzing sensation like a thousand cicadas taking flight fills my body. The color drains from my face. Ice picks hammer into my stomach. No. There is no way. That is not... He can't be... But as my gaze widens to take in his whole face, a buzzing sensation like a thousand cicadas taking flight fills my body. The color drains from my face. Ice picks hammer into my stomach. No. There is no way. That is not... He can't be...

"Amelia?... Amelia Murphy?" The auburn-haired man asks, squinting into the gloom of the low-lit barn. I duck my head down further behind Aunt Margie with a quiet squeak, hiding like a frightened child. God I'm awkward. But what else am I supposed to do? I never wanted to engage with Rhett Hebert ever again. And yet here he is, materializing in front of me while I'm covered in literal horse shit.

Aunt Margie looks from him, back to me, then back to him again with a furrowed brow and growing suspicion. Jacob is doing the same thing, trying—and failing—to grasp what connects the two of us.

"As I said. We'll see you boys in a few minutes at the entrance to the corn maze." Aunt Margie knows me well enough to know it's time to take control of the situation. With those words, she shoos them through the barn door in a neat dismissal. She closes the door before fixing me in her gaze and marching straight toward me. I radiate with the heat of the blush I feel creeping up my neck and into my cheeks.

"What…" she hesitates. She tries again, more soothingly, "Lia. Darling. What the hell was that all about?"

"I don't know what you mean," I squeak out, my heart thundering loudly in my ears.

Aunt Margie levels me with the glare she used to turn on me when I was a child and up to no good. "Is that right? Do you greet most people by ducking behind someone else, or is that something you reserve just for reporters?"

"Aunt Margie, my boobs are covered in dirt!" I wave in the general vicinity of my destroyed shirt. "My foot is covered in poop! What else am I supposed to do?" I say unconvincingly as my blush creeps higher until it nearly consumes my entire face.

"Uh-huh. Well, if you ask me, I think there is more to it than looking like you lost a fight with a flock of angry chickens."

I stare at my aunt in embarrassed horror.

"Out with it. I thought you said you knew that reporter was coming to talk to you," Aunt Margie says, folding her arms against her chest.

"I do. I mean, I did. I, well, I…" I stutter, turning and shoving my hands deep into my pockets, trying to collect myself. Sweat is breaking out across my face, my arms, my chest.

In a rush, before I can think too much about it, words start flying out of my mouth. "I knew Jacob would be out here to talk about the festival. I expected him. I mean, not right at this particular moment, but he wasn't a surprise. I just wish I would have…" I stop myself realizing I'm rambling. I inhale and slowly let the breath out.

"It's just that I thought it would just be Jacob." I lift my arm to wipe away the sweat on my brow.

"And?" Margie has a hand on her hip now. An icy pit forms in my stomach, miners hammering away at it. Shameful memories I've fought to suppress over the past decade threaten to emerge from a long-buried place inside of me. I want to bury it, to hide from facing those old memories. But this is Aunt Margie and I know there is no way I'm getting out of this one.

Growling in frustration, I let out a string of words that blend into one another. "And that other man with Jacob was the guy who made my whole high school hate me, okay?" I say, a touch of hurt lingering in my voice. "He was the reason people accused me of being 'a nerdy slut,' and waved tampons at me when I walked the halls between classes."

My voice wobbles and grows louder as I continue. "I know none of that should matter now. But I'm not gonna lie. I'd be happy to never see him again. I've become an expert at avoiding him around this small town for a decade. I mean I could put hiding behind bushes and ducking around grocery store aisles on my resume at this point. And now I've got to go out there and just talk to him like nothing ever happened? No, thank you."

Margie huffs, dropping her hands to her sides. Wordlessly, she walks over to me and wraps me in a tight embrace. The dirt and poop still clinging to me don't even phase her. It reminds me so much of how she helped me manage my anxiety as a child that I feel tears well up.

"It's okay now, darling." She releases me, placing her hands on both of my shoulders and catching my eyes. She takes in my red eyes and unshed tears. Her warm hands smooth out the dark curls of my ponytail, knocking aside some of the dirt.

"Do you want me to go out there and tell Jacob to come back another day?" she asks.

I close my eyes and breathe in, enjoying the comfort of her earthy, lavender scent. I inhale her confidence, willing it to embed itself in my arms, legs, chest and, finally, my soul. I exhale and reopen my eyes, and look into hers. Their warm, brown depths exude the love of the woman who raised me to battle my fears and come out victorious on the other side.

I will that confidence into my voice. "No, let's do this. Janet will kill me if I botch this interview. I have an extra t-shirt in my car. Not ideal, but better than this," I say, looking down and waving my hand at my ruined shirt.

"You could always try to play that off as a coffee spill," she says.

"Maybe if I dropped an entire pot of coffee on myself… and if that happened, we'd have much bigger problems than a ruined shirt."

As if on cue, we both look up and lock eyes. Aunt Margie presses her lips together and tries desperately to stifle a giggle, but she's finally lost the battle. A loud cackle erupts from her, then she clasps her hands over her mouth as if she can physically hold her laughter inside her body. But now her whole body shakes with the effort and it's too late. It's taken hold of her.

"Oh Lia," she gasps out between laughs. "You should see your face right now. *And your boobs*." She guffaws again.

I try to stare her down, to show her that I am deeply offended. But I can't help myself. Aunt Margie's laughter has always been my kryptonite. It's contagious. And before I even realize what's happening, I've "caught a fit of giggles." And trying to stop them only makes it worse. Soon tears roll down both our cheeks as we belly laugh and gasp for breath. We hold on to one another's shoulders to try and wrestle the hysteria back down. Tucker stares at us, cocking his head to one side, his one eye staring at us like we've lost our minds. He might be right.

"Okay. Okay," I say, dragging in oxygen and wiping at my watering eyes. My sides are heaving with the pain of uncontrolled laughter, giving me the dopamine surge I need to keep going. "You go talk to those two for a few minutes while I change shirts. I'll meet you by the corn maze entrance in just a few."

Aunt Margie fans her face with her hands and tries to put her serious face back. Periodic giggles bubble out of her as we exit the barn and leave the splintered table behind. She makes a beeline for Jacob and Rhett, and I try to walk confidently to my car. I open the door, and the Louisiana heat that's been nesting and growing inside the cab over the past few hours whooshes out, blowing my hair back like some corporate-grade hair dryer. I know my hair must be curling, but I'm a woman on a mission. I dive in and grab my t-shirt, quickly changing as I duck down low.

Staring down at the dog rescue t-shirt I've wrestled on, I think that while it's not professional, at least it's not offensive. It might even be endearing. "Local animal rescue advocate plans this year's fall festival." That would be a nice, empathetic headline, right?

Then my mind fixates on Rhett again. Maybe Tucker could chase him into the corn maze while I do the interview? Too bad that dog is only good for treats, snuggles, and bird chasing. And I don't think I'd want to read the headline if something like that happened. *Time to woman up, Lia. Pull yourself together.*

I stand, raise my chin and channel Aunt Margie's confidence as I stride towards the corn maze, discreetly swiping my boot along the grass to make sure all traces of horse dung are gone. Sliding my hands over my hair, I attempt to flatten my flyaways. I have to hope I look confident because my insides feel like they're tied in a knot and being tugged between two rambunctious labradors.

When I finally make it to the entrance of the corn maze, my nerves ease when I see that Jacob is the only one standing there. I scope the horizon and peer into the corn maze entrance for signs of Aunt Margie or Rhett—or even Tucker—but it's just Jacob. He has his recorder in hand and is in full reporter mode. His mega-watt grin slides into place and he nods his head towards the corn maze.

"They went in there. Your aunt told Rhett she would give him the grand tour while you and I chatted for the interview," Jacob said.

Wearily I peer into the maze entrance, but can't see them. I relax at the reprieve I've been granted. *I hope Aunt Margie leaves him in that dead-end near the swamp where it smells of mold, decay, and dying crawfish.* But then I realize that Rhett being stuck in a corn maze with an indignant Aunt Margie is its own form of punishment.

I look back at Jacob and plaster on a friendly smile. "I apologize for startling you earlier. We didn't expect you quite this early, and we ran into a bit of trouble inside the barn."

"Nothing too serious, I hope?" Jacob says, dialing up the charm.

"Nothing that can't be solved with a little gorilla glue and duct tape," I quip back.

We walk together to the shade of the barn, chatting all the while about the Chamber of Commerce and its upcoming initiatives. Conversation flows naturally as we move into the interview. I tell Jacob about our new plans for the festival, making sure to include my list of buzzwords like "warm," "inviting," and "inventive." This, at least, I manage to get right.

As we wrap up the interview, I lean in. "Off the record, I'd love to have a band this year for the weekends. Any chance you know someone who might be able to help us out? Someone family-friendly. Even better if they can play some Halloween songs like 'Monster Mash.'"

"I think I do," Jacob says, Cheshire-cat grin spreading across his face again. "I'll reach out to my friend and let you know." Then his brows furrow. "You know, it's been a while since they entered that corn maze. I hope everything is okay." Jacob shades his eyes with his hand and squints at the maze entrance.

I realize he's right. We've been chatting for nearly an hour and haven't heard a peep from anyone. A typical walk through the maze— even for our patrons who have had a few too many drinks before entering—usually takes no more than forty-five minutes. And I can almost always hear Aunt Margie's loud voice if she's within shouting distance.

"Maybe we should go in after them?" I ask reluctantly.

Together we walk towards the maze, ears straining for signs of life. Suddenly Tucker bursts through the entrance, barking and chasing after a squirrel. We both startle back, my hand-pressed over my now racing heart. With an awkward laugh, we step inside the corn maze.

As we walk, we try to peer through the towering stalks, searching for our missing companions.

After twenty minutes, we're both drenched in sweat, and I'm seriously beginning to worry that something has happened to them. Maybe I wished a little *too* hard for Rhett to take a dive in the nearby swamp. I reach for my phone to call Aunt Margie when I hear her distinctive, wild laugh and spot her untamed, reddish-gray hair. She and Rhett are sitting together on a hay bail pushed back into the shade of the corn stalks, passing … a flask? And laughing.

Jacob and I slowly turn to look at one another.. .and then back at Rhett and Margie. An ache fists my heart at the scene. *How can Aunt Margie sit there comfortably and laugh with this man who I just told her ruined my life in high school?*

The hot-cold sensation of adrenaline pulses through my body as I struggle with the urge to stand and fight or take flight. But as those ten-year-old memories pass across my vision, I'm suddenly certain that I never want to take flight when it comes to Rhett Hebert again.

"I think that's enough," I say, stepping forward, a cold seriousness frosting my tone.

They both look up, finally noticing us. My gaze locks with Rhett's. I expect to see him sneer at me, or maybe even look at me like he has no clue who I am – but neither of those things happen. His brows knit and he opens his mouth as if to say something, then, thinking better of it, he stops. A sizzling connection passes between us that sets those Labradors in my stomach tugging rope again.

"Done already?" Aunt Margie asks, interrupting the strained silence. She tucks the flask neatly back into her cargo shorts. "Rhett and I were just sharing stories of you chasing those animals in the field next to our house as a child, Lia. Tearing through the brush, lost in your own world, convinced you would catch an armadillo to keep for your very own. And that nest of baby rabbits you found and hid in your room that time, convinced you could raise them on cow's milk and a medicine dropper…"

It takes me a moment to process what Aunt Margie is saying. I blink, and a blush finds its way up my cheeks. "Aunt Margie! He does not want to hear about that!"

"*Au contraire*, my dear. His grandparents lived across the street when you were out in that field. I'm sure he has some of his own tales to share," she says, bourbon warming her cheeks and mischief lighting her smile.

Now it's Rhett's turn to blush. I gawp at him, mouth hanging open, indignation and embarrassment are competing storms raging through my body.

I rally, letting my indignation take the lead. "Well, now that you are both done making fun of me. I'll leave you to your…" I trail off, waving my hand, struggling to find the right words. "Your own amusements. Jacob and I are done with the interview, and Tucker and I are going home."

"Amelia, wait," I hear Rhett say as I turn around and stalk out of the maze, taking the memorized twists and turns as fast as I can. When I finally see my car, I call Tucker. I don't look back. I can't.

This time when I open the sweltering car, I don't care. I allow Tucker to jump in the backseat before I slide in, wincing as the leather seats burn the backs of my short-clad thighs. I crank up the a/c. It blows hot air straight at my face as burning tears of betrayal spill down my cheeks. Finally, the air begins to cool and I collect myself. *I guess I'll still take flight after all.* I wipe angrily at my face with the back of my hand and then put the car in drive.

Chapter 4

RHETT

Amelia. Amelia. Amelia. Her name is a drumbeat in my mind as I sit in the newspaper's archive room. My eyes blur as I stare blankly through the yellow haze into the pages of old newspapers.

My mind plays a reel of yesterday's events on repeat, thoughts snagging on those last moments before Amelia fled down the narrow paths of the corn maze. It was so like her single-minded escape from the high school hallway all those years ago…

When Amelia suddenly appeared with Jacob in front of me in the corn maze, my brain warred between staring dumbly and wondering how she'd gotten even more beautiful over the last decade, and that she and Jacob were together. I mean, I know they weren't *together together.* But those swigs of bourbon freed jealousy that I had no right to feel from the cage inside my heart where I had stuffed it and buried it a long time ago.

And then she was storming off, marching angrily out of my life… *again.*

I force myself to focus on what's in front of me, reaching out idly to reassure myself that my notebook, pencil, and laptop are still there. I tab through the grainy pages of old newspapers, willing myself to digest what I see. But as I scan the pages, decades worth of old city council meetings, obituaries, and wedding announcements sift through my vision in a muddy cloud.

Really, I shouldn't be all that surprised at the lack of any big, earth-shattering news in our city's history. We live in a small, sleepy town where high school football games blaze across the leading headlines, and the death of a town matriarch is front-page news. But I know there have been major investigative stories in the past–I just need to find them.

I pull another dusty volume off the shelf, "October 2002" is printed on its spine. As I slide the bound tome onto the table, an eerie feeling crawls across my skin, raising goosebumps on my arms and prickling my scalp. Old superstition, maybe, but curiosity and the barest twinge of hope fill my chest as I open the large volume. At first, I see the usual stories–volunteers helping those in need, a list of high school graduates, obituaries. My heart sinks. My hunch, it seems, was nothing more than indigestion.

But as I start to close the volume, something catches my eye. I pause, staring at the grainy, faded photo of a young boy, maybe six or seven, standing outside, hair mussed, holding a stuffed butterfly. Deja Vous zings through me as the uncanny feeling of having seen this before settles in my bones. *Do I know this boy?*

Roberts Boy Missing

The headline hits me like a punch in the gut. Memories flicker through my brain, teasing the edges of... something. I close my eyes, squinting, trying to grasp at them, but they drift away like the scattering seeds of a dandelion. I pull out my phone and take a photo of the story. I do a quick mental calculation and realize I was only seven when the boy went missing. I wonder if mom and dad know anything? Surely something like this, in a town this size, would be permanently lodged in their memories.

I slide my phone into my pocket and shelve the archived papers, my mind still trying and failing to conjure up a connection with the Roberts boy. Maybe I'm just so desperate for a good story that I'm imagining some past connection or superimposing myself on one of my old Boxcar mystery books.

I step outside my office building and call my parents. I picture their yellow landline phone mounted to the kitchen wall ringing, mom and dad arguing over whose turn it is to answer. Dad calling out that it's probably some sales call. Mom finally huffing and strolling over to the receiver.

"Hello?" Mom's comforting voice rings in my ear.

"Hey, mom. It's Rhett."

"I know who it is, dear. Is everything okay? You don't usually call this time of day." I can feel her worry wrap itself around me, pulling me into a long-distance hug through the phone. I close my eyes, seeing the newspaper story in my head again.

"Yea, yea. Everything's fine. Actually I have a work-related question for you."

"Okay…"

"I was looking through the newspaper archives today and ran across an old story of a boy who went missing back in 2002." I pause, waiting to see if Mom says anything. When she doesn't, I continue. "His last name was Roberts. The story says he was seven when he went missing, the same age I was at that time. I didn't know if you remembered anything about it or…"

A long pause.

"Mom? You there?"

"Yes. I'm here. It's just. That was…" she stumbles. "It was a difficult time," she says, taking a deep breath, and when she exhales I can hear the pain in her voice. "The whole city was in an uproar. Search parties were going around the clock. Your dad and I would stare at you and imagine ourselves in Jennifer's, in his mom's, place. You know this city, Rhett, nothing like that happens here. It was a shock. You must remember some of it?"

As she says this, fleeting memories solidify in my mind. Dad leaving the house to go look for someone. Mom trying to smile through tears. Teachers at school trying to explain to second graders what happened to Jimmy. And there it is. A concrete memory—one that could have only come from my own mind.

"I think I remember some things," I finally say to Mom.

"It was horrible. Happened on Halloween night, too, during the fall festival when everyone was out celebrating and having fun. I think that event will forever be imprinted on the minds of the people here."

"Thanks for telling me, Mom. I'm sorry. But, thank you. I love you. Tell dad I said hi."

"See you for dinner Sunday," she says.

"Yea, see ya," I say, ending the call.

Opening my phone back up, I zoom in on the photos I snapped of the newspaper pages, reading the old story more closely this time. Mom's right. Halloween night at the fall festival. I distantly wonder if this is the real reason the festival has slowly diminished over the decades. Which reminds me of Amelia. I shake my head, banishing the thought of her to focus on what I've learned.

I open my laptop and navigate our newspaper database, searching for "Jimmy Roberts." A series of old news articles appear on my screen, each more desolate than the last:

Roberts Boy Missing
Boy Feared Dead After Search Turns Up Nothing
No Evidence of Kidnapping in Roberts Case
After Six Months, Roberts Case Goes Cold

I push my chair back, imagining what that night must have been like for Jimmy's family. The anticipation of trick-or-treating, festival rides, and playing with friends. Then the spike of hot fear and agonizing desolation. And then the awful burden of not knowing what happened as the case continued to drag on for days, weeks, months.

The story is digging its claws into my mind. I remember this feeling, the thrill that fills my body when a story latches itself on to me and won't let go. Picking up the phone, I call Jacob.

"Hey, Jacob. Feel like a drive back out to the festival site?"

"Are you trying to scoop me?" It's more an incredulous demand than a question.

"No, nothing like that. It's just a hunch," I say. "A feeling I have about a different story."

"I'll grab my keys," he says as he hangs up the phone.

34

Chapter 5

AMELIA

"I thought you had this under control, Amelia." The voice leaking out of my phone drips with disdain.

I hit mute, letting out a groan of frustration as I try to push down my rising anxiety and stare from my car at the barren festival site. My boss is in the midst of one of her infamous tirades, gearing up to tell me all the ways I've failed in my job, my life, and my existence. I close my eyes, lean back in the seat of my parked car. I direct the a/c directly into my face, hoping its frigid blast will ease the sting of Janet's inevitable barrage.

As I prepare to defend myself, I search deep for a source of controlled confidence. If I don't sound like I know what I'm doing, Janet will steamroll me. I briefly consider letting her, of offering to let someone else take charge of the festival this year. But my conversations with Aunt Margie float to the surface. I can't let her down. Taking a deep breath I will self-assuredness into my voice. "I have it under control, Janet. I've already increased our number of vendors by fifteen percent over last year and.."

"That is not what I'm talking about." She cuts my words off like a hot knife through butter and my anxiety responds in kind, lancing through my gut.

My mind takes a quick inventory of all the possible things she could be referring to. *The dilapidated signage? Not enough early news coverage? The shit in the barn? Wait, did Rhett call and complain about how rude I was to him?* I feel dread well in my stomach. My body temperature flashes to hot, then cold.

"That's what I thought," she continues cooly.

"I can explain," I stutter.

"You don't need to explain. You just need to handle the problem. If I hear one more complaint, one more rumor about that nasty old woman who lives on the edge of the festival property, we may have to shut the festival down this year."

"Wait? What?" Relief and confusion war within me.

"Don't pretend like you don't know. That mad old witch has been calling our offices every day telling us to shut the festival down. She's threatened to file a police report about noise ordinances and disturbing her property. She's even harassing our vendors, telling them she'll spread rumors that their coffee has mold or some other nonsense."

The light bulb goes off in my head. *So that's why I've had vendors backing out of verbal agreements.*

"I'll handle it," I say before I can talk myself out of it. I turn to study the old house at the edge of the festival property line.

"You better. We don't need any more bad publicity," she says.

I only have a moment to wonder what she means before I hear the phone disconnect. Sighing, I decide that there's no moment like the present to handle this. I hate confrontation, and if I give myself even a few more seconds to think about it, I'll chicken out. Shutting the car off, I grab my pumpkin spice latte for fortification and step out of the car. I hold my head high and give myself a mental pep talk as I prepare to stride across the long, overgrown field to her house.

You are a badass. You are in charge of this festival. No bitter old woman who lives with her cats – and cauldron? And bats? – is going to crush all the hard work you've put into this. Not even if she threatens to hex you.

I channel my inner Aunt Margie, puff my chest out and march with feigned confidence up to the old house. My heart is pounding in my ears, and I mentally rehearse what I'm going to say. Anyone can be won over with kindness, right?

As I get nearer to the house, I slow down, taking in my surroundings. The house is old, no doubt about that. Boards from the front porch stick up at angles, nails exposed. A rusty old rocking chair made from horseshoes sits collecting dust and adorned by spider webs. Dead plants sit in terra cotta pots and weeds sprout out from the small amount of dirt that hasn't been eroded by wind, rain, and time. I hear mewling and look over to see a lean black cat slither its way through the wooden swing that's fallen from its roof anchors and now sits forgotten on the crumbling porch.

"Okay then," I say under my breath as I walk to the front door. *Just do it already*, I chide myself. I rap my knuckles on the door, then step back and wait. A minute passes, but nothing happens. I start to leave and celebrate escaping my near brush with the town witch when the door creaks open. I turn around, heart pounding, and see… not quite what I expected. A woman stands there. She can't be older than sixty-five, but life has not treated her well. Dark circles and heavy bags have taken up residency under her gray eyes. Her hair is mussed, but she's, surprisingly, wearing a lavender-colored cardigan–despite the sweltering temperature. She really must be a witch to be able to wear long sleeves in this weather.

"Well, what do you want?" she demands, slowly taking in my cropped leggings, tunic length tank top, baseball cap, and ponytail.

Forcing a smile to my lips, I reply, "Hi. I'm Amelia. I'm in charge of the fall festival this year and wanted to take a moment to stop by and introduce myself. I'd like to offer you complimentary entry and food tickets since you live nearby." I give her my most enthusiastic smile. *There! That wasn't so bad.*

She finally looks up at my face, and her frown deepens. "Now why, on God's green earth, would you think I want tickets to that demon festival?" she says, in what could arguably be called a hiss.

I scramble for a response as I feel my confusion begin to show on my face. I glance around, noticing the black cat has crept nearer to us and is now sitting on top of the broken swing, taking in our conversation like the old woman and I are playing starring roles in its favorite soap opera.

Struggling to recover, I press on. "Oh no, it's nothing like that," I say, forcing a smile and willing her to understand. She must think the festival is some kind of Halloween haunted horror event with chainsaws and fake blood and ouija boards.

"It's a family-friendly event. Nothing demonic about it. We'll have music, a hayride, apple cider, and trick-or-treating. Stuff like that. It's for all ages. Nothing scary—well, except for the little ghouls and goblins who dress up in costumes," I say with a smile. *Surely she can't object to cute little kids in Halloween costumes.*

If possible, she loses even more color from her pale face. Desperate to find a chink her her surly armor, I reach into the tote bag slung over my arm and grab the peach jam (with a zing!) that Aunt Margie gave me. I offer it up to her. "We'll be selling some amazing locally made goods. Here, take this one and give it a try. This whole event has the potential to really give our local economy a boost."

When she doesn't reach to take the jam, I stretch my arm out a little further, nodding with encouragement. She looks at the jar, then back to my face. In that one glance, she's shown me exactly what she thinks of my gift. My smile waivers and my confidence slips.

Like a shark, she senses blood in the water and moves in for the kill. "Listen. I am only going to say this once. I want nothing to do with this so-called festival of yours. No one in this town should. It's evil, and it disturbs the peaceful life I've created for myself here. If you persist in talking to me or having this event—*Amelia*, was it?—I will make it my personal mission, with the time I have left on this earth, to make sure you lose your job."

And without further ado, she slams the door in my face. The loud clash and creaky door hinges startle the cat perched on the old swing. It leaps in panic just as I startle back. We collide in one giant tumbleweed of arms, legs, and claws. In its mad scramble, the cat kicks off my arms with a yowl. My hands squeeze into fists reflexively and my pumpkin spice latte explodes with the ferocity of a volcano. It's contents land all over my face, my shirt, and my dignity.

I stand there, mouth agape, staring down at the remains of the broken jam jar mixing with coffee on the porch in front of me. I feel the latte dripping down my face. In this heat it's already starting to dry into a tacky second skin. I weakly shake my hands to try to get some of it off. When I shift, I feel the warm liquid slide down my bra. *Great. Just freaking great.*

Turning with an angry groan, I storm back to my car, furiously thinking of ways to get my vengeance on that awful old woman. *Maybe dropping off a dead skunk on her front doorstep would do the trick. It would certainly smell as bad as her attitude.* I fish my keys out of my tote bag and glance up and into my car, noticing that they are still in the ignition. And my car is locked. *Nothing is ever. Fucking. Easy. Not even my undignified retreat.*

All the day's frustrations bubble up and out, and I finally let it all out. I yell as loud as I can, channeling all my anger and frustration out into the universe. And then I start kicking my tire, hammering my fists on the hood of my car, letting out a stream of unintelligible curse words. And it is cathartic, this unleashing of anger upon *my locked car with the keys still inside.*

I don't even stop to consider what I must look like, throwing my temper tantrum in the middle of a parking lot. I just let myself go. Let the anger surge up and out. It's been a horrible day, and nothing I could do at this point would make it worse.

And just as I look up and let out another loud growl of anger at the universe, I see Rhett running out of the nearby woods, straight towards me. You have *got* to be kidding me. *Universe 1, Amelia 0.*

Chapter 6

RHETT

Forty-five minutes earlier

"You've been awfully quiet," Jacob says as I park my truck in the festival parking lot.

"I told you. I have a story direction, or er, hunch or something." Reaching into my folder, I pull out copies I've made of newspaper clippings related to the missing Roberts boy and hand them to Jacob.

Scanning them, he says. "Okay…. and what does this have to do with us taking a random day trip out to the festival site? Need to find Margie and have a couple more shots from her flask?" he asks with a grin.

My brows furrowed in irritation.

"What? She's kinda hot," he says.

"She's like sixty years old."

"Yeah, so? Some guys are into that kind of thing. And, look, I'm not here to judge you. If that lady and her whisky flask put some pep in your step again, I'll personally buy the next bottle for you two as a congratulations gift. Maybe even get you a matching flask set."

"Don't let her hear you say that," I smirk. "She'll slap a ring on my finger and march me up the aisle before I can say 'Yes, ma'am.'"

Jacob stares at me in shock.

"What? I was just joking."

"It's not that, it's… Rhett. You just *made a joke*. And you smiled!"

he says, grinning at me. "Look at you! Who knew all it would take was a few minutes alone in a cornfield with your dream woman." He waggles his eyebrows.

"Yeah, I guess I did," I say, smirking slightly. "Joke, I mean."

"Alright, that's it. I'm getting her number for you," Jacob says.

I open the truck door, shaking my head. This feels good. Almost how things used to be.

SLAP.

"Fucking mosquitoes," Jacob snarls as we make our way through the woods. "What are we looking for exactly? Because right now, the only thing I think we've successfully located is the prime location to contract West Nile Virus."

"I don't know exactly. I just wanted to get a feel for the area where the Roberts boy disappeared," I say.

I scan the ground as we walk, kicking aside the dried, brown pine straw, patches of mushrooms, and dense brush. I don't really know what I'm looking for. It's not like there would be any clues just lying around. The boy's disappearance happened more than twenty years ago, and the people of this city combed every inch of this forest when he went missing. But I can't help myself. I search, hoping my intuition led me out here for a reason.

"You better buy me a Griff's burger to make up for this impromptu hike," Jacob grumbles. "Ugh! What the hell?" I turn to see Jacob, glistening palms turned up, looking for all the world like he just stuck his hand in roadkill. He leans down and sniffs. "Ugh. Sap. Damnit. This shit is impossible to get off."

My hands are coated with the sticky, stubborn pine tree blood, too. And when yet another mosquito lands on my face, I decide that this is probably a waste of time. "I'm not seeing anything. Let's head back to the truck."

"Oh, thank the sweet Baby Jesus," Jacob says.

Together we make our way back through the brush. We've been walking for about thirty minutes when I hear loud screaming. My heart rate picks up, and Jacob and I look at each other.

"What the hell?" we say at the same time.

And without another word, we take off, running towards the screams as fast as the forest allows.

When we finally stumble out of the woods a few minutes later, I zero in on the source of the screaming. I see Amelia standing by her car, and she's flailing. Kicking something? *Oh God*, I think. *Is she being attacked? Stung by bees? Hornets? Bitten by a copperhead snake?* My heart kicks into high gear, adrenaline pumping. I don't even hesitate. I run straight towards her.

"AMELIA! WHAT IS IT? Are you okay?" I search our surroundings frantically, taking in the car and the concrete parking lot. I'm still trying to figure out the source of danger when Jacob catches up to me. We're both out of breath. I finally realize Amelia is leaning against her car, hands pressed over her face. She's breathing heavily and ignoring me. At least she's not screaming anymore.

"Are you okay? Are you hurt?" I ask tentatively, stepping closer to her, scanning her for an injury. Her white tank top has stains all over it, and the cold grip of fear tightens around my stomach as I wonder if she's unable to respond. She keeps her hands over her face and doesn't say a word. I reach for her, cautiously brushing her cheek with my hand so she'll pull her hands away. When she doesn't flinch from my touch, I slide my other hand up, cupping her face lightly in my palms. She finally drops her hands, and I'm preparing myself to see blood, a bruise, swelling from a snake bite, something. But her face is just flushed and… sticky? *What the hell?*

"Amelia? Are you okay? Did something attack you?" My eyes dart over her again, looking for injury. I notice some red scratch marks on her throat and follow their lines until I get to the edge of her tank top and halt. Her cleavage is spilling over the low-slung tank, instantly drawing up mortifying memories from a decade ago.

"Is there a reason you're staring at my boobs?" she finally croaks out, voice clouded with emotion.

I realize my hands are still on her cheeks, and I jump back like I've been electrocuted. "I'm sorry. I didn't mean to look... I was looking at your neck. No, wait, I mean. I just..."

I take a breath, trying to push my innate shyness aside, knowing my cheeks are burning. I stare directly at the ground. I can't even look at her. "I was just making sure you weren't injured. We heard screaming, and I thought you were being attacked by something."

I start mentally beating myself up. *Here I thought I would save Amelia, and now I'm apologizing for staring at her boobs?*

I dare a glance up at Amelia, but she's looking past me, eyes wide. "Tucker! Tucker! No! Bad dog! Stop!"

I look over my shoulder and see a cream-colored, thickly built terrier-ish dog running straight at us, barking and growling. My brain does weird gymnastics then, compressing many thoughts into a few brief seconds as I try to grasp on what's happening. *Did this dog attack Amelia earlier? Is it about to attack her again? But why does she know its name? Oh shit, it's about to attack me.*

I keep my back to the dog, ready to protect Amelia and tense for a blow. The dog plows at top speed directly into my ass, forcing my knees to buckle. And before I can stop myself, the forward momentum has me falling forward, effectively smashing Amelia between my body and her car.

"Tucker! Damn you, dog!" Amelia yells directly into my ear, and I briefly wonder if my eardrum just exploded. But the pup has already ricocheted off me and trotted up to her, licking her hand like a prized ice cream cone. He appears to be quite proud of himself.

I slowly emerge from the haze of adrenaline and shock and lock onto the soft, curvy body now pressed directly into my own—a body I've dreamed about for a very, very long time. I turn my head slowly, and I look her in the eyes. I inhale and smell...pumpkin spice? *Do they even make perfume out of that stuff now?* I wonder distantly. But another thought is quickly taking over–our faces, our lips are very, very close together. Our bodies are pressed into one another. And neither one of us is moving. We stare at each other, her brows dipping low. I glance down at those perfect, pouty lips, unable to stop myself.

A throat clears, startling us both. I forgot Jacob was even here. I scramble off of Amelia, stepping back as fast as I can. Jacob, looking utterly baffled, walks closer to us. "So, are you okay?" he asks Amelia.

She looks at Jacob, then at me, red-faced. "What are you doing here?" Anger and shame lace her tone.

"Like I said, we heard screaming and thought you were being attacked," I say.

She looks around and down at the parking lot. "By what? The wind?" she says with enough sarcasm to curl paint off a house.

"We heard screaming," I say for what feels like the hundredth time. I couldn't have imagined it. Jacob heard it, too.

She groans, ducking her face back into her hands. "I'm fine. I was just angry."

"Angry?" I answer back, confused.

She pulls her hands away, staring at them in disgust. "And my keys are locked in my car. And I am covered in pumpkin spice latte, which means I've had *zero* caffeine today. Oh, and I was mauled by a feral cat and probably have rabies. And I'll probably die from said rabies because I can't get into my car. So… yea. Angry."

She tilts her chin up in defiance, and what I now realize is the sticky remnant of a pumpkin spice latte sparkles in the unforgiving southern sun above us. Amelia stares at me, daring me to challenge what she just said.

I glance at Jacob and see his lips quirk, trying to stifle a laugh. I roll my eyes and look back at Amelia, prepared to offer her a ride home. But I can practically see her vibrating with hurt, anger, and embarrassment. And those beautiful, dark brown eyes are leveled directly at me, "throwing daggers," as mom would say.

"Why does this always happen?" she demands, her hands forming fists at her sides. I can practically see indignation take hold of her body.

I stare at her in confusion. "What?"

"Why am I such a *joke* to you? You think I can't see the two of you laughing at me like I'm not even here?" Her tone is dripping with condemnation and hurt. I glance at Jacob nervously. "What about *me* screams *joke* to *you*?" I feel the point of her index finger jab into my chest. I look down, fixated on the perfectly polished orange fingernail.

"You and your buddy must have no lives if you have nothing better to do than make fun of stupid, clumsy Amelia. High school wasn't enough for you? Me avoiding you for the last ten years wasn't enough? You just had to come out to the one place that I've worked nonstop to make a success and turn me into a joke. *Again.*"

Her words punch me in the gut, blow after blow, as I realize we just reenacted a version of that whole embarrassing scene from a decade ago: Clumsily crashing into one another, my friend laughing at us. "No." I try. "This wasn't like that, I.."

"You what? Saw me standing here minding my own business, and it wasn't enough for you to just keep going? Big, handsome, muscly man gets to show his friend how macho he can be by attempting to rescue some helpless little nerd girl? Grow up!"

She turns and marches off to the barn, the dog offering a quick sniff of my shoes before turning to follow in her wake. I start to go after her, but when I call her name, she flips me the bird and keeps walking.

"Yeah, I'd let that go if I were you," Jacob says as he steps up next to me and watches her storm off, dirt clouding up behind her.

"You don't think we should offer to give her a ride since she's stuck here?"

"Just a hunch," Jacob says dryly. "But I think she'd rather walk barefoot over pecan shells and magnolia cones to wherever she wants to go than catch a ride with one of us right now."

I look down at the ground again, desperately wishing for a place to disappear. Fate, it seems, is never going to let me have a normal interaction with Amelia Murphy.

Chapter 7

AMELIA

Safely ensconced inside the barn, I call my best friend Beth. After two rings, she answers the phone. "Hey, you!" she says. Always enthusiastic, my Beth. Always ready to help everyone around her. I can't believe there was a time I once loathed my best friend and closest coworker.

"Hey. I have a sort of big favor to ask," I hedge.

"Anything for you, babe. Need wine? A gossip sesh? Oooo, do you need to vent about Janet? I heard she was furious about that old woman near the festival grounds."

I can just picture the glee on her perfect face, framed by the black hair she inherited from her Japanese mother. Beth is one of those people I would have hated in high school and tried to hate when we started working together. She's got a killer body, is married to a doctor, and seems to have her whole life together. But, damn it, she's also nice. And not artificially nice, like really, genuinely loves to help people nice. Which is the only reason her Junior League membership wasn't a deal-breaker in our friendship. Well, that and the fact that we bonded over our mutual dislike of our boss and shared interest in romance novels.

"Ha, if only that were all. I'm sort of... stuck out at the festival grounds. I locked my keys in my car."

"Say no more. Captain Beth to the rescue! I'll be there in twenty."

I EASE OPEN THE BARN DOOR when I see Beth's text on my phone screen letting me know she's in the parking lot. I scan the perimeter to see if anyone else is here, but Jacob and Rhett are gone. Sighing with relief, I make my way to Beth's car, parked next to mine.

Beth rolls down the window and gawks at me. "What happened to you? You look like you got into a fight with a feral possum and all her babies, and they won."

Rolling my eyes, I walk around to her passenger side door. I open the back door so Tucker can hop in and then slide into the front. Sweet, blessed air conditioning fills the inside of the car, and I swear I've never felt anything this refreshing in my life.

"It was a cat, a mean old shrew, an exploding latte, Tucker, and my archnemesis."

Beth blinks at me. "Are you for real?"

"You have no idea how very real I am right now."

"I'll drive. You talk."

And so I talk. I tell her everything from the barn debacle to the old witch's cat and Rhett's "rescue attempt." In true Beth fashion, she listens with rapt interest, occasionally offering feedback like "Oh, that awful old hag!" and "She owes you a year's worth of coffee." But when I get to the part about Rhett turning me into a Lia sandwich against my car, Beth smiles with wicked delight.

"Oh Lia, that sounds so romantic," she coos. "Is he hot?"

I blink at her. "Are you serious right now?"

"Tell me! Is. He. *Hot?*"

"Um. Maybe?" I say it like a question. This is not where I want this conversation to go right nowveven if the jerk is kind of hot.

"Oooo. Annnnndddddd? Tell me more. What does he look like?"

"And he has this wavy auburn hair and green eyes that look like they were photoshopped or something because they are so freaking green. And forearm muscles that are like woah. And his lips are full—but not like in a super freaky inflatable pool toy way kind of full. Like Brad Pitt full."

"Oh, Lia! He sounds like he's frying eggs on the sidewalk in July, sizzling. And you had him on top of you." She pretends to fan herself with her hand.

"You're losing sight of the problem here, Beth. This is the same guy who mortified me in front of half of our high school. Besides, this was not sexy. I mean, it was hot, but only because my face was on fire with embarrassment and it was one million degrees outside. But Tucker knocked him into me, and I was covered in coffee. And then he and his friend laughed at me. Who does that?"

"I mean, no offense, babe, but if a dog just shoved my ass into your sticky, latte-covered face, I'd probably laugh at you, too. Methinks you protest too much. A hot man with a damsel in distress rescue complex? Sign me up! Look me in the eyes and tell me you didn't enjoy it… just a little."

I roll my eyes at her and don't respond, but a little voice in my head chirps up and says, okay, maybe just a little.

THAT EVENING, I STAND IN my kitchen hammering at the top of a half-gallon of Blue Bell cookies and cream ice cream with my spoon. It's frozen solid. Because, of course it is. It's the *coup de gras* of my day. I stick it in the microwave for 30 seconds, then scoop a bountiful serving into my bowl to eat my problems away. Sliding into my favorite oversized chair, I tuck my blanket around me and call Aunt Margie.

"So we're talking again, are we?" Aunt Margie answers the phone without any formality. I guess my distance hasn't gone unnoticed.

"I'm sorry, Aunt Margie. My feelings were hurt. I saw you sitting in that corn maze, *my* corn maze, with the man who basically turned my high school experience into a giant shame fest. And the two of you were chumming it up like you were lifelong best friends. It felt like you were taking his side."

Saying that out loud, I realize how ridiculous I sound. When she doesn't respond, I say, "I know. That was dumb. I'm sorry. Forgive me?"

"I forgave you the moment it happened," Aunt Margie says. And in my head, I see her making her serious face at me, the one she uses when she wants me to understand, deep in my soul, that what she's saying means something. At least I know that, no matter what happens between us, Aunt Margie and I will always have each other's back.

"So what else is eating at you?" Aunt Margie asks. She always knows.

I relate the day's events to her, from Janet and the crazy old lady in the house near the festival site to the cats, the spilled coffee, and, finally, I get the courage to tell her about my encounter with Rhett.

"The whole thing was so awful and embarrassing. How am I ever supposed to meet with Jacob about interviews again? And am I just destined to have Rhett Hebert falling on top of me for the rest of my life or something?"

I pause when Aunt Margie doesn't say anything.

"Are you… Aunt Margie, *are you laughing?*"

Raucous guffaws erupt from my phone as I stare at it in horror.

"Oh, Lia," Aunt Margie manages to gasp out between laughs. "I'm sorry, but just the thought of you with a cat jumping in your face, covered in coffee with those poor boys thinking they would rescue you. What I wouldn't give to have been a fly on the wall, or I guess I should say, car, when that happened. God bless that poor boy for trying. Oh, don't get your feelings hurt, girl. You know I love you, but maybe you're wrong about this. He did apologize to you, and it sounds like he got mud on his face, too, so to speak. Did you ever stop and think that maybe the whole scenario was pretty funny? I mean, Tucker even shoved Rhett's ass into you!" She lets out another loud chuckle.

I'm taken aback at first, but then I let that settle in, replaying today in my mind, trying to imagine how I'd feel if I witnessed Aunt Margie or Beth go through the same thing. I start to smile, but then, like a knee-jerk reaction, I recall that painful day in high school again.

"But Rhett did almost the same thing to me ten years ago," I protest.

"And maybe it was an accident then, too. Ever think of that?"

"Why are you suddenly on his side now? Sharing a slug of whisky in the corn maze makes you best friends?" I demand, hurt ringing my voice.

"Lia, I'm not on anyone's side. I just think you should consider acting with the same generosity towards him that you expect from others. After all, that was ten years ago. A lot can happen in a decade."

"I'll think about it." I allow.

"And, don't you worry about that old witch, Ms. Clark. I'll talk to her the next time I'm over that way. Surely she can't stand the might of two Murphy women."

I wince, imagining the hurricane-force winds that are sure to result from that confrontation. I wonder if I could turn it into a fundraiser. Murphy vs. Clark. Place your bets now! Ten dollars says Murphy gets the first hit in, and Clark threatens to tell the entire population of Ruston that Margie's peach jam is laced with arsenic. Warning: Not liable for injuries caused by flying cats… or broomsticks.

"If you say so."

"There's my girl," she says. I smile as we tell each other goodnight and I end the call.

Stretching, I get up and deliver my ice cream bowl to the sink, stepping around the piles of books I've left lying around my favorite reading spots. Tucker trails me along the way, hoping I'll share the spoon with him. When I hear the knock on the door, I smile and make my way to the front of the house, swinging the door wide. Beth stands there in her PJs with a bottle of wine in one hand and a bag of nail polish in the other.

"I come bearing gifts!" she says, raising her arms to display her offerings and walking inside. Tucker greets her, and she leans down to kiss his nose. "How's my favorite boy?" she asks him, giving his snoot a rub. She pours us each a glass of wine, and we make our way to the couch, settling in under my favorite fuzzy blankets.

"Dan is working tonight," she says. "Some sort of emergency surgery the ER called him in for."

"The exciting life of a podiatrist," I nod sagely.

"Call him what he is—a foot doctor. The man examines bunions for a living," Beth laughs.

"Hey, at least he has a steady job and thinks the world of you!"

"Eh, maybe a very tiny island, but not the world."

"Better than the men I've encountered," I say with an eye roll.

Beth turns serious. "Lia, I know you haven't had the best luck in the man department, but you'll find the right one."

"Not the best luck? Beth, every man I've dated used me to help them sober up, quit gambling, or as a way to get over his ex-girlfriend. They then promptly dumped me when they recovered and no longer needed me as their healing fairy godmother. That's more than just bad luck. That's a series of tragic train wrecks." I try to say this light-heartedly, but my voice quavers, thoughts lingering on my last ex and his scary obsession with me. I stare down at my blanket, picking a piece of dog hair off of it and tossing it to the floor.

"They were all idiots," Beth says, like I knew she would. "They didn't appreciate the treasure that you are, Lia. Your kind heart and generosity deserve more than the sad deck of men who have fallen into your lap thus far."

"I feel like a band-aid: patching their wounds until they heal and I'm discarded in the trash covered in someone else's dried blood. I'm sick of it. I know there are good men out there, Beth. Hell, you have a good man—even if he does look at bunions all day." I smile. "But I need an extended break on the dating front." I look down at my dog. "Tucker is the only man I need in my life." He thumps his tail in agreement. "All of my energy right now needs to be focused on the large volume of work that I have to do to make this fall festival a success."

Beth sighs but lets me change the subject. "Speaking of, I have ideas! Want to hear them?"

This is exactly what I need. Beth can plan a $100,000 fundraiser with a string of Christmas lights, a $10 budget, and an army of Junior Leaguers.

By the time midnight rolls around, we're a bottle of prosecco in with orange fingernails and a game plan. With my best friend giggly and tipsy next to me, my dog curled up at my feet, and the warm haze of bubbly coursing through my system, I let myself be happy. I submerge myself into the determined optimism that this festival plan we put together tonight will go off without a hitch and be exactly what we need for unprecedented success. And I am determined to believe it.

Chapter 8

RHETT

Watching my ceiling fan's blades spin around as I lay in bed, I wonder how I always manage to screw things up so spectacularly. I can't stop my mind from replaying the details of every single way my encounter with Amelia went horribly wrong today in slow motion—like a kicker who missed the game-winning field goal. I can just hear the announcer commentating on my life now: "He falls!" *Rewind. Play.* Falling onto Amelia, her look of horror. *Rewind. Play.* Dog hitting me in the ass. *Rewind. Play.* Enjoying the feel of her body pressed into mine despite everything. *Rewind. Play.* The announcer: "Can you believe it, John? That has got to hurt."

I toss and turn, desperate to shut off the play-by-play blaring through my brain at top volume, but it's no use. With a yell of frustration, I throw my covers off and grab my gray sweatpants before making my way to my home office. If I can't sleep, I might as well get some work done.

Opening my laptop, I pull up the newspaper archives site and re-read the old articles. I'm scanning, searching for something, anything I might have missed. I fixate on the missing person report. Halloween 2002. Missing from the fall festival. I try to hold all the puzzle pieces in my mind. I blur them together, hoping they'll congeal into something helpful.

I keep thinking about my trek through the nearby woods. *What did I think I'd find? A twenty-year-old piece of ripped Halloween costume or some sign that says, "Oh, look! A clue!"?* There's no way we could cover that giant space in any detail anyway. It would take a satellite, metal detector, and an entire team to find even a hint of a clue, on a long cold trail. I shake my head, and, not for the first time, I admit that pursuing this is probably a huge waste of my time.

That's when my eyes snag on something else in my inbox: An article Dr. Crystal Black sent me recently. She is my former history professor turned story fact-checker on all things archival and archeological. We've maintained our friendship over the years. Occasionally she works on a project she thinks would make a good story and sends it my way. And, she's unerringly right. Dr. Black has become quite the community figure, giving talks at the university, the library, and the local bookstore. Every story I write about her is a rousing success. I know if I reach out to her for help, she'll say yes.

The article she sent me is about a project she's involved with—a local excavation of an old graveyard where they are looking for the alleged gravesite of some of the city's founders. They have clues to help them pinpoint the general area but couldn't dig up an entire cemetery, so they are using modern technology to help them. It's some kind of geothermal something. Opening the email, I click the link she sent me—and there it is: Ground penetrating radar, GPR.

My brief internet research on the topic tells me that GPR is basically a machine that sends energy into the ground and records echoes off of objects that lie beneath. I wonder if that works on bones? Surely it does if they are using it in their research. I cringe inwardly at the thought, recognizing how morbid it is. But still… I set a reminder on my phone to call Dr. Black in the morning and ask her opinion. Maybe we can utilize the technology to scan the woods near the festival site.

I glance at the clock. 2 a.m. I squeeze my eyes shut, the computer screen's glow imprinted on the back of my eyelids. Tomorrow is going to hurt. Maybe if I lay in bed and read something super monotonous, like the history of barnacles or a war treatise, I can finally fall asleep.

As I make my way upstairs, my mind wanders to Amelia. Again. I fixate on those brief moments our bodies were pressed together. For a moment, I thought she felt the buzz of connection radiating between us, too. *Did I imagine the way she looked at me?* Yes, I definitely imagined it. There's no way I'll ever earn her forgiveness, let alone her affection. But I can't help myself. It's been ten years, and my heart still yearns for her. So what if I can't earn her forgiveness. I can at least show her that I'm not a total ass. Which, incidentally, is something I should have done in high school. But I couldn't then. I was a prisoner of my own anxiety and shyness. But now? Well, my therapist would tell me that I could and should try. Apology sincerely. Heal past hurts and all that.

I'm already trying to figure out a way I can see Amelia again without seeming like I'm some kind of creepy weirdo. I owe her an apology for today. I can do that. I *will* do that. Tomorrow. I'll figure out a way to get in touch with her… if she'll even listen to me.

THE NEXT MORNING AT WORK, I make my way over to Jacob's cubical. He's completely focused on his computer screen, earbuds in, typing steadily. When he notices me, he holds up a finger, signaling for me to wait a moment. I slide into a chair across from his desk and stare at my phone until I hear him say, "What's up?"

"Hey, you know how you interviewed Amelia Murphy for that fall fest story? You wouldn't happen to have her number, would you?"

He levels his gaze at me. "Um, Rhett, I'm pretty sure that someone flipping you the bird is a universal signal that she is not interested in swapping phone numbers with you," he says.

My cheeks heat, but I don't give up. "I just want to apologize," I say.

"I have a better idea," he smiles, mischief lighting his eyes. "When I was out there for the interview, Amelia asked me if I knew of any bands who might be interested in playing during a couple of the festival weekends. I told her I *might* know someone." He looks at me knowingly.

"What? You mean *me*?" I say incredulously.

"Why not? You and your dad have been playing together forever."

"We're not a band, though. No way would someone want to see us play in public, like on a stage or something professional," I say, horrified. "We'd be a joke."

"Oh, come on, you're good! Y'all can play just about anything. I bet if you spent a couple of nights a week together over the next two weeks, you could even play 'Monster Mash' with the best of them. Plus, that would make for an *epic* apology to Amelia."

I fall silent and glare at him. He has me, and he knows it. Damnit.

"Come on. I'm headed out there to meet with her this afternoon and look at the stage setup. I'll tell her I'm ready to introduce her to the band. You walk in to save the day—for real this time—apologize, and bam! Just like that, you've gone from zero to hero."

"That's wishful thinking," I mutter.

"No, that's positive thinking. Maybe you can bring your guitar and woo her with an apology serenade."

I just shake my head. "Fine. I'll come with you. But no guitars and no serenades." He lights up at my easy acquiescence.

Already my gut is churning – I'm about to see Amelia again and offer to play my guitar. In public. Voluntarily. I shudder. It's not that I don't like to play. I love it, actually. It's one of the few things that helps me center my churning thoughts and brings me peace. But playing in public? There's no peace in that. But as I picture Amelia's embarrassed tears from ten years ago, her distraught face yesterday, I know I can do this. I can offer up my own insecurity in sacrifice for easing her discomfort. I owe her this much. More even. But I can start by sharing this piece of me.

Chapter 9

AMELIA

Beth and I stand shoulder to shoulder, eyeing the wooden platform stage that now occupies the once empty field. It's not perfect, but it has a rustic charm that fits with our fall festival site.

"That's it. You're a genius," I tell Beth as I admire my vision come to life. In just two days' time, she pulled some of her networking strings and recruited the Fathers Team at her church to erect the wooden platform, complete with a trellis of boards overhead to string twinkle lights through.

"We won't have the sound system until the day of the event, but I think it will work," she says. "We just need to double-check with the band to make sure we have everything they need. Who did you book?"

"Your guess is as good as mine," I say with a slight wince. I watch Beth's eyes grow wide and then close slightly as she attempts to hide her dismay. I press on.

"That reporter, Jacob, the one I've been working with on festival coverage, told me he knows a band who would be willing to perform within our budget. I'm supposed to meet them out here in a few minutes."

"Wait, you mean that guy who was laughing at you?" she asks as we continue circling the stage. Beth resumes taking notes on how she can improve its appearance. However she's also using the opportunity to avoid looking at me directly.

"Um, yea," I shrug my shoulders, relieved that Beth's focus seems to have shifted to her note-taking. She's talking out loud now. "Pumpkins, skeletons, oh maybe hay bales for families to sit on while they enjoy the show!" She's writing frantically now, caught up in her imagination of the perfect autumn day. Or at least she's pretending to be.

"Hey, ladies!" I hear Jacob say as he walks up to us. I tense, but he gives no indication that he was affected by my fit of anger yesterday. His grin is kicked up into high gear, radiating vibes of *everything is fine. We are all good. I'm not upset. You're not upset.* "Nice stage! This is going to be perfect!"

Still feeling awkward and a bit embarrassed, I pretend I didn't throw a temper tantrum yesterday. "Thank you. And thank you for helping us find a band." I clear my throat. "Did you say they were going to meet us here today?" My voice squeaks despite my attempt to play it cool.

"I did indeed," he looks down at his phone and sends a text. "In fact, he's here now." He turns to face the parking lot, using a hand to shade his eyes. I see a man walking up, and my inner hormonal teenager pokes up her head at the sight of him. Jeans slung low over his hips, a t-shirt that does nothing to hide the broad chest and defined shoulders underneath. Tall with hands tucked into pockets as he strides forward. He's looking down, a baseball cap shielding his eyes, but I can see the defined jaw underneath. And those forearms. *What is it about a man with defined forearms?* Today is most definitely looking up. Maybe all of last night's prosecco-induced enthusiasm wasn't just wishful thinking. Already I can envision him playing guitar at the festival, assuming he's a guitar player, that is. And, hey, this, *he,* might be an unexpected festival draw. I wonder if I can ask him to play a couple of sample songs.

But when he gets closer and finally looks up... my insides quickly build a coffin, crawl inside, close the lid and *die.* I think I might vomit because this deliciously sexy man with the out-of-this-world forearms is *Rhett. Why is he here?* I can already feel an angry flush creeping up my neck and cheeks. I glance around in a panic to find a hay bale or a pile of pumpkins to hide behind. A ghost sheet would be even better.

Beth turns and looks at me, noting my complexion is turning into something resembling a tomato, and her brows deepen in confusion. I try to communicate who this is and why I'm being an awkward ostrich with just my expression, but neither of us says anything.

Finally, Rhett looks at me, tilting his lips into a shy half-smile. "Hey, Amelia." He turns to Beth and extends his hand in greeting. "I'm Rhett Hebert. Nice to meet you."

Beth's expression goes from confused, to shocked, to *holy shit this is the guy who had you pressed up against your car? He IS hot. You majorly undersold him. We are gonna talk later.*

Eyes alight and grin wide, she responds. "Well hello there, Rhett. I'm Beth. So nice to meet you."

I am frozen, mentally digging a hole underneath me and burying myself in it, or maybe just my head. Perfect for my awkward ostrich brain, with its head in the sand and butt in the air. Gah. Even my fantasies are insecure and awkward.

"I'm sorry," I finally manage to squeak out. "What are you doing here, exactly?"

"I'm the band," Rhett says with an uncomfortable shrug. "That is, if you'll have me. And, um, I also wanted to apologize for yesterday."

Jacob and Beth watch us like they're ready to pull out the popcorn, sit back and enjoy the show. Rhett looks at both of them, then back at me.

"Just you? Are the band, I mean?" I say, refusing to acknowledge the apology. I've got to figure out how to put an end to this.

"Oh, um, it's not just me. My dad and my sister will be part of it, too. Kind of like the Von Trapp Family singers… without the yodeling goats." I just blink back at him. *Did he just make a Sound of Music reference?*

When I say nothing, he lowers his voice and asks earnestly, "Can we talk? Alone?" His green eyes silently beg me to say yes, like a cute little lost puppy. And those forearms are flexing as he shifts uncomfortably. Damnit.

"Yeah, okay, let's go for a walk," I say, resigned as I pointedly ignore Beth's raised eyebrows.

I watch Rhett's shoulders relax, and he bobs his head. I try to rally all the anger I felt towards him yesterday. Hell, I try to draw on all the resentment I've harbored towards him for a decade, but Aunt Margie knows how to plant the seeds of doubt in my mind, and her words about giving him the benefit of the doubt have found their mark. So I take a deep breath and decide to at least hear what he has to say.

Together we walk towards the trail that runs through the nearby woods, shuffling in awkward silence. He's tall, I notice again as he plods along next to me. He stands at least a good five inches over my own tall frame. I try to discreetly take him in, noticing the edges of corded muscles through his light t-shirt. And he's in a band *with his family*. This last detail reminds me again of my conversation with Aunt Margie. Can anyone who plays guitar with his dad really be an awful person? My mind starts to fall through time back to high school, but then I breathe in deep, taking in the smells of the pine trees surrounding me and… laundry detergent, a spicy, soapy scent, and coffee. I exhale, realizing that we are walking and definitely not talking.

"I'm sorry," we both say at the same time. "Go ahead. No, you go ahead," our words stumbling over one another. We both let out an awkward half chuckle.

"I'm sorry," he says with determination. "About yesterday. I didn't mean to fall into you and your car, which was probably a million freaking degrees in this ridiculous heat. I mean it. I thought I was helping you. And Jacob was laughing at me being a total idiot, not you. I guess what I'm trying to say is that the whole thing was an accident, and I never intentionally laughed at you or made fun of you. It was just my stupidassery."

When he stops talking, I glance over at him, amused. My mouth quirks before I can school my features. "Stupidassery? That's not even a real word," I say, extending an olive branch.

"I guess it is now," he keeps looking straight ahead, but a smile quirks at the edge of his mouth.

"I'm sorry, too." I finally say. "Before you got there, I had a terrible run-in with that crazy, old witch woman who lives in the haunted house that borders the festival site. And her cat attacked me, knocked my latte all over me, and scratched me up. And then I locked my keys in the car. Plus, my boss had just read me the riot act. And then my dog went rogue and jumped on you. I was super embarrassed, and… you caught me at a bad time. A very bad time. And I'm sorry my dog isn't better trained. He really is a good boy. He just gets excited. And once he's in full throttle derp mode, I have a really hard time snapping him out of it."

"Wait, her cat attacked you?" he says, finally looking at me, eyebrows knitting together. "What like he pulled out a sword and went all Aragorn on you?"

"Did you just make a *Lord of the Rings* reference? About a cat?" I say incredulously. "Because there are no cats in *Lord of the Rings*. A better reference would have been, I don't know, like *Puss in Boots*."

"You shall not pass!" he says in a goofy, feigned Gandalf voice. It takes me a minute to process what he just said. I'm utterly surprised by this glint of humor Rhett has shown me. And then I *laugh* at the man I staunchly resolved to hate over the past ten years.

"Who knew that one of Ruston High School's best baseball players had a thing for orcs and wizards?" And just like that, I've thrown a bucket of ice water over the cautiously joyful mood we've built. It dies as we both remember that day in high school. It seems I can't stop remembering it.

"Amelia. Look, that day in high school, in the hall," he begins with determination. But his words send panic barreling down my spine.

"Please don't," I say, cutting him off. I can't do this. Not now, maybe not ever. I stare determinedly at his t-shirt, my eyes tracing a loose thread on his sleeve. I'm surprised he remembers anything even happened. I assumed I was barely a blip on his radar, an insignificant nerd who momentarily interrupted his life as a popular baseball player.

"Let's just pretend I never brought up high school, okay?" I look up at his face, silently begging him to drop it. Finally, he nods, and my breath exits me in a whoosh. I turn and continue walking. He steps beside me, and we follow the trail in silence again.

"So, you play in a family band, huh?" I say, knowing I can't lose him as my one and only band option and desperately trying to steer the subject to more comfortable territory. I spot a wooden bench tucked off the side of the trail and motion for us to sit down.

"Well..." he says shyly as he slides onto the bench next to me. "I play guitar." My mind simultaneously pats itself on the back for guessing correctly and balks at being excited. A frown flits across my face, but I quickly shove it behind a forced smile.

Rhett continues, not noticing. "And my dad plays keyboard. I sing a little, and my sister is an amazing singer, but don't tell her I said that. She's a total diva, and it will go straight to her head," he says with dry affection, his lips tilting up. "Plus, Jacob plays drums a couple of days a week at Sundown Grill. I'm not sure you'd call us a band, but Jay thinks we could perform a couple of weekends for you. And we'll practice to make sure we've got it down ahead of time. I know we're not some amazing, professional group or anything, but..."

"But you sound perfect. I mean, your band does," I say with a smile. Plus, I really, really need a band, and it's last minute, though there is no way I'm going to let him know that I'm teetering on desperation here. And then I remember that not thirty minutes ago, I was trying to figure out how to backpedal out of this deal, but damn. I really do need a band. *Plus, Lord of the Rings and those forearms?* Rhett is not fighting fair.

He's been staring ahead of us into the surrounding forest during this whole exchange, but Rhett finally turns to look at me. My heart stammers a little - in anxiousness or something else, I'm not sure.

"It's the least we can do to help. Plus, we can play *The Lord of the Rings* theme song," he says, lips tilting again in wry amusement.

"No way!" I say with genuine enthusiasm, half leaping off the bench. "That is so cool."

He lets out a surprised chuckle. "So nerdy, you mean," he says, embarrassment caressing his words.

"No, it's amazing. I mean, it *will* be Halloween. I think you should all dress up as hobbits for the show," I say, laughing as I picture the scene in my head: feet bare, vests on, curly-haired wigs, daggers. When I turn to look at Rhett and gauge his response, he's staring at me and looks a little dazed. He seems to realize he's staring, shakes his head, and looks straight ahead again.

""So, um, what else does your band play?" I ask, desperate to avoid any awkward silence. He takes a deep breath, closes his eyes, and then looks at me again. I take in his green eyes, tousled auburn curls, and the five o'clock shadow of his beard starting to grow in. My eyes find his lips and get stuck there for a moment, my stomach line dancing inside me. He leans toward me slightly, and I panic. My inner dramatic teenage girl decides to cannonball directly into the hormonal deep end. And quite frankly, I feel betrayed by her. *Remember Lia, you can't stand this man even if he does like* The Lord of the Rings. *And plays guitar. Snap out of it.*

But he's seemingly oblivious to my awkwardness. "We mostly play classic rock when we jam together in the garage. Those are the songs my grandfather taught me to play on his guitar. Dad and my sister, Katie, know them, too. But we can learn to play almost anything."

I relax, grateful Rhett didn't pick up on my bout of momentary weirdness. *I totally made this into something it is not.*

"Sounds like you're pretty good on the guitar– least for a hobbit, anyway," I say slyly. He leans back against the bench and surprises me with a laugh. And it's a full-throated, warm belly laugh that warms me from head to toe. The deep-dimpled smile transforms him, and I can't look away.

He turns to look at me, eyes gleaming. "Well, I guess we better get back to the festival site. I wouldn't want to miss Second Breakfast," he says without missing a beat. *Who knew my high school nemesis would be so in tune with hobbits?*

I nod, and together we stand and make our way back through the woods. I can tell something has shifted between us. Some of our mutual tension has eased, and my traitorous teenage girl brain wonders what Rhett would do if I reached out and grabbed his hand. *I squash that thought. I am the worst judge of character when it comes to men. Hello, Amelia. Remember your last couple of boyfriends?* Plus, I don't even like this guy. In fact, I can't stand him. But all attempts to convince myself are slowly being smothered by something low and warm fighting its way to the front of my brain.

We continue talking about his band, what they can play, and what sound equipment they'll need. And then, suddenly, time has moved at warp speed, and we're already back at the festival site, walking up to Jacob and Beth. Before we reach them, though, Rhett asks if we can exchange numbers to work out all the details for the band. I can feel the warmth spread through my bones, and it's not just the Louisiana sunshine this time. I let myself soak in this moment of peace, relishing that something is *finally* going right with this festival.

And that's when I hear shouting.

ALL FOUR OF US TURN our heads to the sounds of yells and… yowls? *What the?* My brain finally zeroes in on the witch's house at the edge of the woods. For just a moment, I debate what I should do. Do I go see if she needs help? Or do I just avoid that whole situation like it's the bubonic plague? But my better nature kicks in, and I start running to the house. Rhett, Jacob, and Beth keep pace beside me.

When the details of the scene come into focus, I halt abruptly, the other three rushing past me to help with… well whatever the hell is happening. So all four of us are there to witness the scene unfolding on the front porch of the witch's house.

I see a full-sized gumbo pot whiz through the air, followed by a screech of, "Get the hell away from my house, you crazy she-demon!"

I flinch back instinctively, and for a moment, I think coming here was a very bad decision. I consider taking cover and realize that the other person on the front porch is Aunt Margie. *Oh shit. This is not good.*

Aunt Margie seems to gather the title of crazy she-demon around her like a cloak of honor, and she's just been crowned Queen of All Demons Great and Small. I watch as Aunt Margie sizes up the angry witch woman before her and deduces that she will come out on top.

"Did you just throw a gumbo pot at me?" she says, voice terrifyingly steady, a weapon charging up for a cataclysmic blast. The old woman, who I now know has a name–Ms. Clark stares back in a defiant challenge. She holds a long wooden spoon above her head like a lightsaber, poised to strike. *Use the Force, Aunt Margie*, I silently encourage.

"Yes, and there's more where that came from," the witch says with icy venom.

Aunt Margie glances over, noticing she has an audience. She spots me, looks me over briefly, and determination settles in her features. Then she turns back to the vibrating woman in front of her.

"Well, you better get down on your knees and start praying that the pot you hurled at my head is well seasoned because I choose to take that as a gift instead of a threat. In fact, I think I'll use it to cook up a batch of chicken and sausage gumbo for the festival." She folds her arms and stares directly into Ms. Clark's eyes. She-demon, indeed.

"Should we do something?" Rhett whispers.

"Hell no. I like my balls right where they're at," Jacob shout whispers.

And I have to agree. I have no desire to get in between the fiery death match underway.

The witch woman turns, leaves her door open, and marches back into her house. Just as I think Aunt Margie has won this round, a cat comes tearing out of the house howling. And then, as if in slow motion, a live chicken is ejected through the front door, wings flapping, straight at Aunt Margie's face. Fortunately, the bird misses its target, though it's a near thing. Without missing a beat, Aunt Margie bends down, plucks the chicken from the ground, and tucks it under her arm, pinning its wings. It appears Aunt Margie's lifelong gift with animals–or at the very least her formidable presence and iron grip -

are enough to settle the bird momentarily.

When Ms. Clark stalks back outside, wielding her wooden spoon like a battle ax and threatening to call the police, Aunt Margie looks her dead in the eyes. ""Thank you for the gumbo pot and," she pauses to look down at the chicken and then eyes the cat hissing at her on the porch, "the ingredients to make my gumbo with." She stares at the cat again pointedly. "After all, you know us Louisianians will eat *anything*."

And with that, she reaches down and scoops up the terrified cat with the confidence of a battle-hardened warrior. With the yowling creature tucked under one arm and a chicken under the other, she turns and marches off toward the festival barn, leaving Ms. Clark at a loss for words.

"Lia, be a dear and grab my gumbo pot, will you?" Aunt Margie calls with intentional casualness over her shoulder.

What else can I do? I walk over, pick up the gumbo pot, shrug, and follow Aunt Margie. I glance over my shoulder to make sure nothing else is going to come whizzing at my head.

"You bring my cat back, you crazy demon!" Ms. Clark yells from her front porch. Aunt Margie pays her no heed. Jacob, Rhett, and Beth finally snap out of their stupor and follow us to the barn. Once we're inside, Aunt Margie slams the door and lets the animals roam free. We all stare at her in silence.

"What?" she finally demands, using her arm to wipe the sweat from her forehead.

"Um," Rhett says cautiously. "What was *that* all about?"

"Hmm? Oh, that?" Aunt Margie says with an unaffected air. "I asked Greta Clark to participate or contribute to the fall festival. And when she told me I was bat-shit crazy, I told her that her house would work nicely as our haunted house this year. One thing led to another, and well, I guess she decided to donate a gumbo pot, a chicken, and a black cat to the event."

Aunt Margie is practically buzzing with adrenaline and mischief. I eye the cat. Aunt Margie watches my face shift and says, "Oh, don't worry, I would never hurt the cat or the chicken…. but she doesn't need to know that."

My mouth drops open as I stare at her. And then a wild collision of chuckles and guffaws erupts behind me. I turn to see Beth, Rhett, and Jacob trying—and failing—to stifle their laughter. When I turn back to Aunt Margie, she's shaking with quiet laughter, too.

"Now, let her give you any more trouble about this festival, Lia. If she does, maybe I'll leave a cup of gumbo on her porch. I'll even put lipstick on and kiss a thank you card to leave with it."

And then laughter is erupts from me, too. Leave it to Aunt Margie to solve my biggest festival issue with the threat of gumbo.

68

Chapter 10

RHETT

"Ever heard of Ground Penetrating Radar?" I ask Jacob as he takes a bite of his burger. While he chews, he looks up at the ceiling in thought. Like he usually does when I ask him an off-the-wall question, Jacob takes it seriously, sifting through his memories and cross-referencing them with stories he has written that might have included that term.

"I don't think so…" he finally says, reaching for a fry.

"It's a technology that lets you look underground without having to dig. My former history professor, Dr. Black, is using it to try and locate the grave site of one of our city's founders. I reached out to her to ask about it. We could use it to scan the grounds around the festival site. Maybe there's something there… you know, relative to the missing Roberts boy cold case."

Jacob sits with this for a moment. "You're really hung up on this old story, huh? You know they searched the area thoroughly when it happened and found nothing."

"I know, but it couldn't hurt, right?"

"I guess not, but.. Rhett? How are you going to pay for something like that? We don't exactly have that in our small town newspaper budget."

"The festival is near Dr. Black's research site. I'm hoping she will do me a solid and give us a couple hours with the GPR. Maybe it could even help her research."

He shrugs, and I can tell he's not convinced that this is worth my time and energy but doesn't want to stifle my newfound enthusiasm. Suddenly a grin darts across his face.

"Did you see the air that lady got on that chicken?" he says.

"Huh?"

"That chicken!" Jacob says, changing the subject and still clearly floored over the previous day's events. "Too bad she's such a recluse. With an arm like that, the seniors at the Y would love to have her on their softball team."

"How in the hell do you know there is a senior softball team at the Y?" I ask incredulously.

"Oh, I covered that story a couple of months ago. Their team captain, Dorothy Boyd, was so charmed by me that she keeps showing up at the office with homemade apple pies and begging me to coach their league," he says as if this is an everyday occurrence. And hell, maybe it is for the always-confident Jacob.

"What a charmed life you lead," I say dryly, reaching for my burger.

"Hey, you wouldn't complain if you had fresh desserts showing up at your office on the regular."

"Fair point." I agree.

"Maybe Margie Murphy will be your patroness of peach jams," he says. "Anything happen after that delightful nip you two shared in the corn maze?" he queries, mischief and humor lighting his face.

I pause before taking another bite of my burger and give him the "Are you a complete idiot?" stare.

"Fine, fine. I guess that would be awkward considering how well you were getting along with her niece yesterday," Jacob says slyly. "You and Amelia looked like you were having an enjoyable time out in the woods. *Alone.*"

I refuse to take the bait. "Speaking of," I say, "When do we start band practice?"

"How would I know?"

"We should probably figure that out soon because I told Amelia that you are our drummer."

Jacob sputters, nearly choking on his burger. "*You did what?*"

"Come on. You've played the drums for forever and used to be a regular at Sundown Grill. This is the least you can do. You're my wingman."

"First, I haven't played since college. Second, this is *your* attempt to make amends to Amelia, not mine."

"You laughed when I fell on her, and she thought you were laughing at her. This is your fault, too," I say, dragging a fry through my ketchup. "Plus, we can't have a band with just a guitar, a keyboard, and a singer. And you know you'll love jamming out at practice sessions in the garage with me, Dad, and Katie. Mom will even make some delicious home-cooked meals for all of us." I'm laying it on thick, but we need a drummer. Otherwise we'll be stuck with some cheesy pre-recorded percussion.

"Well, when you put it that way…" he trails off. "Your mom does make the best chocolate chip cookies I've ever eaten. I'll try the rehearsals if you can guarantee those will make an appearance. But I make no promises. I'm rusty."

"All you have to do is bang on drums with some sticks. Maybe sing backup. I'm the one putting my dignity on the line here."

"Ah, my favorite pair of troublemakers," a deep feminine voice cuts in. I look up to see The Boss, our editor-in-chief, Lauren, leaning over the edge of my cubicle. As always, she dominates any space she's in. Her dark hair is pulled into a low ponytail, not a hair out of place. With one crisp eyebrow raised, she says, "Hebert, I have a story for you. I need you to get down to the Chamber of Commerce in an hour. They have been lobbying for a grant to support the Allendale neighborhood park initiative and they finally landed it. Press conference starts at two. Bring a recorder. And Edwards," she says, turning to look at Jacob. "Grab a camera. You're going with him. I expect the story on my desk by four."

"You got it, boss," Jacob says.

She smirks, heels clicking as she continues her pass through the room, stopping by cubicles and checking in with reporters. We finish our burgers, and Jacob and I agree to meet at my car in thirty minutes. Once he leaves, I pull out my phone. I've typed up a text to Amelia but haven't mustered the courage to send it yet. Now or never. I close my eyes and hit "send," my stomach feeling like it's being yanked through the phone and flying through the wifi with the message.

Rhett: Looking forward to playing at the festival. Can we go to lunch to talk about the details?

Those three dots pop up on my screen, letting me know she's typing something back. And then they disappear. My heart drops. I'm pushing my luck. And just as I start to place my phone in my pocket in defeat, the screen lights up.

Amelia: Are you sure you wouldn't rather have Second Breakfast instead of lunch? :)

I smile, relief washing over me.

Rhett: Why don't we try for Elevenses? Lattes and Lagniappe tomorrow at 11?

Amelia: See you there.

I place my phone in my pocket, and for the first time, in a long time, I feel ... hopeful.

Chapter 11

AMELIA

Beth and I sit next to each other on a leather sofa in Janet's surgically clean office, careful not to so much as ruffle the designer rug under our feet. We're updating our boss on where we're at with the fall festival. Our plan for this meeting is to go in strong, highlighting our successes and downplaying anything that's not quite where it should be yet. With any luck, we'll avoid the infamous "Janet Jabs."

I begin by going over the list of new vendors who have agreed to be part of the event this year, noting the addition of several local businesses to the roster—fulfilling one of the Chamber of Commerce's major annual goals.

Per Aunt Margie's suggestion, I've channeled my creativity into seeking unexpected and exciting vendors. My first move was signing on a local farmer who brings petting zoos to children's birthday parties. This ensures that we not only have goats, but also miniature ponies and bunnies for the kids to pet and take photos with. The local Wildlife Refuge has also agreed to bring two owls and a falcon and give talks on area wildlife. (And bonus, they are already funded by a grant and have to do community educational programs to fulfill its terms!). And when Rhett and I have coffee tomorrow to finalize the band's needs, I plan to ask the owner of Lattes and Lagniappes to supply coffee and hot apple cider via their food truck. I smile, looking over what I've accomplished, my inner ostrich doing an awkward little flapping happy dance.

Beth's update is equally exciting. She's secured donations to give a dramatic facelift to the festival site with new signage and enhanced autumn decor, including scarecrows, hay bales, and even a staged area where festival-goers can stop for photo ops and selfies. My bestie has even presented an entire social media strategy, complete with a hashtag unique to the event.

We review our publicity budget and the most efficient and successful use of advertising funds so far. Janet sits through our entire presentation without a word, ice blue eyes impassive. I sigh inwardly, thinking we've done it. We've made it through and *actually impressed her*.

And then Janet levels her gaze at me. "And what about that Clark woman? Will she continue to be a problem?" A hint of intimidation lingers behind her cool words.

My stomach somersaults. I wonder if word has gotten back to her about our disastrous encounter or, even worse, the Great Chicken Tossing Battle between Ms. Clark and Aunt Margie. I steady myself, deciding then and there to proceed like Janet knows nothing. "We've, er, spoken to her. And although she's, um, certainly not pleasant, I don't think she will be a problem." Beth nudges my foot with hers in a show of solidarity. We're in this together, and knowing that gives me confidence.

After a beat, Janet pushes her platinum blonde hair behind her ear, looks at us, and nods. "Excellent progress. Let's meet again Monday to discuss advertising progress, ticketing, volunteers, security, and any other final details. We'll be ready to launch next weekend."

I can't believe that went so well, but I dare not let my astonishment show on my face. Beth keeps her poker face steady, as well. She subtly gives my hand a light squeeze as we stand and exit Janet's office together. Once we enter the elevator and the doors close, I let out a deep breath, look at Beth and say, "That went surprisingly well."

She grins in return. "I knew it would. Well, I hoped it would. I heard Janet was in a good mood about the success of the grant and good media showing at the press conference today. Plus, you are doing an amazing job, Lia. Wanna grab a PSL to celebrate?"

"You know me so well," I say, already tasting the sweet, spicy autumn goodness. Even better since the blazing Louisiana heat is finally starting to give way to hints of "pumpkin weather." These are my favorite days when the humidity drops and a cool breeze sifts through the air telling the leaves it's time to prepare for their fiery autumn transformation.

As we exit the elevator, I feel giddy with success. Just as we step into the lobby, the press conference ends, and we spy Rhett and Jacob across the wide space. They must be here covering it for the newspaper. Years of habit send me turning in the opposite direction when I see Rhett, but I pause. I promised I would try. And even though it's hard to stifle the habit of fleeing any time I've spotted Rhett around town in the past decade, I force myself to focus on the here and now - not the past, not the future. I focus on points of touch: my blazer resting on my shoulders, my ballet flats tapping the floor beneath my feet. *I can do this.* When they wave, Beth grabs my arm, and we navigate through the other reporters and people milling about the vast lobby to make our way over to them. As we walk, I realize that this actually isn't so bad. In fact, I might even be happy to see him. Hell hath officially frozen over.

"You were at the press conference? How did it go?" Beth asks when we finally get close to them.

"Oh, fine. Nothing outside of the ordinary," Rhett responds, hand reaching up to rub the back of his neck. "Though the neighborhood housing initiative receiving the grant sounds amazing. I can't wait to see how the Allendale neighborhood benefits from this."

And then he looks directly at me, and the side of his mouth lifts slightly, turning my heart into a hive of buzzing bees. I remember our brief time together yesterday and cautiously return the grin. I meet his gaze and say hesitantly, "We were just meeting with our boss to go over the festival details. I'm supposed to give all the band details to her on Monday. I can't thank you both enough for volunteering to perform."

"It's our pleasure," Jacob declares with a small theatrical bow. Rhett rolls his eyes at his friend and shakes his head good-naturedly.

"We're on our way to get pumpkin spice lattes to celebrate. Want to join?" Beth asks. But before they can answer, I hear an aggressive, masculine voice that sends nauseating chills up and down my spine until they collide in my gut.

"AMELIA! I knew you were here! Dammit, woman. Why have you been ignoring my calls and texts?"

Shit. Oh Shit. Not him. Not here. Not now.

Matt, my ex-boyfriend, is storming toward me with anger and righteous indignation coloring his features and veins bulging out of his neck. The same ex-boyfriend who was an alcoholic and went on drinking binges and then plowed his fists into coffee tables. The man who once grabbed me and threw me against a wall. The ex who found AA, sobered up, promised me a future together, and then left me.

It wasn't until months later, with the help of therapy and the support of Aunt Margie and Beth, that I realized how lucky I was to be free from that relationship. And that was about the time he started begging me to take him back. It started sweetly with flowers delivered to work and texts telling me how much he regretted what happened between us. Telling me how much he loved me. And when I didn't answer, the calls and texts turned threatening. I finally responded and told him I was seeing someone else—even though I wasn't—and to please leave me alone. I blocked his number, and I thought it was *finally* over. But now I watch in horror as this madman pushes past the receptionist at the welcome desk, yelling at me across the lobby. His voice echoes and fills the space. And I realize my assumption was very, *very* wrong.

I hear Beth whisper, "Shit," and watch as she bravely maneuvers herself in front of me. I begin to panic and look for an escape—any way out of this confrontation. It feels like a racehorse is pounding through my chest, crushing my lungs beneath its hooves. Blackness creeps in at the edges of my vision. When I turn, I notice Rhett has moved to stand beside me, concern clouding his features.

A wild idea born out of desperation and false promises leaps through my synapses. And before I can stop to think it through, I lean into him and whisper urgently, "Can I kiss you?"

Confusion darts across his face, and then he nods. Leaning in, I tilt my head up and press my lips to his. He doesn't hesitate, wrapping one arm around my back and placing his other hand on my cheek. The kiss is soft, warm, sweetsweet—a minty tang coasts on the wave of his breath and floods into my own.

I intend for this kiss to be quick, a way to prove to Matt that I've moved on, that he and I are unequivocally over. But then Rhett's lips begin moving in earnest against mine, *kissing me*. Really kissing, the kind that is filled with passion and fire and a hint of things to come if we let this ember between us simmer any longer.

"What the actual fuck?" I hear Matt grate out, an angry rumble I've heard many times before rounding out the edges of his words. I can't help it. I wince and pull away from Rhett, shaking as fear and adrenaline slam into my veins. Instinctually, I fall into old habits, anxious to do anything to calm Matt down and diffuse the situation. I have to look at him over the shoulders of Beth and Jacob, both of whom have formed a protective barricade. Rhett lets go of me and pushes through the two of them to step directly up to Matt, anger and passion fueling the fire in his gaze and assertiveness in his posture. I've never seen Rhett like this before, and his protectiveness makes my heart thud heavily in my chest.

"Do you have a problem?" I hear Rhett say with quiet resolve.

"Hell yeah, I have a problem!" Matt threatens, leaning uncomfortably into Rhett's space. "My girl Amelia here has been ignoring my phone calls and texts!" His yelling is draws a crowd of bystanders who glance at one another nervously. I see Rita, our receptionist, hit the security button.

Rhett glances back at me, his eyes darting to take in my appearance. He notices my trembling hands and the tears I'm struggling to keep down. As he turns back to Matt, his posture becomes more assertive, his body expanding to take up more space. "I don't think she wants to talk to you," Rhett says with deadly calm. "I think you should leave before we call the police."

Jacob steps up beside Rhett, folding his arms in solidarity. Rhett is tall, well-built, and intimidating, but Jacob stands several inches above him. And while I'm used to seeing Jacob with an easy disposition and smile on his face, seeing him angry makes me want to turn tail and run. Matt looks back and forth between the two of them. His face is flushed, his hair mussed, and he's struggling to keep upright. The smell of Scotch wafts off of him like he fell into a barrel of the stuff. I cover my nose and close my eyes, trying to bury my head in the sand again. I start choking on sobs as memories of Matt's rage toward me comes flooding back. I fold into myself behind the protective wall of my friends and hate myself for my cowardice.

Matt leans toward Rhett like he's about to confide some great secret and nearly falls over. He catches himself on Rhett's shoulder and then says viciously, voice slurring, "I'd stay away from that little bitch if I were you. She may fuck well, but that's about all she's good for."

Between one breath and the next, Rhett slams his fist into Matt's face. I look on in silent shock as Matt hits the marble floor, grabbing his nose and screaming as blood gushes out. Two security officers show up then, jogging over to where we stand.

"What's happening here?" the tall Hispanic male officer asks, taking in the screaming man rolling on the floor.

"This.." Rhett motions to Matt screaming on the floor, "Person… walked into the lobby screaming and threatening Amelia. He's drunk and belligerent. And when he became increasingly threatening, I, well, I acted in self-defense and subdued him." His voice is serious and confident. A distant part of my mind can't believe this is the same man I've been joking with about *Lord of the Rings*. The security officer eyes Rhett closely, looks down and notices the blood on his knuckles.

"It's true," an older man chimes in. "That fella came in here screaming and cursing. He scared all of us half to death." Several others nod in affirmation. The security guards bend down and work together to lift Matt, escorting him outside as he writhes in their arms.

Despite my best efforts to swallow back the tears, I tremble and quietly sob. I feel a hand gently rub my lower back and look up through swollen eyes to see Rhett beside me.

"Hey, it's going to be okay. They got him out of here," he whispers as he presses a light, soothing kiss into my temple. I turn into him, seeking comfort, a place to hide from the embarrassing scene playing out around me. His arms come up around me, his strong body and warm, spicy pine scent enveloping me. And then I feel Beth's small arms wrap around my back, the two of them forming a Lia sandwich. The three of us stand together, me sobbing and the two of them cradling me, offering a small moment of privacy and comfort. I don't know how they understand that this is exactly what I need, but I take it, take them both.

"Ma'am, are you okay?" The words sound far away, like someone trying to speak to me while I'm underwater. I blink a couple of times as Rhett and Beth step back. The fluorescent lights of the lobby and all the people standing around murmuring are jarring. The security officer stands there, waiting for my answer. I nod slowly. "Do you want to press charges?" he asks.

"I, I don't know," I say, folding my arms and pressing them to my center, my stomach in knots. He nods and hands me a business card. "We're going to take him down to the station for public drunkenness and further questioning. Call this number if you want to move forward with charges."

I take the card from him and stick it in my pocket.

"Come on. I'll drive you home," Beth says soothingly, taking me gently by the arm and guiding me out the side door. My entire body is coiled tight, and tears form slow rivers down my cheeks, but I glance back. I can't help it. Rhett and Jacob are watching us, sympathy showing in the turn of their mouths and dips of their eyebrows. They are debating whether or not they should follow us, but Beth says, "I've got her." I let her guide me. It's easier that way, and right now, I just want something, anything, to be easy.

TUCKER IS WAITING TO GREET US at the door when we get home. My faithful, furry friend always knows when I need him most. I collapse on my couch, and he crawls into my lap, resting his head on my chest, just like he used to when he was a puppy. I hear Beth in the kitchen, and a few minutes later, she walks into the living room with a pair of steaming mugs of coffee. Sitting next to me on the couch, she hands one over. Tucker retreats from my personal space, settling into the space between Beth and me to soak up optimal dog pats. Both of us take comfort in his soothing presence. "I don't deserve you," I finally say to Beth.

"Oh honey, give yourself a little more credit than that. We deserve each other."

Beth and I have sat like this on my couch more times than I can count. She has listened to me pour my heart out about my troubled relationships with patience and kindness, always ready to offer comfort and coffee. Over the years, I've been tempted to believe good men don't exist. Between my absent father and string of terrible ex-boyfriends, kind and supportive men seem to only exist in Hallmark movies and romance novels. But when I hear Beth talk about Dan, it gives me hope. And, after today, I'm happy to latch on to that small glimmer.

Finally, Beth breaks the silence. "Okay… That was intense."

I see Matt's aggressive posture and filthy words in my mind and shudder. "I know. I can't believe he showed up at my work like that, screaming and cursing…" I trail off.

Beth shudders, casting her eyes down as her mouth tightens. She's furious. Inside her small frame is an angry ninja waiting to unleash on my ex. But, as she always does, she puts my needs above her own desire to rant about all the ways she wants to end him.

As I discreetly study my friend, I see the moment she shoves aside her fury. Closing her eyes, she visibly relaxes. And when she opens them again, there's nothing but love there. I really don't deserve her.

She smiles with determination. "I mean, yeah, that *was* intense, but I'm talking about that smoking hot kiss with Rhett! Where did that come from? What did I miss?"

"Um," I stutter, feeling embarrassed. But I know what she's doing —she's distracting us both from Matt and the clusterfuck that just went down at work. And even though kissing Rhett is the last thing I want to contemplate right now, I let her steer the conversation. "Oh, that was nothing. I needed him to help me convince Matt that I had moved on. That's all." I don't even sound convincing to myself.

"Honey, you could have done that with a peck on the cheek. *That* was passion." Her eyes are alight. "And for what it's worth, I've met all the men in your life over the past several years. And the only one I've ever approved of before today was Tucker here." Tucker looks up, tail thumping at the mention of his name. "But Rhett? I do believe I approve."

"There is nothing to approve of," I say a little too quickly, cheeks coloring.

"Lia, don't be embarrassed. If I weren't already hitched to Dr. Sasquatch, I'd be making the moves on him myself! He's cute. But, more importantly, he's kind and looks at you like you're a cold glass of iced tea on the Fourth of July. And when he went all Hulk smash and punched Matt in the nose, I nearly swooned and kissed him myself."

"It's not like that with us," I demure. "At least, I don't think so. Lord knows I'm not a good judge of character when it comes to men, but anyone who knows the eating schedule of hobbits can't be all that bad." I say with false courage, a half-smile tilting my lips.

"What the hell is the eating schedule of hobbits?" she asks in confusion. "Are those some kind of wild animals?"

I laugh. "Oh, Beth. Do you live under a rock? One of these days, I'll get you to marathon *The Lord of the Rings* movies with me. Until then, you'll have to trust me on this one."

Chapter 12

RHETT

Plop. A glob of crunchy peanut butter falls off my spoon and right onto the middle of my t-shirt. *Damnit.* I scoop it up with my spoon and shove it in my mouth before leaning forward and sitting the jar on my coffee table. Leaning back into my second-hand couch – thanks, mom and dad – I try to focus on the college football recaps on the screen in front of me. Usually, the purple and gold LSU jerseys hold my attention better than nearly anything else on the planet, but not tonight.

No, tonight I'm still buzzing with the adrenaline from my confrontation with that guy at the Chamber of Commerce. *What the hell even was that?* And why was he after Amelia like he was ready to grab her by the hair and drag her out of there caveman style? He fucking terrified her – transforming Amelia into a shell of herself. I want to punch him again.

Without warning, thoughts and emotions of my past explode in my mind… the way Chels used to scream at me lash across my brain. And with it comes all the lingering shame, hurt and crippling depression. I can't stop digging my finger into that old wound, replaying how she would get so angry with me for no real reason. How she'd scream, rage, and cry until I was begging for her to forgive me just to get her to chill the fuck down. Just so I could escape the barrage of hysterics and find a quiet place to stare out a window, strum my guitar, and exist in peace for a while.

Giving up on watching football, I turn the TV off and briefly consider picking up my guitar and playing some screaming heavy metal. But then I remember that it's nearly midnight, and my downstairs neighbors would likely call the police. Instead, I head to the second bedroom of my apartment, where I keep my workout equipment. There's a treadmill, weight bench, and free weights. Lying down on the weight bench, I go for low weights and high reps so I don't hurt myself lifting while I'm upset. I let my mind drift to counting the reps, the seconds of rest in between, then starting over again. When I finally wear myself out, I get up, arms shaking with fatigue, and hit the shower.

By the time I finally make it to bed, I've burned all of my adrenaline off, and my mind can settle and sift through the day's events a little better. I replay it all, and that's when I finally let go of all the built-up anger and frustration to focus on the most amazing part of my day: that kiss.

When Amelia asked if she could kiss me, I wasn't sure why she wanted to at first, but there was no way in hell I was going to tell her no. I have been dreaming about kissing her since I was eleven, and I'm still not entirely sure that I didn't hallucinate that whole part of the day. Because even though it only lasted a moment, it was hot. Her lips felt better than every fantasy I've ever had of us together. And did I imagine her melting into me?

I revisit every second – the feel of my hand against her back, the press of her cheek. She must have been chewing gum recently because she tasted minty and sweet. I feel heat pull low in my abdomen and grab a cool pillow, pressing it into my face. I reluctantly admit that she probably only kissed me to keep that asshole away, not because she *wanted* me. I don't blame her, though. And even though I would love to kiss her again, I'm glad I could at least do something to help her today.

Feeling self-indulgent, I sink into the fantasy of a future with Amelia: Holding her hand, watching movies together, laughing over morning coffee, sharing a bed… Maybe one day I can win her over. I remember that we have plans to chat over coffee tomorrow, and I wonder if she still wants to meet up. Maybe she still needs time to recover from the trauma of today. Hell, I can't blame her for that. I reach over and grab my phone off my nightstand. *Is it weird if I text her? It's normal if I check on her, right? I mean, I was there when it happened.* Before I can talk myself out of it, I pull up her number.

Rhett: Hey, there, hobbit. You ok?

Those little dots pop up almost immediately, and desire and elation fill my chest.

Amelia: Who's calling who a hobbit? Pretty sure you're the one who knows how to play the LoTR theme song Samwise.

Rhett: First, I am not a chubby sidekick. Second, you are definitely a hobbit, short stuff.

A moment passes before she responds.

Amelia: Thank you for today. It was kind of you to stand up for me.

Rhett: It was nothing. Anyone with half a heart would have done the same.

Amelia: I guess I'm lucky that you have at least half a heart.

Rhett: You wound me.

Amelia: Seriously, though. Thank you.

Rhett: You're welcome. Are we still on for coffee tomorrow?

Amelia: Of course. Need to get this band stuff settled.

My heart sinks a little at that. Just band stuff. But I can practically hear her wry tone through her texts, and it reassures me.

Amelia: See you at 11. Good night.

Chapter 13

AMELIA

The temperatures are finally starting to ease into a semblance of autumn as I stand outside Lattes and Lagniappe. The breeze dances through my hair. I left it down today, letting my natural chestnut waves do what they will. I even took the extra time to put on a little bit of makeup. But that has nothing to do with kissing Rhett yesterday. Or our texts last night. Absolutely nothing. And, yea, I'm in full-on awkward ostrich mode in my head. *Don't be weird, Lia.*

I walk into the coffee shop taking in the white textured walls and gray floors, eyes lingering on the art and photography contributed by local artists that bring bright spots of color to the space. As I scan the room, my gaze snags on Rhett already seated at a small table, laptop open. He looks up and spots me, his lips quirking in a half smile. And oh my gosh, he has *a dimple.* My heartbeat ticks up a notch. *Stop it, Lia. Stop it. You are here to talk about his band, not fixate on dimples. No, a single, perfect, delicious dimple.*

He closes his computer and stands, tucking a hand in one pocket. He walks over, gaze darting between the floor and me. I'm not the only one who feels awkward today.

"Hey there, hobbit. What can I get you?" He smiles a bit bashfully. I can tell he's relishing calling me "hobbit" but unsure how it will go over face-to-face. I don't make him wait long, however.

"Nice to see you again, Samwise. I'll have a pumpkin spice latte, of course." I hope he doesn't hear the slight tremor in my voice. When his grin broadens to encompass his entire face, my inner ostrich starts running around, flapping her gigantic wings inside my body. *Do not be awkward, Lia.* I coach myself again. *The kiss wasn't even a real kiss. He probably hasn't even thought about it since it happened. Do NOT think about the kiss.*

"What's your poison?" I ask.

"Cappuccino for me. And one of their amazing chocolate croissants."

We wait in line to place our orders in silence, and I can't stand it. I try to fill the space. "So, have you figured out your setlist for the festival weekends yet?"

"Not exactly," he replies, shoulders shrugging. My eyes snag on his shoulder muscles pressing against his t-shirt before I quickly look away. "But I'm working on it. We'll be ready. Any requests?"

"Hmmm." I have to rein my focus back to the topic at hand and clear my throat. "Well, the usuals. 'Monster Mash' is always a hit. 'Werewolves of London.' Any fun, spooky stuff the kids can dance to. Feel free to mix in popular songs, too."

"I should be taking notes."

"Probably," I deadpan.

He looks at me to see if I'm joking, and when he realizes I am, he relaxes a bit. Then, in a mock serious tone that matches my own, I hear him quietly say, "Sure thing, boss."

Once our orders are ready, we make our way back to Rhett's table. We settle into the small two-person space, knees bumping as we pull our chairs in. The contact is a little unsettling. I simultaneously want to jerk away and press my leg into his and hold it there.

He starts to show me the list of sound equipment he needs on his laptop, but I cut him off.

"Before we talk about the logistics for the festival, I want to apologize for what happened with Matt yesterday. I mean, that guy who… um." I stumble over my words, anxious to get this over with. I hate talking or even thinking about Matt, but I have to do this. Rhett starts to respond, but I stop him. "Let me just get this out, please." He nods and sits back. I continue, "I had no idea he would show up at my work. After I blocked his calls and texts, I thought he got the freaking hint, and I'm sorry that I put you in the position of feeling like you had to confront him. And, um, well, I'm sorry about the kiss."

There. I got it all out. I look down at my fidgeting hands, studying my freshly painted fingernails as I wait for his response.

"Why?" he starts, and my stomach lurches.

"Why are you apologizing? You did nothing wrong. If anything, I should probably be apologizing to you for decking the guy, but I don't feel sorry. He deserved it. Anyone who would assault you, or anyone else for that matter, and make you feel that way deserves worse."

I look up, staring at the color infusing his cheeks. I'm stunned at the quiet passion behind his words. He swallows, closes his eyes, takes a deep breath then looks at me steadily.

"Speaking of apologies and people who made you feel terrible. I owe you a long-overdue one. An apology, I mean." I watch him steady himself, and then my brain finally catches up with what he's saying.

"Oh no, please, Rhett. You don't…"

"No, I do. I should have done this years ago." My heart drums in my ears. I do not want to revisit that day, but he listened to me. Hell, he let me kiss him. I can listen to this. I think. Already I feel embarrassment and shame snaking their way through my veins, urging me to run out of the coffee shop. I start focusing on my points of touch: thighs on the chair, wrists on the table, fingertips on the coffee mug.

"Here goes nothing," he whispers to himself as if in prayer. Then, with sincerity wrapping around each of his words, he looks me straight in the eyes and continues. "I am so sorry for what happened between us in high school. I never meant to run into you, or for everything that came after. I am a complete cowardly asshole for letting you take the heat and embarrassment. I should have stood up to the guys and," he gulps, swallows, tries again. "And to Chels." He pales but continues. "You deserved more than that awful school gave you. I failed you that day and the year that followed, and I've regretted it every day since. I don't deserve your forgiveness, but I hope you'll let me try to make it up to you."

My emotions churn, a kicked anthill with its colony of insects teeming in chaotic, frantic patterns. That day was one of those defining moments where every single detail is imprinted permanently in the folds of my brain. How Rhett knocked me over, landed on top of me and basically felt me up. The moment when the entire high school population zeroed in on us. How all his baseball buddies laughed as they scooped up my scattered tampons that flew across the hallway and pretended they were guns, mock shooting at each other. What Chelsea, the head cheerleader, said to me before taking Rhett on her arm and guiding him away. How I fled to the sound of catcalling and laughter…

I'm struggling to process what Rhett just said to me as all those long-buried memories simultaneously flood my mind. He seems entirely sincere, and it's… unexpected. I thought that was just another day for him, one that happened, and he instantly forgot as he went on with his life. Those thoughts of his complete ambivalence to my humiliation are what continued to fuel my anger and resentment towards him over the years. I never imagined he felt guilty or even cared how I might feel. A heavy silence has settled between us.

"Well… say something," he whispers across the table.

"I don't know what to say."

He dips his head and nods.

"But, for what it's worth, I *don't* think you're an asshole." He looks up at me, eyebrows furrowed, expression teetering on hopeful. "I mean, I totally did back then. And honestly, I have ever since. I actually thought you were a huge asshole when you fell into me again last week and laughed at me." He winces.

"But the other day, with you falling on me, was actually my overly enthusiastic dog's fault." I wince with this admission but press on.

"And volunteering to play at the festival, standing up for me yesterday, checking on me last night… I think you might actually have a big, soft heart somewhere in that big body of yours. And." I gulp, take a deep breath and start again. "And maybe it would be good for us to start with a clean slate. We're will be working together over the next few weeks after all."

"Thank you," he finally says. "For giving me a chance." I feel his knee press against mine under the table, and my heart leaps into my throat. I'm not sure if the touch is accidental, but it feels oddly comforting. So I leave my leg where it is, just barely pressing back.

I nod and take a sip of my latte, my eyes lingering on the way his jaw clenches and releases, the column of his throat as he swallows. I clear my throat, forcing myself to focus on why we're here. "Now that that's settled. Let's talk about what you need in terms of sound equipment."

Over the next thirty minutes, he shares what the band needs while I take notes. Then we chat about a potential set list while he types it up to share with Jacob, his dad, and his sister. He's a fan of rock classics that hint at witches and ghosts. I try to convince him to take on some cheesy Halloween classics like "Monster Mash" and "Witch Doctor."

We fall into easy conversation, laughing at song suggestions, wincing at others. Attempting to make his case for song choices, Rhett sings a few bars from "Witchy Woman." And the sounds of his rich, raspy baritone melts through the clanging dishes and whooshing of espresso machines around us. I'm transfixed, his voice sliding from the depths of his soul and straight into my body. It wraps around my shoulders like a warm winter scarf, sliding down into my gut like a smoldering ember until its heat pulses through my whole body. No one this handsome has the right to sound this good.

When he stops singing, he looks at me. "Do you think something like that would work for the festival?"

I close my mouth, realizing that it's been hanging open the entire time he sang. I try to swallow and half choke. *Awkward ostrich. Dammit.*

"I can go with something else if that doesn't work," he says. But I frantically shake my head no.

Clearing my throat, I try again. "Sorry. Choked on my, um…" I glance around desperately, eyes landing on my cup. "I choked on my coffee. Anyway. You're perfect. I mean, that sounded perfect. For the festival, I mean." I can feel all my insecurities trying to claw their way back into my chest again as I sit across the table from this man with a voice made of smoke and magic.

"That's a relief," he says with a half smile. And there goes that damn dimple again.

As our meeting draws to its natural close, I feel confident that the band portion of the festival will be a success. Just as I'm about to push out of my chair to leave, Rhett says, "One more thing before you go. I wanted to let you know that I'm working on a story for the newspaper. I'm looking at an old cold case about a boy who went missing from the fall festival nearly twenty years ago. Who knows if anything will come of it all these years later, but I just wanted you to know because I'll be out at the festival site from time to time as I research."

"Oh. I've never heard of that case," I say, intrigued. "That shouldn't be a problem. Good luck with your research."

"Thanks," he says as we get up from the table. As he packs his laptop away, he looks at me and says, "I'll actually be out there tomorrow. I'm meeting my colleague, Dr. Black, near the woods. Maybe I'll see you?"

"Maybe," I say. He walks toward the door and then realizes I'm not with him. When he looks back, confused, I say, "Oh, I'm hanging back to talk to the owner about having a food truck at the festival."

"I guess I'll see you around then," he says with a hesitant smile, the bell above the door tinkling as he opens it and steps outside into the golden sunshine.

"I hope so," I whisper to myself as I continue to stare at the door long after he's gone.

Chapter 14

RHETT

As soon as I park at the festival site the next day, I scan the grounds for Amelia and look for her car, but no luck. I'm meeting Dr. Black in a little over an hour to try out the GPR and get her opinion on the old case, but I thought I'd get here and walk around a bit first, clear my head… maybe bump into Amelia.

Turning off my truck, I open the door, climb out and stretch my arms above my head. I'm sore from my workout, so I roll my shoulders and decide to hike around a bit to loosen up. As I walk, I notice a lot of work has been done in preparation for the festival launch. A new hand-painted, wooden sign hangs above the barn doors with "Boutique Barn" written in a bold, black script. The barn doors have been painted, and lights hang around them.

As I approach the barn, I see a dog poke its nose out of the doors and bellow at me. I recognize that dog as the one who shoved me into his owner a couple of days ago and smile. She's here. "Tucker! Come here, boy!" a voice calls from inside the barn. Leaning down to pet the pup's head, I peer inside and I'm amazed at what I see.

The festival team has been busy. All of the muck has been cleaned off the barn floors, and string lights have been draped along the walls where they meet the ceiling. Even the horse stalls that line the back wall have signs hanging off them, denoting vendor names. I can't remember the last time I've seen this place look this sharp—probably because it's *never* looked this good.

"Oh, Rhett, hey!" I hear someone call. I see Beth up on a ladder hanging more string lights, a tall, dark-haired man holding it, so she doesn't fall. She waves me over. "This is my husband, Dan," she says with a grin. He reaches out to shake my hand.

"Here to help hang lights?" Beth asks. It comes out more of a demand than a question.

"I can if you need me to," I reply.

"Good. There's a box of them in the corner and another ladder in the back. Amelia is setting up vendor booths in the old horse stalls. The two of you can work together to hang the lights above them."

Eager for any excuse to see Amelia, I grab the box and make my way to the back of the barn, looking for her. I hear her humming to herself as I spot movement in one of the stalls. Walking over, I peer inside and see that she's bent over a box, digging for something. Her earbuds are in, and she's humming and sort of dancing, butt in the air. She is completely oblivious to my presence. I pause and take in the scene before me, admiring her beautiful, curvy behind. Bent over like that, my mind immediately goes to a place it probably shouldn't.

"Oh shit, Rhett! You scared me to death!" she yells as she turns and spots me. She is blushing, big time. "How long were you standing there?" she squeaks.

"I just got here. I was, uh, trying to figure out how to get your attention without scaring you."

"Well, major fail," she says, irritated, a blush flaring in her cheeks.

I chuckle at the sight of her all flushed and rumpled, breathing hard. I let my gaze slide over her, then check myself. I hold up the box of lights and fix my eyes on hers.

"I stopped by to work on that story but got here early. When I poked my head in the barn, Beth asked me to help. Actually, I don't think she would have accepted 'no' as an answer. So... want to hang some lights?"

I watch Amelia collect herself and nod, dusting her hands off on her denim shorts. "Um, sure. Let me grab the ladder."

I follow her to the end of the line of stalls and pick up the ladder leaning there. As I set it up, she asks, "Do you want to hang lights or pass them up to me and hold the ladder?" she asks.

You're the decorator, not me. I'll stay on the ground and catch you if you fall."

"So chivalrous of you," she deadpans.

I set the ladder up at the beginning of the row. She climbs up, and I hand her the staple gun and the beginning of the light strand. What I didn't anticipate, though, is that the stalls are much lower to the ground than the edge of the barn walls. So when Amelia climbs up the ladder to start hanging lights, her ass is directly at my eye level. *Well shit.*

I try to be a gentleman. Mostly. I divert my eyes as I bend down to gather more lights, but every time I rise to hand them up to Amelia, I come face to face with that beautiful behind. For her part, Amelia seems completely oblivious, stapling lights to the tops of the stalls, moving the ladder, climbing down and back up again. But I'm struggling to avert my eyes and to hide my desire. When we finally get to the end of the line of stalls, I look down at my watch and realize it's nearly time to meet Dr. Black.

"Got somewhere to be?" Amelia asks.

"Meeting my former history professor today to discuss this ground penetrating radar technology. Shouldn't take more than an hour, though. Will you still be here afterward?"

"I don't think I'm going anywhere for a while," she laments. "Too much to do before the festival opens next weekend."

"I'll stop by before I leave and see if you need any more help," I offer.

"Oh, that sounds great," she says, a little surprised.

DR. BLACK AND I STAND out in the field near the woods with a machine that looks like a suped-up lawnmower.

"I'm not sure if this will help your research," she says. "But I'll let you give it a try." She walks me through the process of how to use the GPR. "The problem is that you really need to have an idea of the location of what you're searching for," she says. She eyes me, dark brown eyes cutting me down just like they did years ago when I sat in her lecture hall. "And it sounds like you have absolutely no idea where or even what you're looking for."

I rub my hand through my hair, abashed.

She continues, "You know I'm only here because I owe you for that big story you published on the work we're doing at the university. Louisiana Tech's history program is growing, and I've been able to share that article with potential students." Then she smiles, her demeanor softening. "So here's what we're going to do. You push the GPR and start talking. Tell me what you're looking for."

And so I do. I tell her about stumbling on the old cold case, about the itchy feeling that ran under my skin when I found it, about the hunch I can't shake. I explain how important this story would be personally and, hopefully, for the community. I go into all the details I know about the case while she listens in silence. When I finally finish, she puts her hand on my shoulder, pausing my work, and turns me to face her. I look down at Dr. Black's serious face, ready for her to tell me that I'm an idiot and she has better things to do with her time, but she surprises me.

"I remember when that happened," she says somberly. "The community was… in mourning." Dr. Black looks down at the ground, lost in her own thoughts for several moments. Finally, she looks up at me, lines deepening around her eyes. "Rhett, I don't think GPR is the answer here—though I'm happy to share all the results of whatever we find."

Disappointment rushes through me in a crushing wave.

"But," she says. "I know something, or should I say *someone*, who might help." I see hesitation written across her face. She glances across the field to the old, ramshackle house at the edge of the festival property line. The home of our resident chicken thrower. "You should talk to Greta Clark," she finally says.

"You mean the crazy old woman who lives in *that* house?" I say incredulously.

"You might be a little crazy too if your grandson went missing without a trace," she says with a cold stare.

My brain goes into a tailspin with those words. *Is she saying what I think she's saying?*

"Wait, you mean, the Roberts boy is, was…"

"Her grandson? Yes. And she was there the night he went missing."

MY MIND IS REELING AS I walk back to the barn. *Ms. Clark was Jimmy Roberts' grandmother? No wonder she hates the fall festival. I have to talk to her… if she'll even consider it. I have to tell Amelia. She needs to know. This explains so much. Ms. Clark's attitude. It may even be connected to the festival's decline. How did she… how did so many of us not realize?*

When I walk into the barn, Amelia, Margie, Beth, and Dan are sorting fall decor into piles. I feel dazed when they all look up, their eyebrows knitting in concern.

"Amelia, can I talk to you?" I manage to ask. I know I need to share this bombshell with someone, and she's the only one I want to talk to right now. Her presence feels right, comforting.

"I'll come with you," Margie says, sitting down the scarecrow she's holding.

"It's okay," Amelia says as she follows me outside the barn.

I stare at Amelia, taking in the concern on her face. "Well, I think I've uncovered the answers to two mysteries. I know why Ms. Clark is so staunchly against this festival, and I think I may know at least one reason it's been difficult to revive."

She looks at me, eyes darting around my face, trying to figure out what I'm talking about.

"I…" I take a deep breath, close my eyes and try again. "I just talked to Dr. Black. Told her everything about the story I'm researching, what I'm hoping to find. And you know what she said?"

Amelia silently shakes her head.

"She told me the missing boy is… was…. Ms. Clark's grandson. Shit. Amelia. That's why she's doing this. Why she's trying to sabotage everything. And I don't blame her. I can't even imagine. She must think–rightfully so–that everyone has forgotten. That no one gives a shit about what happened to her grandson twenty years ago."

"Oh," she says, hand rising to her mouth. "I should tell Aunt Margie and Beth. I don't know if I should tell Janet, though. Rhett, are you going to try to talk to Ms. Clark for your story?"

I gaze into those beautiful, big, brown eyes full of curiosity and empathy for the woman woman who yelled at her, who tried to sabotage her work. A woman everyone has misread. I nod.

"Are you sure that's a good idea?" she whispers. My mind replays Amelia screaming at her car. I remember the gumbo pot and the angrily thrown chicken. This is going to suck. I'll be lucky if I walk away from the encounter with my balls still in place.

"Yes. I have to," I finally say.

Her eyes continue to search my face, looking for some truth that I don't understand. Finally, she nods. "Okay. I want to go with you… if you want me to, that is. But first, let's go sit down somewhere and talk this through. You have to tell me what you know."

I nod in agreement and follow her back inside.

THIS TRUCE AMELIA AND I have formed is fragile. But she listens intently as we sit in one of the old horse stalls. I wonder aloud, "Do I just show up on Ms. Clark's doorstep and say, 'Hi, you don't know me, but I'd like to talk to you about your grandson who went missing twenty years ago?' How stupid am I to *not even consider* the Roberts boy might still have family here. That's base-level research."

"Rhett," she says, reaching out to lightly touch my forearm and catch my gaze. The jolt of her skin on mine zips through me. I look into her eyes and see the encouragement there. So different from Chels, who would have made fun of me. I can just hear her now. "*Well of course he still has family here, ya dumbass.*" The words rolling off her tongue with contempt and a hint of false humor. But with Amelia, there's no belittling, no taunting. I drag myself out of the past, planting myself into the here and now.

"Don't beat yourself up," she says. "This is a lead. This is *good news.* Your intuition was right. It helped guide you here." She says it with so much certainty that I almost believe her.

She stares at me a little longer, a question lighting her eyes. Amelia seems to come to a decision, and, slowly, she eases forward and wraps her arms around me in a tight hug. It takes me a moment to recognize that she's offering me support. I close my eyes and settle into her embrace, letting the comfort she offers seep into my skin, my bones. I lean forward and rest my nose in her hair and inhale. Coffee, pumpkin spice, sweat, and hay. Amelia. My heartbeat slows as I sink into the hug, wrapping my arms around her in return. But the longer we sit here embracing, the more aware I become of all the places her body presses into mine. And while it's a welcome distraction, I am better than this, bigger than this. I push back and look at her. "Thank you," I whisper.

And then she glances around the corner of the horse stall. I realize that she's listening to someone talk. And it's not Beth, Dan, or Margie. I turn my head and listen intently. I recognize the voice—and my stomach drops.

Chapter 15

AMELIA

"What is it?" I notice Rhett paling at the sound of the voice outside the horse stall. I lean over and see a woman talking to Aunt Margie. She's gorgeous, tall, dark hair just beginning to turn gray, slicked back into a low ponytail. She's dressed pristinely in a suit and looks slightly out of place in a barn next to Aunt Margie in dust-coated overalls. But she's smiling at Aunt Margie.

"We have to get out of here," Rhett whispers urgently.

"What? Why?"

"That's my boss," Rhett says. "And I may have told her that I was sick today so I could bail on an evening story and help out here instead," he says sheepishly.

"Amelia? Are you still here?" Aunt Margie calls out. I look at Rhett, and he shakes his head in an emphatic no. I grab his hand, and we duck down to escape out the back exit of the barn. But the footsteps are approaching quickly now. There is no way we are making an escape without being seen, so I aim for the nearby equipment closet. I duck in, pulling Rhett in behind me. I ease the door closed, leaving only a small crack so we can both hear what's happening outside it.

I forgot how small this space is, though. Its only purpose is to hold mucking equipment and a few spare cleaning supplies. With both of us in here, there is barely any room to move. We are pressed up tightly against one another, chest to chest, legs to legs, hips to hips. We're breathing loudly, both trying to stifle any noise. I lean into Rhett so I can see through the crack in the door.

"Amelia?" Aunt Margie calls, confused as she emerges from where we were just sitting in the horse stall. "That's weird. I could have sworn she was just here. I guess she stepped out for something."

"It's okay," the other voice says, reassuring. "I can meet her another day."

"What's happening?" Rhett whispers. I shush him.

"Don't look so upset, Margie. This story we're working on is about you. I feel honored that you want me to meet your niece. But it's okay, really. We'll figure it out another time. I'm sure I'll be back out here at some point."

They move closer to us. I hold my breath, my head pressed to Rhett's chest. I can hear his heart thundering against my ear, and I know mine is doing the same. My nose is filled with his soapy, woodsy scent, masculine and earthy, and I allow myself to breathe it in and enjoy it for a moment. Then I feel him bury his nose in my hair, and my entire body locks up, rigid as a mannequin.

Their conversation continues outside the closet door. "Thank you for coming by, Lauren," I hear Aunt Margie say. "I know this place isn't really your style."

"It's fine!" she says. "I've been reporting a long time and been to every place you can imagine. This barn feels homey—like the perfect place for your big official launch." *What the hell is she talking about?* I think. *Launch what? And what could Aunt Margie possibly be doing to draw the newspaper's editor out here? I'm half tempted to burst out of the closet and run up to them to demand answers, but the way I'm pressed against Rhett right now... well, I'd be lying to myself if I said I wanted to leave.*

I feel Rhett's arms cautiously wrap around my back, pressing me even closer to him. I respond in reflex, wrapping my arms around him. I'm not sure what we're doing, but I like how it feels.

"Don't move yet," I whisper. "I can still see them, and we need to make sure they're gone." He nods into my hair. We stay like that, locked in an embrace for several more minutes.

He leans down and whispers, "Probably just a little longer." I nod. The feeling of his warm breath whispering against my ear combined with his body pressed into mine sends waves of desire coursing through my body. My mind logs every point of contact: my breasts pressed against his solid chest, his hips pressed to mine, the slow circles he's rubbing on my lower back. Fire sears through my veins. I feel his nose press against the side of my neck, and I tilt my head to the side, inviting him in. He accepts the invitation, and I feel his lips graze the side of my neck, making a slow, barely there, trail up to my pulse point. I turn my head into him, and his nose bumps mine. We're both breathing heavily, and I can feel his exhales brush my lips. We're so close like this. One move, and our lips would touch. But he doesn't move and I am incapable of shifting my body, unsure of what he wants, what I want.

I feel his hand come up to press against my cheek, his thumb tracing my cheekbone. He's slow, deliberate, giving me time to pull away if I want to. "Can I kiss you?" he whispers, echoing my question from two days ago. And my mouth answers before I have time to think it through. "Yes," I say on an exhale.

And then his lips are on mine, slow at first, brushing my mouth lightly. I adjust to their feel under his gentle exploration. It's cautious and teasing, and it's driving me crazy. I can tell he's hesitating, not wanting to scare me, so I lean into him, pressing my lips firmly against his own. He groans, and then our mouths are moving together, hunger fueling our movements. His teeth lightly nip my lower lip, and I let out a moan, opening for him. He gently tilts my head back, deepening the kiss, tongue stroking mine in warm, luxurious movements. He leans into me, pressing me against the wall.

I let my hands roam up his back, feeling the hard muscles beneath his shirt, just as his other hand runs down my side, gripping my thigh and lifting my leg slightly. I follow his lead and lift it the rest of the way, letting it rest in his grip. I can feel him pressing against his jeans as he leans into me. I am aching for him, desperate for friction. I line my hips up so that the hardest part of him is pressed against the softest part of me, and I groan into his mouth. He's pressing the inseam of my jeans into me, and it is creating a chain reaction of sensations in my body.

He breaks the kiss and moves down the side of my neck with his lips. I'm losing control, and it's making me impulsive. I let my hand slide under his shirt and up the skin of his back. He groans, slowly grinding against me. I feel my desire building, low and hot. I should probably stop this. *But, I don't want to stop this.* My body is electric, demanding more, more, more.

Sunlight suddenly rips the closet, blinding us both as the door is pushed open. I feel Rhett pull back from me, hastily pulling his shirt down. The sudden loss of his warmth is disorienting. In a panic, I glance over to see who's found us, but I don't see anyone when I look at the door. And then I hear a woof. Looking down, I see Tucker wagging his tail at me, proud of winning this round of hide n' seek. I sigh in relief and groan in frustration at the interruption.

I look cautiously at Rhett and see lust glazing his features. His hair is rumpled where I ran my hands through it, his shirt is a wrinkled mess, and he is straining against his jeans. But the moment is broken and I can feel my awkward inner ostrich lifting her head to say something stupid.

"Um," I finally get out. "Um. I should probably go." *Ugh. Why am I like this?*

"Oh, okay. No problem," he says awkwardly, reaching down to adjust himself. "I'll walk you to your car."

"Um, well, I rode here with Beth and Dan. I'll just... go find them." He nods his head in agreement. And then he stares at my lips, glances up to my eyes, and smiles, biting his lower lip. And holy hell, he is devastating like this. Ruffled, unguarded, hungry for more. I notice that dimple in one cheek, covered by the scruff of a couple days' beard growth. I take in those pine green eyes and russet, mussed curls and lips swollen from kissing.

Waves of desire are coursing through me like an incoming ocean tide. I feel its push and sudden withdrawal, certain the tide is about to pull me under. My inevitable drowning will be the perfect torture.

I start to ask him to stay longer, and see where this goes. But then he rubs his hand through his hair and says, "You're right. I need to head out. Band practice this evening."

I nod, knowing I'm blushing. We walk towards the back doors of the barn together in silence. I turn to leave, but he reaches out and grabs my hand. I pause, turning back to look at him. "Amelia," he fumbles with his words. "Can I call you tomorrow? Maybe we can figure out the best way to move forward?" He coughs. "With Ms. Clark?"

A twinge of disappointment lances my gut. Right, business. All business. But I drag up my confident mask and pull it forcefully over my features. "Yea, that would be great," I say, shoving the insecurity out of my voice. He releases my hand, reaching out as if he's going to trace his hand along my jaw, but pauses, unsure. I tense. I want to step away. I want him to touch me. I breathe, preparing to step into his touch. But I wait too long. He drops his hand and nods, answering his own unspoken question.

"Well, I'll talk to you soon." Rhett waves awkwardly before turning to walk outside. I watch him retreat, locked in place. When he exits the barn, I remain standing there, dazed. It's quiet, the sun is setting, casting the surrounding field just outside the doors in a golden glow. The last twenty minutes feel like a fever dream. The longing, our mutual desire, the sizzling chemistry. And it was Rhett! *Rhett.*

I need sleep. And a cold shower. Both, I decide. Definitely both.

Chapter 16

RHETT

Years of fantasizing and it actually happened. Shock and lust rocket through me. The heady reactions are liquid metal, coursing through my veins and branding me with her feel, her scent, her touch. I realize I'm still staring at my hand on the handle to my truck door, unmoving.

I shake myself from my stupor and climb into the truck. As soon as I crank it up, I turn the a/c on full blast and make sure all the vents are aimed directly at my face, hoping my makeshift cold shower works. Fuck. That equipment closet will be the setting of my fantasies for the rest of the week. Hell, for the rest of my life.

I start driving and know I have to reel in the lust coursing through my body before I get to my parents' house for band practice. I focus on mood-killers: cold showers, rotten food in my fridge, roadkill, that time I caught my parents making out on the couch. *Shudder.*

I park at my childhood home and then walk up to the front door and let myself in. I'm welcomed by the smell of roasted chicken, potatoes, and Mom's famous chocolate chip cookies. She's always happy when she has a full home. I hear the soft shuffle of socks in the hallway and then Mom turns the corner, her eyes creasing with joy at my arrival.

"Rhett! You're here!" She wraps her thin arms around me, stretching up to kiss my bearded cheek.

"Hey, mom," I say, hugging her back and looking down into green eyes and auburn hair that mirror my own. I study her face, noting the concern that's always etched there when she looks at me these days. I know she has been worried about me over the past year during my separation from Chels. Hell, longer than that. She never approved of my wife, though she never let Chels see that. And I know, even now, she's trying to hide how glad she is that we aren't together anymore, though it has pained her to see me hurting.

"About time you showed up!" a rich female voice calls from the kitchen. My little sister, Katie, two years younger than me, pops her head around the corner and sticks her tongue out.

"I didn't know this was a family affair," I say, then stick my tongue out at her in return. Some things never change.

"It's been too long since we had the whole family together," Mom says. "Now, you go do your band practice, and I'll have dinner ready for the crew when you're done."

I start walking toward the garage. "Hey, wait up," Katie says, stepping up next to me and yanking on my shirt. "Admit it. I know you're glad to have me in the band." Like me, my sister has Mom's dark red hair and green eyes. She has an easy way about her, always up for whatever steps in her path.

"Oh, and what is it you'll be playing?" I ask her.

"It's a surprise," she says with a wink.

We step into the garage, and Dad and Jacob are already there, talking about the LSU game. They look up as we walk in. "There he is," Dad says, his Burl Ives voice an instant comfort. "What took you so long?"

Roadkill. Moldy food. Cold showers. I think on repeat. "Found out some crazy things about a story I'm working on," I say. Jacob looks at me with interest. "I'll tell you about it at dinner. Mom will kill us all if we run late." They all nod knowingly.

We spend the next hour getting acquainted with each others'

playing styles. Dad and I jam from time to time–he on the keyboards and me on the guitar–so we pick up on each other's cues quickly. Jacob is a bit rusty on the drums, but after about ten minutes, he falls into the rhythm of playing again. Katie will be our lead singer and has even brought her instrument of choice: a tambourine. When our hour of practice is up, I'm relieved, excited even. We're no major headliner, but we sound good. We make plans to practice several more times before our opening night performance.

"We need a band name," Katie says, looking at each of us in turn. "How about The Graveyard Gators?" she says, grinning wildly. She's obviously already put some thought into this and I can't tell my sister no. None of us can. I look up and notice Jacob eyeing my sister appreciatively. I frown at him, but then Mom's voice calls out, "Dinner time! Wash your hands and come to the kitchen!"

As we walk to the kitchen, Jacob falls in step beside me, speaking quietly. "Everything okay, man?"

"Yea, why?"

"You seem… different. I can't put my finger on what it is. There's just something…." he trails off, staring at me like I've suddenly sprouted horns.

"I'm good, man. I promise."

IT'S NICE SITTING AROUND THE dinner table in my childhood home with my family and Jacob. I haven't felt this comfortable with them in a long time. For so long, I always felt like they were pitying me. And before that, I felt compelled to be the buffer between Chels and all of them. But this feels easy. Katie tells us about yet another new job. Mom talks about her garden. Dad talks football.

Finally, I bring up the Roberts boy case. I remember how Mom reacted the last time I talked to her about him, so I ease into the conversation. After bringing everyone up to speed, I look at Jacob and tell him what I learned about Ms. Clark today. He's stunned.

"You mean that crazy woman who *threw a chicken* at Margie? She was the boy's grandmother? Man, you can't make this stuff up," he shakes his head and snags a cookie from the plate in the middle of the table.

"Wait, who threw a chicken? Do I need to call PETA?" Katie gasps out.

"I could have told you that," Mom says, cutting off Katie before she can launch into an indignant rant. All eyes turn to her. "What? You never asked," she says defensively. "And when you called me that day, I was surprised. It's been a long time since that happened. But Rhett, Greta Clark and your grandmother were dear friends. You probably don't remember because you were so young, but you and Jimmy used to play together at her house."

There go those chills again creeping up and down my spine again. "Mom, why didn't you say something when I called you?"

"I, well, like I said. I was just surprised. I hadn't thought about that case in a long time."

And then I realize maybe this is why I felt a connection to the boy's story. Maybe it wasn't some premonition at all, just my subconscious remembering the past.

WHEN I GET TO MY APARTMENT, I'm so exhausted from the day's adrenaline rushes that I bypass my workout and head to bed. Sliding under the covers, I kick my arms back behind my head and close my eyes. I'm immediately back in the equipment closet. I can still feel Amelia's hands tracing up and down my back, diving under my shirt, her tongue in my mouth, her soft sighs of pleasure in my ear. Maybe I should hit the weights after all…

My phone buzzes. I'm tempted to ignore it. Sure it's my sister teasing me about "feeling the music," and "channeling Carlos Santana on the guitar," like she did at the dinner table tonight. But sometimes I get late-night work texts, so I open one eye, and I look down to see…. a meme of Sam the hobbit saying "PO-TAY-TOES."

A huge grin spreads across my face as my heart picks up speed.

Rhett: Miss me already, hobbit?

Amelia: Got a chocolate croissant from L&L. You're right. These are amazing.

Rhett: Told you. That is some magic in a flaky package.

Amelia: Any story updates?

Rhett: Turns out Ms. Clark and my grandma were best friends... and I played with Jimmy when we were kids.

Amelia: Oh. ... That's... Interesting.

Rhett: Right? I think we should talk to her in person tomorrow.

Amelia: We?

I stare at the text screen to make sure… and yea, I definitely typed "we." Like we're detective partners or something. Old insecurities flare. She must think I'm an idiot.

Rhett: ME. I. Myself. Unless you want to come.

Three dots appear and disappear as I re-read what I just sent. If you want to come? Mortification rips through me and I quickly hammer out another text.

Rhett: I mean if you want to join me in talking to her.

There go those damn dots again.

Amelia: I told you I wanted to come with you. And never fear. I'll be your knight in shining armor. ;) I'll even bring my shield. What animals do you think she will throw at us this time?

I was already drafting an apology text, so it takes me a minute to understand that she wants to join me in facing this. Or maybe she thinks I need moral support. Or maybe she's just practical and willing to serve as a witness in case things totally go off the rails. I delete my apology and start again.

Rhett: Surely she hasn't already run out of chickens...

Amelia: Noted. I'll bring a face shield too.

Rhett: Maybe we can bring a peace offering. Think she'll take that chicken back?

Amelia: Tried the peace offering thing already. And we both know how that turned out. And have mercy on that chicken. I'm sure it's happy to not live in fear of being thrown at someone's face.

I laugh to myself, imagining some poor chicken spending its entire life in a vicious cycle of being hurled through a front door, only to return home and have it happen all over again. Its whole perception of humanity being one of startled faces and flailing hands.

Rhett: Fair point.

Amelia: Let's bring something that doesn't remind her of Aunt Margie.

Rhett: Chocolate croissants?

Amelia: Great idea. Maybe pick up some extras for me.

My heart beats a little faster, knowing she wants to see me—that maybe today wasn't a fluke brought on by impulsivity and being trapped together in a closed space. That maybe, just maybe, she enjoyed it as much as I did.

Rhett: I think I can manage that. See you at 1?

Amelia: I'll be there setting up all morning. We have a lot to do. But I should be able to take a break around then.

Rhett: I feel honored.

A long pause. I see the three dots appear, then disappear. It happens two more times. Finally, my screen lights up.

Amelia: Good night, Rhett.

114

Chapter 17

AMELIA

Six Days Until the Festival

Only six days until the festival opens, and anxiety is a seagull pecking at the shells of my nervous system. The festival site is a beehive of activity with trucks arriving and unloading and people walking by with decorations. At one point, I turn and make sure that I actually saw a witch fly past me. And yep, Dan is carrying a near-life-sized reproduction of a witch to her perch above the corn maze. Text messages from Beth's team continue to stream in as they show up and unload more hay bails, faux spider webs, and scarecrows than I can shake a stick at. My mind is going through the lists of everything I still need to do before Saturday. My cell phone is ringing nonstop as vendors call to confirm contracts.

And to top it all off? I should be ten times more focused on this final push… but my eyes keep darting over to the barn and that damn equipment closet. And as soon as my eyes snag on the space, I'm replaying my seven minutes in heaven session with Rhett over and over again, my whole body heating.

"Amelia? Are you okay?" I look away from the closet and notice Beth standing there. She's expecting some sort of answer from me.

"Yeah. I'm fine. Why?"

"Oh, I don't know," Beth says dryly, "Probably because I've asked you three times where we should set up the selfie station, and you, apparently, have cotton in your ears."

I wince.

"Sorry. There is just a lot on my mind right now," I say distractedly.

She softens. "Of course. There's so much to manage right now. But don't worry, Lia, we'll get through this together." She puts her plastic pumpkins down and wraps her arms around me.

"Maybe we should meet up for Happy Hour later," I say as she pulls away. There's so much to catch her up on. I need a healthy dose of Beth's no-nonsense approach to work through my conflicting emotions surrounding what happened with Rhett.

"It's a date! That is if we can get all this organized by Happy Hour," she frowns, eying the giant U-Haul packed full of decorations that just pulled into the parking lot.

"Come on. I'll show you where we can unload the stuff for the selfie station." The weather has maintained its near autumn-ish temperatures, at least the Louisiana version of autumn-ish temperatures, which makes working outside tolerable. We spend the morning unloading supplies and work together to lift hay bales, mums, and scarecrows.

The day has been flying by at light speed, so I'm surprised when someone taps me on the shoulder and quietly says, "Hey, hobbit." I spin around, and Rhett is standing there, hands behind his back, half-smile lighting his face. I'm utterly captivated by him as my eyes roam his handsome face, snagging on that dimple.

Then I realize I must look like I took a literal roll in the hay after all the physical labor I've done today. "Hey," I say, attempting to discreetly pull random pieces of hay and pine straw out of my ponytail and dust the dirt off my overalls. "You're early."

"Not that early," he says. "It's already noon. And… I thought you might be hungry." He pulls his hands out from behind his back, and produces a PSL and a bag of something that smells like chocolate and butter.

"Are those…?"

"Chocolate croissants? Yep! And… I thought you might need something a little more substantial too, so I picked up a couple of breakfast sandwiches. I thought we could share breakfast for lunch."

I take Rhett in as he stands there holding my favorite coffee and lunch, his auburn waves tucked haphazardly under a baseball cap, wearing a Better Than Ezra t-shirt and faded jeans. I can just see the edge of a tattoo on his bicep, peeking out from beneath his sleeve. My fingers twitch, aching to trace it. His half-smile makes his single dimple deepen, and it sends my heart skittering like a stone across a pond. I was worried about things being awkward between us after yesterday, but all I want to do right now is wrap my arms around him and drag him back to that damn closet. I swallow and take a slow breath so I don't say or do something stupid. Reaching out, I take the latte and crumpled white bag from him.

"Thank you," I say, the corners of my mouth lifting cautiously. I'm not used to men being attentive to me, and my long-held grudge against Rhett is hard to shake. But his kindness feels genuine, and every part of me longs to comfort others—to overly thank them for any kind gesture, even to my own detriment. It's my fatal flaw, but the impulse is too strong for me to tamp down.

"Hey, where's mine?" I hear Beth say from behind me. She jolts me out of my Rhett-induced stupor, but I recover quickly.

"Oh no, you don't. These are my goodies," I say, hugging Rhett's gifts close to my chest, my heart. Beth raises one eyebrow at me. "Plus, I know Dan is bringing you lunch."

"Well, that is true," she says, eying Rhett and me suspiciously. "But Lia, what did you do to get such special treatment?"

I hear Rhett try to muffle a laugh with a cough. I scramble to say something, anything. "I am going with Rhett to face down Ms. Clark. *Again*. I need a little caffeine if I'm going to survive my next encounter." I stare at Beth, silently begging her not to press this right now.

"I'll bring more croissants by tomorrow on my lunch break," Rhett offers.

Beth relents. "Fine. But you're buying me a drink tonight," she demands, poking me in the shoulder. And then she's off to work again, marching over to the U-Haul.

"I'm starved," Rhett says with gusto. "And you deserve a break and a little special treatment. Let's eat." Those words make me want to press into him like a cat in need of affection. *Cool it, Lia. He's just being nice. Don't read into it.*

I follow him to his truck, and we climb in. He turns it on, cranking up the air conditioner. The cool air feels good after all the energy I've exerted over the past several hours. I know I'm sweaty and probably smell gross. I try to ease into the path of the car vent to dry off without Rhett noticing.

"Thank you so much for bringing this. I didn't even realize how hungry I was. It's been crazy today." I'm anxious to avoid any awkward silence.

"No problem. I'm out of the office for the rest of the afternoon. I've got a story to write up, but I plan to finish it from my apartment."

I open the grease-stained bag and hand Rhett one of the warm breakfast sandwiches as the smell of bacon fills the inside of the truck. I inhale deeply and sigh, instantly transported to mornings spent in our kitchen with Aunt Margie as she cooked bacon on the stove top for mom and me.

We dig into our breakfast sandwiches. Hunger is tearing at my insides, but I try not to devour my food like a starving alligator because I am also fully aware of the man sitting next to me. The one I can't stop thinking about. We reach for our drinks at the same time, bumping hands. Even that small collision of skin is enough to send a shock through my system, reminding me of how much touching we did yesterday. *I've got it bad.* The thought hits me like a slap across the face—fast, hot, and blindingly uncomfortable.

"Everything is looking great out here," Rhett finally says, breaking the silence filling the truck's cab.

"Oh, thanks," I say a bit awkwardly. "We've been working nonstop. I mean, well, obviously, which is why I'm sort of a mess right now," I say, waving in the general vicinity of my hair, which I know must be shooting out in all directions.

"Nah, you look great," he says casually.

I glare at him, incredulity radiating from my expression.

"Okay, okay," he laughs, his deep chuckle reverberating down my spine and rippling down into my gut. Lower. "But you don't look bad, Lia. You just look like you've been hard at work. And I admire that."

I stare at him.

"What?"

"You called me Lia."

"Oh, is that okay? I heard Margie and Beth call you that, but I shouldn't have assumed…"

"I mean, that's what my family and friends call me."

"Aren't we… friends?" he asks cautiously. And he's so earnest. I try to stifle the blush I know is threatening to creep up my neck because I so want to be friends. More than friends. Wait, do I? I am the worst at relationships. Even when I think they're going well, they always come back and bite me in the ass in the end. But yesterday was… well, we had a moment– a really, really good moment. But anyone in a situation like that would. Right? Don't be weird. Act casual. I swallow my food and look at him. I know my heated thoughts must show on my face, but I push on.

"Yeah. Friends," I say. Some emotion crosses his face. *Does he look like he's in pain? Doesn't he want to be friends?* I wonder, feeling a little hurt. *God, I am reading too much into this.*

"Good. Because I need someone who has my back to talk to Ms. Clark with me today," he says.

"Yeah, sure, anytime," I say, trying to sound confident and not like I'm fantasizing about Rhett and the equipment closet. "Before we do that, I'm going to duck in the barn and freshen up. Grab her chicken so we can return it as a peace offering. Plus, that thing is pooping and laying eggs everywhere. It needs to go home."

Rhett laughs. "I'll walk over to the barn with you. Maybe giving the chicken back to her will come better from me since I may be the only person left on the planet she hasn't thrown something at or spilled coffee on… yet."

"To be fair, she technically didn't spill coffee on me. Her cat managed that all on its own. But I get your point. I'll let you charm your way into her good graces. I'll do my part. I'm prepared to gaze at you like you're a trustworthy gentleman who likes to walk old women across the street and rescue injured animals and… stuff. And I'm still committed to being your backup if a fight breaks out."

"Fists of fury, eh?"

"Something like that. At the very least, I'll be prepared to catch whatever is thrown our way this time."

"It's a deal then." He extends his hand, and I reach out and shake it. He has a firm, warm grip. His fingertips are calloused from playing the guitar, but I like the way they feel against the back of my hand. We sit there for a moment, hands clasped.

"Amelia, I want to ask you something," he says as he lets go of my hand.

"Okay," I say hesitantly.

"Will…" and then my phone starts ringing. I scramble for it and look down at the screen. It's Janet.

"I'm sorry. I have to take this. It's my boss." He nods, and I step out of his car, making my way back to the barn as I fill Janet in on the day's progress.

Chapter 18

RHETT

Leaning against the outside of the barn, I scroll through my phone, re-reading my potential interview questions for Ms. Clark–if she'll even give us the time of day, that is. I'm preparing for how she might react when we show up on her front porch. This includes the best ways to respond to anything from yelling to chicken hurling.

"Hey there, handsome," a familiar voice says from behind me. I turn and see Margie walking up to me. I like this woman. She's full of fire and grit, and she loves Amelia–Lia–fiercely.

"Hi there," I say back, quirking my lips.

"I hear you're going to talk to the Witch of the Woods," she says, nodding at Ms. Clark's house. "Better you than me."

"She's been through some rough shit," I say, folding my arms across my chest and leaning my shoulder back into the barn.

"Haven't we all?" Margie says, never beating around the bush. It makes me wonder what kind of rough shit Margie's seen in her life. "Still no reason to be an awful old hag to everyone who tries to show you kindness or even just talk to you," she says. I can see the anger over their last encounter still thrumming through her veins. It's charging her up like an electric car that's ready to hit the pedal and go barreling straight through Ms. Clark's front door, taking down every chicken and cat in the near vicinity.

"And I know what you're thinking. You think I'm still pissed about her throwing that chicken at my face."

"Well, aren't you?" I say, watching her as she stares at the house on the property's perimeter.

"A little. But I've experienced far worse from people in my life. And let's face it. I'm not exactly rainbows and sunshine either," she says dryly.

"But I can let that childish shit go. Well, mostly. I may still do something petty like serve her up a pot of gumbo of questionable origin in that giant ass pot she threw *at my head*. But I'm case hardened. I've seen a lot of ugliness in my life. I can handle myself."

No doubt there. If I ever go into battle, I want this woman at my side.

"Lia, though, she wants to see the best in everyone, and she has worked so damn hard to make this festival a success. Hell, she even brought that old broad a *gift* after all the shit that witch stirred up to make sure the festival failed. And that's a helluva lot nicer than most people would be."

She pauses and then turns to look at me. "Grief is a bitch, I get that. But isolating yourself from the entire world, creating a den of anger and regret… it's not healthy. And Lia deserves much better than what that woman gave her. She deserves better than being humiliated and treated like she's nothing."

Margie looks straight into my eyes when she says this, and I realize we're not just talking about Ms. Clark anymore. She must know what happened between Amelia and me in high school. She likely suspects something is happening between us now.

"Are you picking up what I'm putting down?" she asks, radiating intimidation and authority.

"Yes, ma'am," I say with all the sincerity I can muster.

She pats me on the shoulder. "I'm glad to know we're on the same page." Margie reaches into her overall pocket and pulls out her flask. "Need a nip before going into the lion's den?"

"Nah. We've got this," I say, pushing confidence and calm into my voice.

Margie nods. "Good. I'll go get that damn chicken then. She can have her shit bird back."

And with that, Margie turns and walks around the side of the barn.

A few minutes later, Amelia walks back outside. She's straightened up her hair and dusted off, though I notice a couple of pieces of hay still sticking out of her wavy brown ponytail. I reach over her shoulder and pull them out, tossing the rogue pieces to the ground. And before I can stop myself, I tuck a stray piece of hair behind her ear, letting my fingers linger for just a beat before pulling them away.

She stares at me for a moment, then seems to remember we have somewhere to be. "Ready?" she asks breathily.

"Here, take this," Margie says, walking up to me and placing the chicken in my arms. "And hold on tight. That bird's a menace. I'll be here if you need backup—just text. Or scream. I'll be ready either way."

I look down at the chicken, and the chicken looks back at me. "Your funeral," it seems to say.

I look at Amelia. "Let's go then."

We set off together across the field towards the old house. After a moment, she reaches out, snags my free hand, and squeezes. I squeeze back.

I PULL BACK THE SCREEN DOOR, knocking on the rotting wooden one behind it. It takes a moment, but we finally hear approaching footsteps. The door swings open, but Ms. Clark leaves the screen door closed. She stares at Amelia, suspicion and mistrust pulsing from her tiny form. "Well, what the hell do you want now?" she barks.

I step into her line of vision before Amelia can answer, "We just want to talk. And I brought your, um, pet back." I hold the chicken out, but she glances at it before staring at me with confusion, eyebrows knitting as she eyes my tall form.

"You look… familiar," she finally says, easing open the screen door to get a better look at my face. "Do I know you from somewhere?"

I swallow, unsure of what to do with the chicken. I tuck the bird back under my arm. "I think you might. I'm Rhett, Millie Hebert's grandson." Recognition lights her face, and then she turns to look at Amelia. "If this is some kind of trick to get my blessing on the festival, it's not going to work."

I start to talk again, but Amelia has had enough. She folds her arms across her chest and rises up to her full height, and I can see how Amelia and Margie come from the same family. Her voice is calm but firm, and damn if watching her confidence rise to the surface like this isn't the sexiest thing I've ever seen.

"Ms. Clark. This is not a trick. None of my attempts to talk to you have been. I have come to you with goodwill and an attempt at being neighborly." Ms. Clark starts to talk, but Amelia cuts her off. "And, quite frankly, you owe me an apology and a pumpkin spice latte. You're lucky I didn't call animal control after *your* cat attacked *me*."

I don't say anything, letting Lia fight her own battle. The air between them crackles with tension. Finally, Ms. Clark breaks the standoff. "I… regret that happened. With the cat, I mean." And it's like the words are being ripped from the depths of her soul. "I just wasn't expecting you. Not then. Not now." She clears her throat and seems mildly surprised that she just uttered those words.

It's not exactly an apology, but it's something, at least.

I clear my throat. "Can we… come in? We just want to talk. That's all." She turns to me, and I see her gaze soften fractionally. She takes me in again, studying my features, memories clouding her eyes. Ms. Clark finally nods her assent. But she hasn't stopped to wait for us.

"And leave that damn chicken outside," she yells from somewhere inside her house. I look at Amelia, and she looks back at me and shrugs. I lean down, gently placing the bird on the porch, and then follow her inside.

The first thing I notice is the nearly overwhelming smell of mothballs and cats with a hint of some citrusy cleaner. As my eyes adjust to the dim light, I look around. The faded orange-tinged photos on the wall, the floral furniture, and the olive green appliances—all look like they came straight out of the 1970s. Curtains shut out the sunlight, and only a few lamps light the space. Heavy emotions invade the room, and it feels like walking into a confessional. But it's pristine – not a pillow cushion out of place.

An orange cat prowls in front of us as we wander down her hallway, finally spotting Ms. Clark in the living room. She gestures at a floral, mustard yellow couch, so Amelia and I take our seats. She doesn't offer us a drink or anything to make us more comfortable. She simply lowers herself into a matching mustard-colored chair across from us, placing the throw pillow in her lap. She stares at us, a frown creasing her wrinkled brow, and says nothing.

I feel Amelia reach for my hand and squeeze. I squeeze hers in return, then let go, focusing my attention on the woman before us. Ms. Clark simply stares at us, and it's unnerving. I wonder briefly if she actually is a witch, or maybe a lonely ghost who still wanders this earthly plane searching for her missing grandson. I shudder slightly. I've got to do or say something to break the thick silence clouding the room.

I let my years of journalism experience take the lead. "Ms. Clark. My mom told me you were friends with my grandmother." *There. I've extended an olive branch.*

"Yes." That's it. That's all she says.

"I was wondering how you two knew each other?"

I see her looking over my features, looking for a hint of her old friend's young grandson in my adult face.

"You're really her grandson?" She asks.

"Yes, ma'am," I say, echoing her short response from earlier.

"Yes. I think you are. All that red hair from your mother," she says distantly. Silence fills the room. I hear Amelia start to speak, but I lightly nudge her leg with mine, and she stops. I give Ms. Clark space and let the silence hang, inviting her to fill it.

"Millie and I met after our husbands died," she finally says. "We went to Trinity Methodist Church, but we didn't really know each other, just knew *of* each other. But when my Tom died in a car wreck and Fred, your grandfather, died of cancer, our meddling children encouraged us to attend a grief group at church." The words come out raspy and covered in cobwebs.

I nod with encouragement. "So the two of you became friends and supported one another?"

She lets out a dry laugh that sounds like it's been sitting in a coffin and covered in dust for a decade. "Oh God, no! Millie and I couldn't stand each other when we met. She was always walking around like some high falutin queen, and, I dare say, she treated most of us like we were there to do her bidding. And grief… Well, grief does weird things to us. It made me angry, belligerent."

No shit, I think.

"But Millie acted completely unaffected by it all. I swear that woman buddied up to any newly grieving man in the group trying to make a match–and hell if they didn't respond. I hated that she seemed to manage her pain so easily and that everyone in the room was drawn to her like she was a fresh batch of beignets dusted in the finest powdered sugar. And me? Well, no one wanted to be around me. Not that I blame them, really. Some tried. A little too hard sometimes. But the pain of losing Tom so suddenly was impossible for me to escape."

"Oh. Mom made it sound like you two were good friends," I finally say, starting to regret this visit. No one wants to hear that their grandmother was the grief group hussy.

She lifts her eyes to the ceiling like she's looking for an answer. "We were. *Eventually.* Turns out Millie didn't like that *I* was the only person in the room not fawning over her when she walked through the door. She made it her personal mission to win me over to her fan club."

I smile to myself. *Now that sounds just like my grandmother.*

"So she started in on me. Sitting by me in all of our grief group meetings. Trying to talk to me about baking cakes and other nonsense I could care less about. When that didn't work, she tried telling me about the time she won the Peach Pageant. As if *that* would impress me. I refused to cave to her poor attempts at friendship. I thought she had finally given up the day she came in and sat by Jasper Fredericks, flirting with him shamelessly. And maybe she had. But after the meeting, I went to the ladies' room. And when I came out, she was the only one still sitting in the room, and she was crying her eyes out like some lost, forlorn kitten."

My heart feels heavy in my chest, imagining my bright grandmother sobbing in a fold-out metal chair alone in a dark room. I swallow my own grief down.

"I wanted to keep going, to walk right past her and show her I didn't care one iota about her. But she didn't even see me there. She was hiding, and I... well, I knew that feeling. I walked over to her, sat down, and said, 'This is shit. This grieving, I mean.' She looked up at me and scowled." Ms. Clark laughs dryly. "And that's when I realized that the crazy old bat had genuine feelings after all."

""I felt stupid for talking to her after rejecting all of her attempts at friendship, but I couldn't very well back out of it. And then, somehow, she invited herself to my house for lunch one day. And what was I supposed to do? I couldn't tell a crying woman no. Not even I am that heartless. At our meetings, she mentioned her grandchildren. I told her that I..." she stops abruptly, emotion catching her voice. A sob rises in her throat, and she barely manages to swallow it back down. "I told her I had a grandson the same age as hers and that she should bring her grandson—you—over to play."

She takes a minute to try and suppress her emotions, but a tear rolls down her cheek, and she dashes it away with the back of her hand. Lia fidgets beside me. I know she is fighting the urge to comfort Ms. Clark. I place my hand on her knee, urging her to remain sitting beside me.

Finally, Ms. Clark looks up. "Millie showed up at my house the next day with that infamous pound cake of hers and you in tow... and then never stopped showing up. Every Wednesday, she'd come, even when I tried to shoo her off. Crazy woman." This time she says it fondly, more tears threatening to spill.

"So," she finally says. "That's how I know... how I knew your grandmother."

"Mom still makes her pound cake," I say. "I could bring you one sometime."

She looks surprised and then laughs a little. "Oh yes. You are definitely Millie's grandson."

I take a deep breath and prepare to ask her about her grandson. I'm weary now that she's struggling with her emotions, and I've seen how much she cared, albeit reluctantly, for my grandmother.

"Ms. Clark, your grandson, the one I played with as a boy. Jimmy, wasn't it?"

She halts, staring at me like I've struck her, and doesn't say a word.

"I was wondering because, um, I just learned recently that he died and…"

"He didn't die," she says with sudden venom, tears still in her eyes. "He disappeared. And not a damn person in this city was competent enough to find him."

Taking her lead, I respond, "I'm sorry. I didn't mean to…," I stumble. "But, you see, I would really like to help find out what happened to him all those years ago."

Gone is the reminiscing woman. In her place sits a viper, ready to lash out and strike. "And what do you think *you* can do? Are you some kind of detective or something?" Any goodwill I had won over from this woman is gone. Amelia pressed her leg against my thigh in a show of support.

"Not a detective, exactly," I say. "But someone who cares. Will you hear me out?"

At first, I think she's going to go find another chicken and hurl it at me. Or maybe punch me. I feel Amelia tense, waiting to see how she will respond.

Finally, Ms. Clark sits back in her chair. "Fine. But only because Millie would come back and haunt me if I was ugly to her grandson." And she actually rolls her eyes.

Damn, I think she's serious. I press on and explain to her how I found the old newspaper articles, learning when and where the disappearance happened and the failed attempt to make a discovery with GPR. I explain that all my leads are dead ends, and she might be my last hope for a new one. She stares at me, listening, occasionally wiping her eyes. I see the anger drip out of her, a scoop of ice cream melting and hitting the ground until all that's left is a sad, soggy cone. I feel Amelia take my hand, and I hold onto it tightly.

When I finish, we sit in silence for a moment. "I… appreciate the effort," she says. "But I don't think I can help."

"I heard that you were with Jimmy the night he went missing. Are there any details about that night that you would be willing to share that might give me another way forward?"

She looks at me, but it's like she's not there. She's trapped in a memory.

"I… I don't think so," she finally says. I debate whether I should push, but Amelia nudges me, and I can tell by how she looks at me that it's time to go.

"Ms. Clark.. Thank you for sharing your memories with me… with us. I know that was hard. If you want to talk some more, or just want a pound cake or anything, call me." I hand her my business card. "My cell phone number is on there." She stares at the card and nods.

"We'll just see our way out then," I say, grabbing Amelia's hand and gently guiding her to the front door. I glance back over my shoulder as we leave. Ms. Clark is a ghost, holding vigil over a life that no longer exists. A shiver runs down my spine.

"Are we just going to leave her there?" Amelia whispers to me.

"I think that's what she wants," I say uncertainly. I just know I need to get out of this house and away from the ghosts of my grandmother and a young boy that seem to be lingering over this place.

AMELIA AND I WALK AWAY from the house and towards the festival barn, still holding hands. It's a lot to process, but the feel of her hand in mind grounds me in the present. We walk in silence for a few moments, taking in the late afternoon sun, the smell of hay and dirt lingering in the country air.

"Well, that was… interesting," I finally say.

"No wonder she's so angry," Amelia replies in acknowledgment.

"Kinda awkward about my grandmother, though… her hitting on all the old widowers."

"Like grandmother, like grandson?" she says with a hint of mischief.

"Nah, I only have an ounce of my grandmother's fire."

"Well, it sounds like you have her empathy and courage… And her pound cake recipe," she says, bumping my side.

I smile down at her, squeezing her hand. Things are easy between us, playful even. When we reach the parking lot, I pause, stopping us both. "Amelia, thank you for going with me today. I know you probably didn't want to risk assault with a deadly chicken by Ms. Clark again." I quirk a half-smile at this. "So I mean it. Thanks."

"It's fine," she says, waving it off. "I needed to scope the situation out anyway, make sure she wasn't going to fly out of her house during the festival on her broomstick. Though I guess that *could* add to the whole Halloween atmosphere."

God, I love it when she does this. How she lightens the mood with a dry joke and a wry grin. As I stare at her, her warm hand still in mine, I think about kissing her again. And before I can stop myself, I ask, "Want to go out tomorrow? Like for dinner? With me?"

She seems surprised. She takes in my expression like she's trying to decide if this is a joke.

"You didn't get enough of me at lunch?" she finally asks. I can tell she's trying to make it sound like a joke, but there's an underlying seriousness there that makes my heart ache.

"I think I could stand a little more time with you," I say, knowing I'm smirking.

She nods her head. "Okay."

"Yeah?"

"Yeah."

"Pick you up at six?"

"I'll be ready," she says.

I go to climb into my truck when she says, "Rhett?" I turn to her. "I never thanked you properly for bringing me a PSL and chocolate croissant."

I start to tell her not to worry about it, but before I get a chance to speak, she walks up to me, stands on tiptoes, and presses her lips to mine. I respond instantly, closing my eyes and leaning into her, my body lighting up with heat everywhere it touches hers. I tease her mouth open, and she doesn't hesitate, kissing me back fiercely, deeply. I want to press pause, and allow us time to luxuriate in our stolen moment. But just as I let my hands start to wander her body, she pulls away. Lia is flushed and breathing hard.

"See you tomorrow," she whispers, a wicked grin stealing across that gorgeous mouth of hers. Then turns and jogs off to the barn. As I stand there and watch her retreat, my heart thrums in my ears, and the ghost of Amelia's kiss haunts my lips.

Chapter 19

AMELIA

I stir my Cape Cod, watching the vodka and cranberry juice swirl around the lime I've squeezed into it. A cacophony of laughter and conversation fills the bar around us. We're sitting at one of the tall tops, slightly sticky from spilled drinks and the sugar of dessert crumbs from previous patrons. I breathe in, feeling content in the familiar and expected. The smell of draft beer has always been a strange comfort to me. It's like bread and sunshine.

"I saw the two of you kissing by his truck today," Beth says, knocking me straight out of my musings and planting me firmly into reality. "Spill it. What's going on there?"

My eyes rise from my cocktail, where I've been gazing idly for a few minutes. I grin a bit sheepishly.

"Oh my gosh, *are you two sleeping together?*" Beth practically shouts.

"Shhhh. Keep your voice down," I say, looking around to make sure no one is eavesdropping. After all, Ruston is a small town, and a comment like that will get back to Aunt Margie before I even make it home tonight. I look back to Beth. "And no. We're not, okay?"

She looks at me skeptically. "Certainly looked like something super spicy was happening between you two."

"I don't really know what's happening," I say uncomfortably. "But no. There's no sex. We've only kissed twice, and the first time was kind of an accident."

"What, you tripped and fell, and your tongue landed in his mouth?" she asks before daintily taking a sip of her gin and tonic.

"Sort of?" I say, embarrassed. Beth levels me with a stare. "Ok, there was active participation from both of us. We were kind of squeezed into a closet together, and it just sort of happened. The kissing, I mean. And yea, I liked it, okay?"

"Well, yea, you did. Lia, Rhett is smokin' hot. And he honestly seems like a really nice guy, too. And you kissed him today *on purpose*. You can't deny it. So now what? Are you two an *item*?"

I fidget. "No, nothing like that, but he did ask me to grab dinner tomorrow. I don't really know if this will go anywhere, though, or if we're just two people who had a moment and want to see if it's worth pursuing." I roll my eyes to the ceiling, looking at the stained, metal-stamped tiles for an answer and coming up with nothing.

Beth is still staring at me expectantly, anxious for more. "The thing is, I like Rhett–a lot. But I'm damaged goods. All of my relationships have been gigantic failures. I don't want to mess this up. And, honestly, I'm having a hard time seeing what a guy like him sees in *me* of all people."

"First, you shut the hell up with that self-conscious bullshit. You are gorgeous, Lia. And you're funny and brilliant. I would never pick just anyone to be my best friend," she says, self-satisfied. "And that's really all that needs to be said about that. My word is law." She cocks a grin at me. What I wouldn't give for her brand of confidence.

"And another thing. You did not fail at your past relationships. You just picked bad people."

"Thanks for the vote of confidence," I reply dryly and take another sip of my cocktail.

"Oh hush Lia, you know I'm right. You are a kind soul and want to see the best in others, the best in your boyfriends. They took advantage of that, but this is the opposite. I mean, you loathed Rhett for a decade, and now you're giving him a chance. Already you're off to a better start!" She says this like she's telling me that my ugly drawing is a masterpiece. Like just by willing it, she can make me believe what she's saying.

"I know this shouldn't matter," I say, tracing my finger along the wood grain of our table. "But Matt told me I never give anything one hundred percent. That I am always happy to do what others tell me. And when I try to do things I enjoy, they always explode in my face. That's why I'm always making a mess of things." My heart feels weighed down with the memory of two years of being told what a failure I am, by all my memories that confirm that assessment. Hell, even Ms. Clark's cat…

"Listen to me right now, Lia Murphy." I look up in surprise at the fierceness in Beth's voice. "Matt was–and still is–a piece of shit. He was an alcoholic who manipulated you into taking care of him and solving his problems. He verbally abused you. Any opinion from that worthless, slimy piece of horse shit is not worth your time or consideration. You're better than that."

I stare back down into the swirling depths of my cocktail. Beth leans down to catch my eyes. When I look at her, she continues. "Lia, look at me. Do you trust my opinions?"

"Well, duh."

"Because I think you are one of the most selfless, caring women I know. You put one hundred and ten percent into everything you do. Matt kept you isolated from your friends and family. You disappeared on us for a year while with him because he controlled you and kept you away from everyone and everything that made you happy. But I know a good person when I see one, and Lia, you are the best of the best. And Rhett? The man offered to bring me chocolate croissants on his lunch break because I'm *your* friend. That is the kind of person you need in your life."

"The kind who brings my friends chocolate croissants?" I ask, trying to lighten the mood.

"Well, yea. But, more importantly, someone who cares about what makes *you* happy. Someone who builds you up, not tears you down."

"So you're saying I should date *you*?" I smile.

She reaches across the table and places her hands over mine. "Honey, if we both played for that team, I'd be all over you. But alas, Dan and I are happily married, and you have a super hot reporter who wants to make out with you in closets. So do us both a favor and go on that date with Rhett and enjoy yourself. Okay?"

"I don't deserve you, Beth."

"Quit saying that, Lia. You have to realize that you deserve all the good things in your life... though I admit I *am* one of the best." She winks at me. "And... just so you know. I totally expect all the hot details of your date."

I roll my eyes. "Wishful thinking, Beth."

"Oh, it's gonna happen. And I've been off the dating market for years. I need to live vicariously through you and Mr. Hot Reporter. Don't you dare let me down, Lia."

I turn my hands over so I can hold hers in my own and squeeze them tightly. "You really are *the* best friend, you know it?"

She pulls her hands away, grabs her cocktail, and motions for me to pick up mine. She taps my glass to hers and says, "Cheers to that!" We both down the last of our drinks. As the warmth of the alcohol slides through my limbs, I imagine what tomorrow evening might bring and allow myself a smile.

Chapter 20

RHETT

Four Days Until the Festival

I park my truck in Lia's driveway, and all the shyness I've struggled with my entire life suddenly rears its ugly head, a bull of shame charging through my body. A piece of my soul yearns to escape our mutual tension and observe her quietly from a distance. Safe, calm, non-confrontational. I sit there, waging an internal war with this old feeling, foot tapping anxiously on my truck's floorboard. I close my eyes, inhale slowly, and focus on Lia, tracing her body's lines, remembering how she stole a kiss from me. Twice. No, three times now.

I open my eyes and look at her house. For some reason the universe has granted me another chance with this girl, and I know, in this moment, that if I don't pull myself together, it will never happen again. Then I realize my gaze has been locked on her house for several minutes, and it's probably going to be really weird if she looks out her window and sees me sitting in her driveway *staring through her windows. Shit.*

I look over at my passenger seat, where the flowers I picked up from the grocery store on my way here still lay in their plastic wrap, their fresh floral scent filling the cab of my truck. Sunflowers... and some kind of... other... flowers? They are orangish and reddish. Whatever they are, they're beautiful and remind me of autumn—of

Lia. I grabbed them on impulse. Even though, staring at them now, it dawns on me that giving them to her will definitely make this whole thing an official date. And yeah, I definitely want it to be a date, but I don't know if Lia does.

Between warring with my apprehension and indecision, I know I've probably sat in my truck for too long already. *What is wrong with me?* I haven't battled with this overwhelming shyness in a decade. This is Lia. I'd do anything for her. My internal pep talk finished, I reach over, grab the flowers and walk up to her front porch. This feels a bit like I'm picking up my high school prom date. Except my high school prom date was Chels, and she always told me what to do and how to do it—and this is already ten times better than that.

Barking comes from the other side of the front door before I even knock, and I know Tucker is heralding my arrival.

"Get back, Tuck, get back," I hear Lia's muffled voice through the closed door. My heart pulls taught, a fishing hook snagged by an oversized catch determined to escape with its prize. Now that I hear her voice, it's all I can do not to give into that tug.

She finally manages to push her dog away and open the door. She looks… wow. I realize this may be the first time I've seen her in something that's not a dirty pair of overalls, a business suit, or a school uniform. Even though she is gorgeous in whatever she wears, tonight she's wearing a navy dress that hugs her in all the right places. I can see her curves and her legs. And yea, there is definitely a fish hook lodged in my gut and Lia is holding the reel. Plus, she smells… amazing. Like pumpkin spice. Do they make pumpkin spice shampoo now, too? Whatever it is, I really, *really* like it.

I realize my gaze has locked onto her legs when I hear Amelia say, "Hey, Rhett. You okay?"

I look up and quirk a smile, trying not to look as embarrassed as I feel. "Yea," I say, my voice husky. "You look amazing." The words are already out of my mouth before I can stop to think of something more eloquent, but I don't regret them. She does look amazing— sexy, beautiful, perfect. I offer up the flowers to her. "I saw these and thought of you. I hope they're okay?" *I should really rethink talking tonight, evidently.*

She smiles warmly, reaching for them. "Sunflowers and gerbera daisies. The flowers of fall. My favorites." She buries her nose in the bouquet. "Want to come in for a minute? I'm almost ready. Just need to feed Tuck."

I follow her into her home. It's an older house and hasn't been updated much, but it's full of warm, earthy colors. Every nook overflows with framed family photos, coffee mugs, greeting cards, and books. It's a little disheveled, but not messy. Amelia pulls out a vase, trims the flower stems, then arranges them. She sits the final arrangement in the center of her worn, wooden kitchen table. They fit there, in this house, with her.

She pours food into Tucker's bowl in her kitchen, and he immediately runs over to bury his nose in the offering. I look around, noticing a pile of novels on a side table in her kitchen. I smile, remembering the girl I used to try to catch glimpses of in high school, nose always buried in a book.

"Okay, I'm ready. You driving?" she asks.

I nod my head, and we walk outside. I follow her to the passenger side, opening the door.

"Such a gentleman," she says, laughter in her eyes.

"My mother wouldn't have it any other way." She reaches out, grabs my keys, then pops them in the ignition, starting the truck as I walk around to the other side. My mom would say *the sign of a keeper*, but I already know that. I just need to convince Lia that I'm worth holding on to. I put my truck in reverse, sliding my right arm behind her seat and looking over my shoulder. I do this all the time, but with Lia in the car next to me, the gesture pulls her into my space, and it feels intimate.

"So," she says. "Where are we headed tonight?"

"It's a surprise." I cut my eyes over to watch her as I drive through her neighborhood.

"As long as you're not a serial killer, I guess that's okay," she responds. I glance to make sure she's joking and see that wry quirk of her lips.

"You have my word that I am definitely not a serial killer, but feel free to text everyone you know and send them your location."

"That's exactly what a serial killer would say. Plus, you could always snatch my phone and toss it in the dumpster of a nearby restaurant."

"Ummm... I think you watch too many true crime shows."

"Never hurts to be prepared." And she says it with a tone so dry that it again makes me wonder whether or not she's joking.

"I guess you'll just have to trust me," I shrug.

"I think I can manage that." And this time, a genuine smile spreads across her face.

When we pull up to Squire Creek Country Club, I hear Amelia say, "Well, this is swanky."

"I aim to please. It doesn't hurt that my boss has a membership here and is willing to share it with her employees from time to time. So don't get any crazy ideas thinking I'm a secret billionaire or something."

She laughs. "'The Secret Billionaire' sounds like some highly watchable reality TV."

"Don't get too excited. No one is waiting around a corner with a camera," I say as I park the truck.

"And to think I got all 'gussied up' for nothing."

I relax into our easy conversation. There's something about Lia's presence. Her soul is a brightly burning campfire, its warmth pushing into my bones and chasing away the cold traces of my insecurity.

We climb out of the truck and start walking towards the restaurant entrance. I can feel our uncertainty dissipate as we continue to joke with one another. Tentatively, I reach out and place my hand on the small of her back. She steps in a little closer. It's a light touch, a small movement, but the connection between us is magnetic.

When we finally step inside, I'm momentarily taken aback by how freaking fancy this place is. I've only been here once before when The Boss hosted the office Christmas party. But even then, it was a group setting, and we were all a little drunk. Tonight the inside is decorated for autumn. There are pumpkins and berries on tables, candles inside glasses, the light warm and low. It even smells like fall, with scents of cranberry, apples, and cinnamon filling the room.

"This is so… perfect," Amelia says dreamily. I look down and can practically see hearts forming in her eyes like some enthusiastic anime character. Inside I fist pump in triumph.

The hostess greets us and walks us to our reserved table, covered in a white tablecloth, a burgundy table runner across it. Once we're seated, she presents us with a wine list and a single-sided menu.

"Are you going to have a drink?" Lia asks cautiously. "I mean, I will if you do, but I don't want to presume anything or make it awkward or…"

"Hell yes," I say and then laugh roughly. "I mean, yea. I'll have a drink."

She relaxes, examining the menu. "So many of my favorites are on here," she says with a groan. "How am I supposed to choose between shrimp and grits and crawfish etouffee?"

When the waiter walks up, she orders a glass of chardonnay, and I opt for a Crown and coke. Once the drinks arrive, we take sips and settle into the cozy atmosphere of the room. The warmth of the alcohol eases our shoulders and conversation.

"I forgot how nice this place is," I confide to Lia. "I mean, even the mounted deer heads look elegant." She looks up to where I'm staring at the line of taxidermied game on the wall, their antlers bedecked with autumn leaves like they just wandered out of the woods, and her eyes widen.

"Nothing like staring at the mounted head of what you're about to eat to make you hungry," she says dryly. I still can't believe I'm sitting here with Lia. On a date. Teenage Rhett is giving me a high five and thanking me for finally managing to do something right.

"I feel like I know you, Rhett," she confides. "But there's so much I don't know about you. What's your family like? Siblings? Pets?" She asks the last question hopefully, making me contemplate adopting a dog before our next date. Damn, I'm so gone for this girl.

My family is an easy subject to talk about, though. I can easily picture Lia at my family's dinner table. I know she would love my mom, and they would be instant friends. So I tell her all about my parents. About Mom's love of cooking and overprotective ways. About Dad's love of football and how he's constantly tinkering around in the garage. I tell her about my little sister, Katie, my polar opposite in every way. Where I'm quiet, Katie is loud. If I go for meat and potatoes, Katie will choose the Vegan option. The only thing we really share is our red hair and sense of humor. She lights up when I tell her that Katie is our band's lead singer.

"It must be wonderful to have a sister! I am an only child, and I desperately wished for a sister. Mom wanted another kid so badly, but miscarried all of them except me. So I took in wild animals for companionship instead," she says proudly. I glance over to the mounted deer heads and wince.

A memory of her as a child, probably seven or eight, flashes across my memory. My grandparents lived across the street from hers, though she probably never knew that. She was always in her own world, exploring the field next to her yard. At that point in my life, I was painfully shy, and it constrained my thoughts and ruled my actions. So when we visited my grandparents, I'd run upstairs into my grandfather's office. I'd play with his guitar while I sat in the window seat, enjoying my bird's eye view of the outside world.

"I know," I say. And she looks at me quizzically.

"Oh, right. Aunt Margie told you that day you two snuck off in the corn maze," she dips her head into her wine glass, taking a sip.

"Actually, I already knew. Before that, I mean," I say awkwardly. She looks at me like a bird just landed on my head and crapped down my face. "Don't freak out. I swear I'm not a creepy stalker or something. My grandparents used to live across the street from your family. I used to hide upstairs, and, every once in a while, I'd see you from the second-story window. One time I watched you drag a raccoon into your garage."

She stares at me, her expression transforming from horror to confusion. "Wait, what?" she finally says. Why don't I remember you?

"I was… awkward. And shy," I grumble out. Even now, even with how comfortable I am with her, I hate admitting how much I've struggled with this over the course of my life. "I spent most of my time inside when we visited my grandparents. Plus, eight-year-old me thought you were crazy brave. No way I had enough courage to venture outside and wrestle raccoons," I say with a smile. "Plus, those things have rabies," I say with faux seriousness.

"I… Wow. I feel terrible that I don't remember you. Are you sure?"

I laugh. "Do you remember the raccoon?"

She ducks her head and grimaces a little. "Oh, my Mom and Aunt Margie aren't likely to ever let me forget that." A beat passes, and she looks up. "You really did see that. You couldn't have known. Unless Aunt Margie told you?"

I shake my head no.

"So you knew who I was in high school? I mean that I used to be your grandparents' neighbor?"

I remember that day like it was yesterday. Hell, probably because I've recalled it every day of my life since it happened. I had my head down in my locker, trying to get a grip on the noise around me. At seventeen, I was still fighting my deeply ingrained shyness, despite the popularity I inherited by being a good baseball player and constantly hanging out with the team.

That day, like every other one before it, I was hoping to catch a glimpse of her, of Amelia. By high school, that puppy love I'd latched on to for the young girl across the street had morphed into something more. Stoked by the fires of teenage hormones, it was a full-blown, infatuated crush. But, back then, there was no way I'd ever be brave enough to act on it.

I tried to play it cool while looking through the cafeteria window across the hall from where I was standing. And there she was, right where I hoped she'd be, where she always was every Monday. The brown waves of her hair skimmed her shoulders. She wore a washed-out pink sweater and an enamel pin fastened over her heart. Unsurprisingly, her nose was tucked firmly behind a book.

I was completely caught up in that stolen moment, watching the way her hand lingered on the pages. When her eyes broke from the page, and she suddenly looked up, she caught me staring at her like some kind of weirdo. I turned back around and stared into the depths of my locker, trying to collect myself. My locker door slammed hard in front of me, and I startled back a couple of steps. And there was Eric, grinning back at me like he just got laid behind the bleachers. Hell, he probably did. He was the captain of our baseball team and always seemed to have a pack of girls throwing themselves at him. I was both jealous and disgusted, even though there was really only one girl I wanted.

I remember talking to him about baseball practice, feigning interest in the girls he kept rambling on about. He was interested in Chelsea, but I didn't care. I was more worried that Chelsea was interested in me, and I didn't know how to tell her no. And Chels was used to getting her way. And she was hot with her blonde ponytail, perky boobs, and short cheerleading skirt. The very epitome of most teenage boys' fantasies. But not mine. Which is why she was so determined to make me like her.

I had finally decided to make my retreat to the locker room, but I was a distracted mess. Between the cacophony of students in the hallway and my raging hormones that flared up like a pile of dry wood soaked in lighter fluid and torched with a flamethrower every time I saw Amelia, I wasn't paying attention. I walked on autopilot as I gazed down at my practice jersey in my hands.

Which is why I didn't see her.

I slammed into something, someone. The breath was knocked out of me as I tumbled forward. It took me a moment to realize I had fallen. Everything was dark and warm and smelled like vanilla, cinnamon, and pencil shavings.

"Get OFF of me!" Even now, recalling that exact moment makes my stomach heave like one of those inflatable dancing things outside car dealerships.

I slowly lifted my head, alarm bells ringing in my subconsciousness.

Because I knew I should have felt like I just got punched in the face by the floor. But I managed to find a soft place to land… a really soft place. As the shock ebbed away, I realized I was on top of… Amelia. And that soft landing? That was my face buried in her ample cleavage.

It was an out-of-body experience, my brain warring between the horror of hurting her and making a scene in front of half the student body… and the distinct pleasure of touching her. Amelia, the girl I had a crush on for years, was beneath me… in the middle of the hallway in our high school. I felt her shove my shoulders and yell again. I looked at her face, where rage and embarrassment were fighting a battle.

At first, I didn't notice laughter filling the hallway… or that my hand was resting on Amelia's bare thigh where her skirt slid up, exposing her underwear. I ripped my hand away like hot coals had just branded me. She grabbed her skirt, yanking it down to cover her underwear and thighs.

Eric's voice still rattles my mind. "Getting frisky in the halls with the nerds there, Rhett?" His yell echoed down the hallway, calling the attention of the rest of the student body. He gave me two overly enthusiastic thumbs up, cementing my guilt and shame.

"Man, I wish the girls would hurl themselves at me like that!" Anthony, another teammate, jeered.

"I wish I had your balls, Hebert, getting it on in the hallway!"

On and on it went. The laughter and teasing came from all sides, a swirling tornado of voices around us. And just like I did earlier this evening, I let my shame and shyness take hold, locking me into place. Even though I was literally on top of Amelia, I couldn't move. My vision tunneled until all I could see were flushed cheeks and eyes brimming with tears. It was enough to shock me back into reality and force me to my feet. But when I leaned over to help her, a voice cut through the noise around us.

"Nice granny panties." Chels stood a few feet away, taking in the scene. "Where'd you find those hideous things? Goodwill?" The clan of girls always following Chels snickered loudly at her insults, but she wasn't done. Oh no. She had pried open the bear trap and needed only to apply a little pressure to spring it.

"Good attempt at humping Rhett in the hallway, by the way. I'll give you that, but he's mine," Chels said, sliding a possessive arm around my back. "Throw yourself at someone else next time."

I was still having a mortifying out-of-body experience, trying to figure out how I went from quietly daydreaming about Amelia to standing above her, Chels's arm stroking my back. Nearly the whole school must have been standing behind me and laughing at her. I knew, at that moment, that every dream I ever had of asking Amelia out, every imagined kiss, would never, ever happen. She looked at me like I not only stole her favorite cat but threw it in a bag and drowned it in the river.

Fueled by panic, I tried to salvage some of Amelia's dignity. I pulled away from Chels, knowing Amelia needed someone to stand with her. But when I tried to get Amelia to take my hand to help her up, she looked at it like it was a hot poker and I was inviting her to scald herself. She scrambled up and surveyed the ground around her. She must have dropped whatever she was carrying because her belongings were scattered. She started grabbing books and pencils gracelessly, shoving them into her backpack.

I reached down to help her pick up her things, but she glared at me. Her look swung a hammer into my gut. "I just want to be left alone," she said through tears. "Is that too much to ask?" And then, as if the universe looked at what was happening and decided it wasn't embarrassing enough, her backpack suddenly ripped, spilling all her books back to the floor. We both stared in horror as her tampons spilled out and bounced, actually fucking bounced, hitting the feet of one of the nearby football players.

The laughter around ratcheted up, catching fire and spreading through the student body, lightning striking a dry tree and leaping across a dead forest. Ty, a football player, reached down and snagged a couple of the tampons, pretended they were guns and fired them at his buddies. "Don't touch me with that shit, man," they said as they jumped away from him.

But that wasn't even the worst part.

"Here, let me help," Chels said coyly as she walked past me and bent down to where Amelia was bent over collecting her books. I watched, locked in place by debilitating shame and shyness, as Chels leaned into Amelia and bumped her hard with her hip, making her stumble, hands slapping the cold tiles. It was like watching a train wreck, and I couldn't stop it. I heard her say, quietly enough that just the three of us could hear her, "You think this little embarrassment was bad? It will be far worse next time if you ever try to throw yourself at Rhett again."

"I didn't... I wasn't," Amelia stammered. And my heart, once aflame with desire, turned into a doused, smoldering pit of ashes.

Chels' lips crooked to the side. "Have a nice day," she says with mock kindness, waggling her fingers at Amelia.

Amelia took one more look at me, eyes filled with anger and tears, cheeks aflame, then ran down the hall, leaving all her things behind. Laughter, catcalls, and whistles chased her out of the hallway. And I knew I was a total piece of shit for it, but when I felt Chels wrap her arm around me again and said, "Come on, Rhett, you've got a big game to practice for," I numbly let her guide me away from the disaster.

"RHETT? RHETT? YOU OKAY?" I snap back into the present and see Amelia across the table, trembling with the desire to jump across the table and comfort me. I was trapped in that terrible memory and now the shame of it washes over me, fresh and raw.

"Amelia. I really am so sorry. You have no idea," I gulp, reaching for my cocktail and knocking back a shot.

Her brows furrow in question.

"About that day in high school," I croak out. I can barely look at her.

"Rhett, you already apologized. I forgave you. A long time ago, if we're being honest. Looking back, I realize now that it was a really, really unfortunate accident.

But I refuse to let her forgive me that easily. "Lia," I say in an embarrassed whisper. "I was such a cowardly dumbass who should have done more."

"No, Rhett. You misunderstand. That's not why I mentioned high school. At all!" She seems to realize that her earlier words brought on my memories and this flood of apologies.

She presses, "I just didn't think you even knew I existed, that's all. I mean, you were cool and on the baseball team, and that popular Chelsea chick was all over you. I was just a big nerd."

I wince, Chels' face flashing across my mind, but tonight is not the night to discuss my history with Chels. I take a few slow, deep breaths and rally. I need this to be a good evening, one that makes Lia want to see me again. "Believe me, Lia. I knew who you were. I just let the stupid teenage boy in me make decisions back then. I've tried hard to be a better, stronger man."

"Rhett, teenagers are stupid. It's a confusing and terrible time in life where we feel like we're grownups, but ruled by hormones and angst. Yes, it was a bad day. A bad high school experience, in general. At least for me. But, I've had a lot of time to step away from that. To build up and discover the person I am, or at least attempt to. Plus, at least high school helped fortify me for dealing with the ugly whims of mean girls."

I cringe, then take her in. She's so earnest and I realize she is trying to comfort me. Ugh. This is not what I wanted for tonight. I shake my head, start to talk. Stop. But she speaks again.

"Plus, what an absolute revelation," she says, lips curving into a grin. "The hot, popular baseball player actually knew the nerdy, little wallflower existed. It's like my whole life's a lie."

She thinks I'm hot? I swallow and wrap that thought up and store it in my pocket to obsess over later. It's well past time to change the subject. "What happened to you anyway?" I say. "You were there, across the street from my grandparents for years, and then one day, there was a new family there."

Her face falls. "My parents divorced. They sold the house and moved into separate places. Mom moved into an apartment with me, and Dad went back to Greenville, Mississippi, which is where he's from originally. But Mom, well, Mom really struggled with depression.

I guess she always did, but the miscarriages and the divorce sent her over the edge. She couldn't take care of me like she needed to, and I missed having a yard, being outside." She pauses to take a sip of her wine.

"Mom needed help, and her sister, Aunt Margie, stepped in," Lia shrugs as if to say, of course, she did. That's the kind of person Aunt Margie is. "She took us both under her wing, and we moved in with her, way out in the country off Farmerville Highway. There were so many changes and adjustments for all three of us, but living with Aunt Margie was the best thing that ever happened to us. It grounded us. And Aunt Margie, she took care of us. She made sure we were both okay, you know? Looking back now, as an adult, I realize how selfless Aunt Margie was with us. She can seem so gruff and dismissive, but she has the best heart under all that grouchy exterior. She loves us so much and sacrificed her life to make sure we were alright. She's a second mom to me."

My heart hurts thinking of that raccoon touting little girl caught up in a broken family. But as I stare at this beautiful, confident woman in front of me, I realize that her family wasn't all that broken. If anything, it was forged into something stronger. Then I smile. "I bet you loved living out in the country with all those wild animals, though, huh?"

And a grin erupts across her face. "Oh, you have no idea. I think Aunt Margie probably regretted letting us move in with her the first time I brought an armadillo home." And a laugh bursts from her, airy and bright. "Those things are blind, and when they startle, they just roll up in a little ball. I went hunting for one with a net when I was, oh, probably ten or eleven. I got up early because they are always out at dawn. I had binoculars and a net like I was a Louisiana Steve Irwin. And when I managed to catch one, I was so proud! I brought it home in my net and told Aunt Margie that I was going to build a cage for it. She took one look at that poor thing and said, 'Amelia Louise Murphy, you turn your ass around and put that thing back where it came from or so help me.'"

And I'm laughing now, too, imagining the whole scene.

"What about you? Surely you got up to no good as a kid?"

The waiter shows up then and takes our orders.

After he leaves, Lia sips her wine and asks, "So? I told you about my armadillo escapade. Dish it. Tell me an embarrassing childhood story."

Taking a sip of my drink, I lean in. "Well, there was this one time…" She leans in closer to listen, and I can smell her: pumpkin spice, wine, laundry detergent. I hold my breath a little longer, letting her scent fill my senses, soothing me. She leans closer. "Yes?"

I smile at her, looking up and down her face. I owe her an embarrassing story a thousand times over. And even though it's hard for me, I offer up an uncomfortable moment from my past to her in supplication.

"Well, when I was fourteen, I thought I was a badass, practically an adult. Occasionally, my dad would come home after a long day, reach for a bottle of gin and make a cocktail. When I asked what he was mixing up, he told me it was an 'adult beverage' and that I wouldn't like it until I was an adult."

"Oh, I think I know where this is going," Lia says, settling back into her chair and taking a sip of wine.

I raise my eyebrows at her. "Do you now? Well then, I guess I'll stop there," I say, leaning away and back into my own seat, mirroring her pose.

She kicks me under the table. "Don't you dare leave me hanging like that!"

I look at her with mock horror. "Okay, fine," I concede, leaning forward conspiratorially.

"One night, a couple of my friends spent the night at my house. I didn't have a lot of friends. I… mostly kept to myself. But I was playing baseball by then and invited my teammates over. I told them about my dad's drinks, which in hindsight, was a terrible idea. But I was trying to be cool. And so, we waited until my parents went to bed and snuck downstairs to make our own 'adult beverages.'"

I look at the drink in my hand now and shake my head.

"We mixed them with all kinds of terrible shit, and they tasted awful, but none of us would admit it. Cool factor and all. In the middle of our attempt at bartending, my little sister, who was twelve at the time, walked in on us and threatened to wake up mom and dad and tell them. To keep her quiet, we offered to let her join us, but told her that only adults actually liked these kinds of drinks. Well, damn if her defiant self didn't chug a whole glass of that awful concoction and put our asses to shame."

"No!" Lia says with horrified delight, hand covering her mouth. Her eyes widen, ready to hear the rest of this tragic tale.

"Oh, yes. And none of us was going to let a twelve-year-old girl show us up, so we all downed them, too…"

I stop talking to take a sip of my cocktail, the heady smell of hard liquor instantly transporting me back to that night.

"Well, what happened?" Lia asks.

"I didn't realize you were so invested?" I tease. She raises an eyebrow.

I laugh. "Okay… So, at first, it was fine. We laughed a lot and said stupid shit. And then we realized dad's gin bottle was nearly empty, so we decided to replace it… with water," I shake my head. "We were so dumb. But then we all started feeling really sick. Katie raced off to the bathroom and locked the door. We heard her start puking, and that was all it took. Just the sound of it…" I shudder.

We all went downhill from there, puking all over ourselves and the floor of dad's office. We tried to clean it up, but we were sloshed. When Mom and Dad woke up and found us, we were all asleep on the floor and smelled like booze and vomit… that is, all of us except for Katie. That sly girl managed to take a shower and go to bed. Mom and Dad were none the wiser, and we never told on her because she said she'd tell Dad we filled his gin bottle up with water—which he had to have figured out anyway. My parents made the three of us tell Jeff's and Eric's parents what happened. Needless to say, we were grounded for months." I shake my head again. "We were so stupid."

I look up at Lia, and she is chuckling to herself. "You really were an idiot. But I think I need to meet your sister. Sounds like a woman I'd like," she says.

"She'd love you," I say instantly, knowing it's true. "But I'm scared of the kind of trouble the two of you could create together. We're all done for if Beth gets in on it too." I'm grinning now, my cocktail helping to relax me.

Our food arrives, and we spend the rest of dinner sharing stories about our family and laughing at each other's childhood antics.

When we step out of the restaurant, it's dark out, and the temperature has dropped. We reach for one another on instinct, smiling when our hands touch. I feel like teenage Rhett again, lost in the sight of Lia's lips, her smile, her eyes, her dress…

When we climb into the truck, I look over, lift an eyebrow and say, "Up for one more adventure this evening?"

"I think I can handle it. Where should I tell my 'I haven't been kidnapped by a serial killer team' we're heading?"

"I don't suppose you'll let me surprise you? You can turn on that GPS tracking thing if you want."

"Nah, I think I'm safe."

Every protective instinct in me perks up at those few words. Lia knows she's safe with me. I momentarily consider pulling her into my lap and cocooning my body around hershers—a space just for the two of us. But yea, that's a weird response, so I focus on our next destination instead. I pull out of the parking lot and make my way to the interstate. Lia looks at me, reaches for my hand resting on the console between us, squeezes it, and holds on.

After about ten minutes, she says, "Um, I may need to let someone know if we're going all the way to Shreveport."

"Not quite that far. Be patient, hobbit." Her mouth twists in a half-grin, and she leans back into the passenger seat, watching the headlights on the interstate. And I can't wait to see her face when she realizes the surprise I have planned for us this evening.

Chapter 21

AMELIA

When Rhett finally pulls off the exit about twenty-five minutes later in Minden, a city even smaller than our own, I am completely confused. Surely everything has been closed down here for at least an hour. I look to Rhett, a secret smile playing across his face, obviously up to something.

"Minden? I thought the only things here were a Baptist church and a bridal shop?"

"There's one other thing," he says, turning down the long, dark country roads until we get to a Methodist church with a field beside it. There's a small fall festival taking place. "Margie told me that this little fall festival has owls and goats. Thought you might like to get a glimpse of the competition," Rhett says.

"Yes!" I say with a fist pump. "Undercover work. *Espionage.* I like it." And I do, so so much. It's thoughtful, intentional and makes me feel seen like what I care about matters to him, too.

He laughs. "Sounds like you've been reading one too many spy books."

"There's no such thing as reading too many spy books," I quip back. "You should know that, Mr. Reporter."

As we step out of the truck, I notice the evening has cooled around us, making it truly feel like autumn outside. Woodsmoke and BBQ fill the air. The comforting smells bringing me back to my childhood at Aunt Margie's. Sitting by a bonfire, bundled in a blanket, while Aunt Margie grilled and we made s'mores. And by the way Rhett sighs with happiness, I know he smells it, too.

He reaches for my hand, and I slide my own into the comfort of his warm, calloused palm. My hand fits perfectly in his, and I love this small public show of affection, like he's proud to have me next to him.

Like our own festival site, there are woods around the space, lending a spooky, night-darkened atmosphere to the evening. Though this festival is much smaller than the one we're planning, it's adorable and perfectly suited to its town. I hear laughter and squealing as kids jump from hay bail to hay bail and chug hot chocolate. There is a whole pen of petting zoo animals, their musky scent mixing with the woodsmoke. There's even a little train pulling carts made from metal barrels around a track. I smile, remembering riding in something very similar as a child.

"Where to first?" Rhett asks.

"Dessert," I say, pointing to the small booth of little old church ladies selling caramel apples.

"A woman after my own heart," he says. As we walk across the field, I step closer to him, basking in this perfect moment. We wait in line behind a mom who is laying out the rules on what her three young children can and can not have to eat as they try to negotiate for more. I watch as she maneuvers around their demands and threatens to walk away with nothing at all. Aunt Margie giving me the same speech rises from my memories, and I share them with Rhett.

He leans in then, presses his lips against my ear, and asks, "So what's it going to be? Are you going for the traditional caramel apple or one of those crazy-looking ones with eight different toppings? I feel we're old enough to decide for ourselves now." He presses a smile into my temple.

I glance up. "You should know by now that I'm always going to take the crazy option." His warm and rich chuckle shudders down my spine.

"I expect nothing less."

We make it to the booth, and one of the ladies takes our order. We both go for the caramel apple with chocolate drizzle and chopped almonds on top, grabbing extra napkins before making our way over to one of the empty wooden picnic tables near the cakewalk. "Monster Mash" is playing on full blast, starting and stopping as the kids jump from one number to the next, attempting to secure an iced confection to take home with them.

Rhett is eying his giant, sugar-coated apple. "How am I supposed to eat this?"

"Don't think too hard about it. Just go in face first," I say. He turns and looks at me, lifts one eyebrow and we both burst out laughing. And I don't know if it's the atmosphere of the festival or the joy I've felt over the course of the evening, but impulsivity kicks in. I don't stop to think about it. I dig my teeth into the sugar and make a huge mess in the process. I try to cover my lips that now have caramel and chocolate smeared across them, but Rhett grabs my hand.

I look up, and he's watching me, heat licking across his gaze. The air sizzles between us, and my stomach lurches. He moves into my space, head bending and pausing, his breath teasing my lips. I ease towards him, inviting him in. And then he kisses me. He sucks my bottom lip into his mouth and licks all the caramel and chocolate off of it. One swipe of his tongue and I ignite, an ocean of lust rising from my core, muting everything else around us.

He leans away and whispers, voice deep and throaty, "Maybe we should have just gotten one to share."

"Maybe we'll just get one to go next time," I say, amazed at my own boldness. His gaze heats further, and he starts to go in for another kiss when a kid runs up to him and shouts, "Hey, Mister! Where did you get that?" He's pointing at the caramel apple. Rhett pulls back from me and points to the caramel apple booth. The kid takes off running, and Rhett ducks his head in a quiet laugh, eyes still smoldering.

"Your turn," I say nodding at his caramel apple, trying to wrestle back my desire. I'm ready to watch his attempt to eat the mess. He pulls out a brown paper bag complete with a paper tray and plastic knife that he must have gotten from the booth when I wasn't looking. He promptly slices up his apple, pops a piece in his mouth, and chews with satisfaction.

"Well, that would have been nice to have before I went face first into chocolate and caramel," I say with mock indignation.

"Nah," he says, a wide grin on display and – damn. There's that delicious dimple again. "I liked watching you try to eat it your way. And... I enjoyed sharing." He presses his leg against mine, and I push back.

"Well, just for that, you have to cut mine up for me."

He makes quick work of it. After we finish our apples, we get up and walk around, hand in hand. We laugh at the old wooden, painted cutouts of scarecrows and candy corn that the church has probably used for this festival since the 1980s.

"Not sure if your festival can beat out this kind of competition. I mean, they have ponies, hobbit, and we both know how much hobbits like their ponies."

I elbow him in the ribs, and he laughs loudly.

"Come on, and I'll take you home."

As we walk back to the truck, I soak in his warmth. And as I replay that stolen kiss on the picnic bench, I wonder how our evening will end.

OUR DRIVE BACK IS FULL of laughter and joking. We somehow manage to avoid talking about work, and it's a break we both need— this moment of existing with one another right here, right now. By the time we pull up to my house, all awkwardness is gone. Our hands are still clasped across the truck console, and Rhett rubs his thumb over mine in slow circles. That single point of contact shooting waves of desire through my whole body. How can one touch make me feel like this? Matt never made me feel this way. No, stop. Do not think about Matt.

Parked in my driveway, I can tell we are both trying to figure out what happens next. The uncertainty fills the air around us. Do I give him a quick goodnight kiss inside the truck and tell him I'll talk to him tomorrow? That feels too casual, like I'm telling him "thanks, but no thanks." But it's too soon to ask him to come inside, right? My stomach is like the inside of a pinball machine, all flipping paddles and metal balls banging around. I can feel my awkward ostrich peek her head up and look around, ready and willing to ruin our perfect evening.

"I had a great time tonight," he finally says, squeezing my hand tight and attempting to pop the balloon of tension hanging around us. I zero in on that small touch, his warm hand holding mine, his calloused palm brushing against my own, his thumb stroking mine. My traitorous brain immediately goes to what else that thumb might do when allowed to explore the rest of my body. I'm struggling between throwing myself at Rhett and jumping out of the car in an awkward panic and running inside.

But when he looks into my eyes, I'm completely caught up in him, and all thoughts of running evaporate. I'm not sure which of us moves first, but suddenly my stomach is pressed against the console of his truck, straining against it to reach him. I feel his lips on mine. He kisses me softly, slowly, brushing his lips over mine again and again. And then our mutual desire takes over, and we are kissing like that day in the barn closet—with a ravenous, insatiable hunger. Our teeth and tongues clash as our desire rises. Rhett pulls back, nips my lip, then trails kisses down my neck. It's the most perfect form of torture.

This is so good, so hot, so right. I try to move in closer, but the truck's console is pressing into the side of my ribs. I fumble around to unbuckle my seatbelt. When it finally releases, I pull away from the kiss to let it retract, then dive into him again. Rhett does the same, and then we are kissing madly, deeply. I feel the scruff of his new beard scraping against my lips and cheeks, and that slight hurt paired with our warm kisses sets me ablaze.

I scramble gracelessly over the console and into his lap, trying to fit in the small space between the steering wheel and his large body.

He reaches down to grab a lever and slides the seat back to give us more room. The sudden jolt of the seat sliding backward startles me, and we bump heads, both laughing breathlessly.

"Is this okay?" he asks softly, thumb tracing my lower lip.

"Yes," I rasp out. And then he's kissing me again, with ferocious passion. I feel his hand slide across my thigh, under my dress, up over my underwear, until he finds the skin of my back. He strokes circles on my lower back, each pass pushing heat further and further into my body.

I reach for his shoulders to stabilize myself on his lap, and my legs slide to either side of his hips so I'm straddling him. I can feel his desire as he pushes up against me, the friction driving me wild. His hands climb higher up my back, feeling along my ribs, higher until they find my bra. My hands return the favor, making their way down his shoulders, feeling his biceps as they work to rub my back. My hands slide to his chest, feeling the muscles beneath the thin fabric of his button-up shirt. I let them drift lower until I find where his shirt is tucked into his pants.

He strokes the clasp of my bra just as I lightly tug on the hem of his shirt, working it free. He pulls away from me and looks into my eyes, his expression fogged with heady desire.

"Lia. Wait."

I freeze. *Oh shit. Is this too much? Does he think I'm desperate?* I feel embarrassment creep up my cheeks. "Oh, I'm sorry," I stutter and start to slide off his lap, but he holds me close to him, lightly stroking my thighs with his thumbs where my dress has risen up.

"Wait, no. I didn't mean." He exhales loudly.

I pause, waiting to see what he says.

"I just. I don't want to rush things, and I don't want to pressure you into anything you're not comfortable with," he says, expression strained as if uttering those words is physically painful.

I let out a throaty laugh. "I think it's pretty obvious that I'm comfortable with what's happening here," I say breathlessly. "But if you want to stop, I understand. I know it's soon and…" but my words have liberated his caution from the last traces of his restraint. His lips are on mine again, and his tongue is dipping into my mouth desperate for more.

And even though we are both still fully clothed, I move against him. Rhett follows my lead, hips lifting in rhythm with my own. I let my hands slide under his shirt and groan when I feel his hard, flat stomach beneath my palms.

"Lia," Rhett whispers desperately. My hands roam, exploring the hidden planes beneath his shirt. I feel his hands start working the clasps of my bra.

"Do you need me to undo it?" I whisper into his mouth. But just then, I feel the tension of my bra release and fall forward. He's managed to unclasp it with one hand. Smooth. As my bra loosens, he moves his hands around to my breasts, thumbs stroking. I gasp. He groans as our hands roam each other's bodies, exploring, touching, lighting up with sensation.

Rhett leans forward to kiss my neck, and then a loud horn blares. We both jump straight up. I hit my head on the roof of the truck. "Shit!" I yell. My heart is pounding, and we are both breathing heavily.

"What the hell?" Rhett exclaims.

"Um, I think I hit the car horn with my butt," I say and start laughing.

Rhett chuckles, and then he leans his forehead into mine. My phone starts ringing, and I groan. "Ignore it," I whisper to him, grazing my greedy lips across his.

He lets out a pained sigh. "You should check it. What if it's Margie? That woman scares me, Lia. She'll come after me with a pitchfork if she thinks I've done anything to you," he says, brushing his lips against mine in reassurance.

He's right. If it is her and I don't respond, I know she has no problem showing up at my house to make sure I made it home safely. And wouldn't that be awkward if things continue down this path?

I grab my phone and look at the screen. Yep, a missed call from Aunt Margie and several texts. She can't help but be a bit overprotective.

Margie: Lia, how did it go tonight?

Margie: You there?

Margie: Do I need to come get you?

Margie: Are you passed out drunk somewhere?

Margie: Shit, I'm coming over.

Missed call.

I frantically text back.

Amelia: I made it home safely. You do NOT need to come over.

Or at least that's what I intend to send, but autocorrect has a mind of its own. I'm convinced that whoever programs autocorrect has a diabolical plan to subtly ruin everyone's lives. Because what I actually send is:

Amelia: I mess it home sanity. You NEED to come over.

Immediately a text appears on my screen.

Margie: I'm on my way.

"Shit shit shit shit," I hiss, and Rhett looks worried. "Is everything okay?" he asks.

"Yes, no. Just a second," I say, calling Aunt Margie. She answers on the first ring.

"Lia, I'm coming. Are you alright? Did he do something to you?"

"No, Aunt Margie, I'm fine. I promise. Autocorrect mistake," I tell her quickly.

"If you're being held hostage, at gunpoint, or need a way out, say our code word," she whispers into the phone.

And God bless my aunt for all the conversations we've had over the years. She has always made sure I've understood consent and safety and had an exit plan if I needed one. My heart aches with how much I love her.

"I promise. I'm fine. Really. We actually had a wonderful time tonight, and I promise to tell you all about it tomorrow."

I hear her exhale through the phone. "Okay, if you're sure."

"I'm sure," I say, trying to push all the calming vibes I can muster through the phone. "Good night Aunt Margie. Love you."

"Love you too, Lia."

When I hang up the phone, I look at Rhett, and I know our lust-fueled make out session is over, at least for tonight.

"I'm really sorry about that," I say, dipping my forehead to press against his. "My aunt is so protective of me. She has a troubled past and…"

"It's okay. You don't have to explain. I'm glad to know someone is watching out for you," he whispers to me in the intimate space we've formed between our bowed heads. He tilts his head, presses a soft, chaste kiss to my lips, then pulls back and looks into my eyes.

"Let's do it again?" he asks hopefully. And I know he's talking about all of it—the dinner, the evening out, the making out.

"Yes, please." I smile. Reaching behind me, I re-clasp my bra, then open the driver's side door next to us and try to slide out of his lap and onto my driveway. But, after several minutes with my legs tucked in tight against my body, my right foot fell asleep. So, when I attempt to exit the truck and land gracefully on the concrete, my leg buckles. As if in slow motion, arms pinwheeling, I fall and land on my ass, hands slapping the concrete. My dress has ridden all the way up my thighs and I am a hot mess. Way to finish this date strong, Lia.

Rhett jumps out of his truck and reaches down to pull me back to my feet.

"You alright?"

I roll my eyes at myself, lifting my hand to inspect the bleeding scrapes. "Yes. My foot just fell asleep. Give me a second. I can already feel the needle-prick sensation of it waking up again."

He kneels down to where I'm still sitting in my driveway and extends a hand. "Must be something about me," Rhett says, pulling me to my feet and wrapping his arms around my waist. "Every time I'm around you, you seem to get weak in the knees." He gives me a shy smile, and I can see that he's still struggling with the guilt of the past. Trying to find a way forward with levity. So, I indulge him, reaching over to poke his ribs.

"Hey now, you don't want me to drop you and let you hit the ground… again," he whispers into my ear.

"That's fine. I'll hop to my front door… with dignity." I pull away from him and start to do a sort-of one-footed zombie lurch to my house when I feel Rhett step up beside me, his arm wrapping around my lower back, and we walk to the front door together. Tucker starts barking as soon as he hears us.

Rhett leans into me and says, "Don't forget to text Beth and let her know you made it home safely. I don't want her and her posse of angry Junior Leaguers showing up on my front doorstep with baseball bats at 2 a.m."

"I think I'll wait a little bit longer. Beth will want a full minute-by-minute report of our date as soon as I tell her I'm home," I say.

"Date. I like the sound of that." He reaches and tucks a strand of my dark hair behind an ear. "Thank you for the best first date I've ever been on," he says. Then leans in and gives me one more long, soft, warm kiss. It's the kind of kiss that promises future cuddles on the couch and laughing over movies together. The kind that says, "I want to hold you. To be with you." I sigh against his lips, and we slowly pull away from each other.

"I'll call tomorrow. I know things are busy with the final push to the festival. Let me know if you can break away one day this week. I can come to you, bring you lunch," Rhett says.

"Okay," I say, warmth filling my soul. I turn and unlock my front door. When I open it, Tucker rushes to me, jumps up, and places his paws on my stomach, tail wagging. He hops back down and rushes to Rhett, sniffing his feet before jumping up on him and licking his hand in greeting.

Rhett leans down, pats his head, and says, "Don't worry. I'll take good care of your Mom, buddy."

With that, Tuck jumps down and runs back inside. I follow him in, then turn around one last time.

"Good night, Lia," Rhett says with warm affection.

"Good night." And I let my eyes linger on his broad frame as he walks back to his truck and climbs in. I wave to him from behind my screen door. Rhett is right. This was my best ever first date, too.

164

Chapter 22

RHETT

Three Days Until the Festival (Wednesday)

I hit send on my email, successfully wrapping my third story of the day and sending it off to the news editor.

"And he's back!" Jacob says enthusiastically as he slides into the chair across from my desk, throwing touchdown hands into the air with a smile. "I heard the story you wrote on the fracking out near Farmerville is going to be front-page news tomorrow," he raises his eyebrows. "I guess this means I have a little healthy competition again."

I try to play it cool, but I can't help it. I'm grinning like an idiot. "Not gonna lie. It feels good to be excited about work again."

"And, just think, after our band performance on Saturday, you will have every seventy-year-old widow in a thirty mile radius giving you her number." He winks. I laugh, and then my smile slowly fades as I remember Ms. Clark and grandma and their widow support group.

"Hey man, no need to look so glum. Some of those old ladies are in great shape and can make a mean apple pie," Jacob says.

"No, no, it's not that. The widow comment just reminded me of my visit to Ms. Clark." I tell Jacob the whole story, and by the time I'm done, he's somber as well.

"So now what? She doesn't want you to pursue it? What are you going to do? Let it drop? I mean, you have your fire back. Wasn't that what this was really all about?"

"Yes. No. I don't know. I guess there's no rush to pursue the story on Jimmy Roberts, but I feel connected to him and to Ms. Clark. Especially since now I know how much Grandma used to check in on her—and that Jimmy and I used to play together as kids. The whole situation is just freaking weird, you know? After discovering all these connections, it seems like dropping the story would be like flipping the bird to the universe" I let out a heavy sigh. "I'll figure something out, I guess."

"But first, we should celebrate getting your groove back. How about a couple of beers at Sundown?" Jacob asks.

I look at my watch, shocked to realize it's already 4:30. I start packing up my things. "Can't today. I promised Lia I'd help her set up for the festival after work the rest of this week. They have so much to do and could use an extra set of hands."

"Help Lia?" he says meaningfully.

There goes my dumb grin again. "Yea, so?"

"And just how will you be helping her?" he asks suggestively, one eyebrow raising.

I roll my eyes. "Why don't you come with me and find out? We could use a big ox like you to help lift crates and mount fancy decorations to walls."

He sits back in his chair. "Nah, I think I'll pass today. I'll go get that beer—in your honor, of course–and let you and Lia have some alone time," he says, voice dripping with innuendo.

"Don't get too sloshed. We need you at the top of your game for our final band practice tomorrow night."

"Okay, Mom," he replies, waving his hand at me as he stands. "I think I can handle myself. You, however… well, don't do anything I wouldn't do." He winks dramatically and then turns and heads back to his desk.

I finish packing up my things and make my way to the truck, already thinking about a way to get some alone time with Lia again.

"RHETT, HONEY, BE A DEAR and come get this crate of spooky shit and carry it out to the corn maze." Margie is a woman on a mission, and she has shown up in full force to help Lia and Beth do all the final festival prep work.

As I hoist up the cardboard box, dirt billows up in my face. I cough and squint through the dust cloud and see large, sequined, fuzzy spider legs sticking out of it. I know better than to question Margie's orders though, so I haul it outside. The sun is beginning her descent and its glow stops me in my tracks. I take a moment to pause and enjoy golden hour—that perfect moment in time when the setting sun sets the world ablaze with warmth and magic.

Two arms slide around my waist from behind and give me a squeeze. Looking over my shoulder, I see a pile of wavy brown hair in a bun and two beautiful big, brown eyes looking up at me. I want to drop my box right then and there and press Lia up against the side of the barn, but I know Janet, her aunt, and, hell, everyone and their mama would see us. So instead, I whisper, "Hey there, hobbit. I missed you, too." She gives me one more tight squeeze and then lets go.

"Give me a second. I'll grab a box and walk with you," she says.

Together we lumber over with arms full to the man stationed at the entrance of the corn maze. He smiles broadly when he sees Lia, and I feel a jealousy surge through me.

"Hey there, Lia!" He reaches and takes the box from her. "Follow me, and I'll show you where Beth's staging all this."

As we walk through the maze, I glance over and see her watching him and have to stifle the temptation to hurl my box of fuzzy spider legs directly into the back of his head. He's about our age, maybe a little older. And I know by the way he looks at Lia that he knows how hot she is and would be all for it if she gave him the go-ahead. But when we make it to the staging area, he puts the box down and Lia simply says, "Thanks for helping, David." He turns around and starts opening the box up.

David pauses a minute, then shrugs and walks back out. It's quiet inside the corn maze, the tall stalks blocking out the sounds of everyone working at the festival site around us. I watch Lia unpack the box, admiring the sight of her bent over… again. She's wearing shorts and I take the opportunity to admire the long expanse of her legs. I walk over to her and place my hand on her lower back.

"Here, let me help you with that," I say, leaning over.

"Is he gone?" she whispers.

"Who, the box carrier?"

"David."

"Yes, he's gone."

"Thank goodness. I was about to make up a task for him to do so he would finally leave."

I only have a moment to bask in her words before Lia grabs my hand and drags me through the corn maze to a quiet dead end. Once there, she collides into me, pressing against my chest. She stands on tiptoe, and presses her lips to mine. Her mouth opens and my body responds without thought, meeting her tongue stroke for stroke. I wrap my arms around her, pulling her in tight against me. I'm desperate to pick up where we left off last night.

She pulls away and whispers, "I missed you" into my mouth.

"I hope you greet me like that every time you miss me," I whisper back, still rubbing her back, wishing we were in a quiet, locked room somewhere. But then she reaches up and nips my neck, and I realize I don't care that we are outside.

"Lia," I whisper and dive back into her, kissing her desperately, my whole body a desert storm swirling with erratic bursts of heat. Even with Chels, even as a teenager, I've never felt anything like this. I'm desperate for Lia's touches, her mouth, her whole, beautiful, soft body. And she responds with the same need. Her hands are roaming. I feel them all over my back, tracing my shoulder blades, pressing my lower back… grabbing my ass.

We're both frantic, and I let my hands loose, caressing her bra through her shirt. "God, I want you," I whisper to her as my hands drift down, caressing the band of her shorts, silently asking for more. "Is this okay?" I whisper.

"More," she whispers back. I explode at her words, every part of me fireworks launching one after the other. I let my hand dip into the waistband of her shorts, slowly stroking her stomach just below her waistband. She rolls her hips against me.

"Do you like that?" I whisper, dipping my hand a little lower.

"You are such a tease," she whispers back.

A loud barking erupts from somewhere in the corn maze. "LIA! Are you in here?"

Dammit. I wrestled down a frustrated yell. It's Beth.

"Maybe if we're quiet, she won't find us," Lia whispers with a smile. There's no hint of embarrassment, just an eager desire for more. But as I watch over her shoulder, I see Tucker turn the corner. Like a heat-seeking missile, the dog finds his mistress, running up to her, tail wagging. I hear more shuffling in the corn, and Lia whispers, "Later," before pulling back and tugging up her shorts in one swift motion. She turns to face the sound, positioning herself in front of me to hide the evidence of what we were just doing… what we were about to do. Beth rounds the corner, gaze zeroing in on the two of us.

"Hey, Beth. All good. Just setting up some of the last corn maze decorations," Lia says a bit breathlessly. Beth looks at us both, taking in our rumpled appearances. Lia's hair is tangled and wild. Her shirt is untucked, and she's flushed. I can't even imagine what I must look like right now, but I know my lips are swollen from kissing. Then Beth looks around us.

"And yet, I see no decorations," she says pointedly.

"Brainstorming," Amelia says.

"Hmmm. Well, brainstorming time is over. We need to get the decorations up. Corn maze needs to be ready by the end of the day today. We have more things to take care of tomorrow," she turns to walk back to our staging area, pauses, and looks over her shoulder. "Oh, and Lia. You may want to tame that hair of yours before Margie sees you and thinks you had an encounter with one of Ms. Clark's cats again."

Chapter 23

AMELIA

By the time we leave the corn maze, we are sweaty and exhausted from unloading and staging decorations throughout the maze, but I barely notice. I'm still fixated on making out with Rhett, on the warmth of his body, how close we got to… yea. And I'm trying to stifle the grin that's found a permanent place on my face. And it's hard, especially when Rhett is right there every time I turn to grab another box or hang another decoration. When he passes, he brushes against my back and lightly tugs my ponytail to get my attention. And I'm doing it right back, tracing my fingers along his biceps, aching for the physical contact, doing my best to get him to show me that dimple. Our little scene in the corn maze is playing on repeat inside my head.

The prep team has mostly stopped for the day and as I look around the inside of the barn, I'm proud of our progress. It looks like the autumn section of Hobby Lobby and Magnolia Magazine made a cocktail, and the blender exploded in here… which means it's perfect!

Thanks to Beth, we have hand-lettered signs adorning all the vendor stalls. We have new signs that direct attendees to food, shopping, games, crafts, music, and activities. Orange, red, and gold shimmer at every corner. Tomorrow we will decorate the stage and make sure the food vendors have everything out at the site. Beth has also rallied the Junior League to manage all the craft tents for the kids.

They can make leaf murals, decorate pumpkins, and get their faces painted. I know I'll see women out here dropping off craft supplies in droves tomorrow. And I smile. We're doing it… we're actually doing it. I feel a set of warm arms wrap around me from behind.

"What's got you smiling like that?"

I reach down and hug his arms wrapped around my waist. "I'm just so pleased with how this is coming together. It's been so much hard work and, for a while there, I wasn't sure I could do it."

"I always knew you could," Rhett says.

"You haven't even known me that long."

"Oh, trust me, I used to watch you in high school… all the time. If Amelia Murphy put her mind to something, it got done."

"Ha, well, a lot of time has passed since then."

"And you have only gotten more resourceful and more beautiful," he says, pressing a kiss to my temple.

We stand together in the quiet, enjoying the feel of one another. A knock comes from the barn door. "I bet someone left their keys," I say, walking to the door. But when I open it, Greta Clark is standing there, dusk fading behind her.

"Oh, hello," I say, slightly startled. "Were we being too loud? I asked the crew to keep it down today, so I hope…"

"No, it's not that. I… I thought of something. About Jimmy, I mean. And, well, if you're still looking into the case, it might be important to know," she says.

"Please, come in and have a seat," Rhett says. "Can I get you some water?"

She nods, and we make our way to the folding chairs in the barn's corner. I study her face, noting the deep wrinkles around her eyes and forehead—lines that time and grief have etched permanently in her expression. When Rhett brings the bottle of water to her, her hand trembles as she reaches for it. He sits next to me, leaning forward slightly, concern darting across his face. I know he feels connected to Ms. Clark, to Greta, now. They share a past, even if it was brief and he was too young to remember.

She starts to talk slowly, unwinding a pile of thoughts she once tangled up like a strand of old Christmas lights, threw in a drawer, and left untouched for decades.

"Jimmy was… special. I know that all grandmothers probably say that about their grandchildren." She smiles to herself. "But I mean that… differently. He was what they call 'on the spectrum.' My boy saw the world differently than other children. He fixated on things. And bugs were one of his… fixations."

The words are halting, painful. I stand up, walk over, and sit beside her, resting my hand lightly on hers. She startles but doesn't pull away. Breathing deeply, she starts again.

"He could look at any bug, any of them, and tell you exactly what it was… what class, its variations, its habitat… anything. And he struggled with people. Talking to them and looking them in the eye was difficult for him. He didn't pick up on social cues. Other kids bullied him."

She looks up then, straight at Rhett. "But never by you. I know you can't possibly remember those days—you were so young—but your grandmother would bring you over, and you just accepted him. You sat and listened to his long explanations of bug legs and the distinctions between arachnids and insects, and… he liked you."

I watch Rhett, who sits across from us now. I can see tears gather in his eyes. I know when he found those old newspaper stories, he could have never anticipated this: the emotions, the history, the family ties.

"And that's why I want to tell you about that night. I don't like to talk about it… or think about it. It hurts so much, and it still keeps me up at night. I failed him that day—the day he disappeared."

Goosebumps ripple up my arms, and I look up to see Rhett staring back at me. We're both anxious about whatever Greta is about to tell us. She grips my hand tightly as if drawing strength from me to keep going.

"I knew Jimmy was different, but I wanted him to have a life like other children, to experience the joy of being a kid. Jen, my daughter, was so protective of him, you see, never took him anywhere. She didn't want to spook him. And I thought the boy didn't need to be locked away, that he could still experience life. I thought maybe he just needed to give it a try, you know?" She looks up to us then, seeking understanding and validation. I squeeze her hand, and Rhett nods solemnly.

"That's why I asked your grandmother to bring you over when she visited. And it went so well. You understood him, and he lit up around you, Rhett. I knew he could do more, so I decided to surprise him and take him to the fall festival. I knew the noise would be a lot, so I took precautions. I got him earplugs. I made his costume out of his favorite materials so he wouldn't be bothered by tags or textures. I thought..." she lets out a sob full of two decades of agony, and my heart bottoms out in my ribcage at the sound. "I thought that I could do this right and let Jimmy have just one normal day."

Tears slide down her cheeks now in slow, steady tracks. She looks up at us. "I loved that boy with all of my heart," she says emphatically. "Please know that I would never have taken him to the festival if I had known..." she gasps out a sob again.

Rhett gets up, reaches into his pocket, and pulls out a handkerchief. I didn't even know people still carried those, yet he offers it to her like some old-world gentleman. Greta takes it, lightly dabbing at her cheeks.

"I didn't tell Jen because I knew she wouldn't allow it. And we live so close to the festival anyway that I thought we could be there and back in a short time. When Jimmy arrived at my house that night, I dressed him up in the costume I made for him—a grasshopper, his favorite insect. I popped the earplugs in his ears, and we walked over to the festival. I was so proud of myself. Jimmy seemed to love it. He even ate a caramel apple for the first time in his life!" She's smiling through the tears now, lost in the memory. "And oh, he loved the petting zoo, cautiously touching the animals. It warmed my heart in a way I hadn't felt in years."

Her expression darkens. "He kept pulling me to the corn maze, and when I saw how well he was doing, I thought, 'Why not?' We went in, and it seemed perfect, quiet even. But then, as we made our way through the maze, he saw a butterfly and started running ahead of me, chasing after it. I couldn't keep up. He was so fast and small." She was pleading with us to understand.

"And then I heard someone shout 'Boo!' and heard him scream in terror. I know that was all in good fun, but Jimmy didn't understand. He must have been terrified."

My heart is a bass drum in my chest as I listen. Empathy grips me, and I'm desperate to stop what I know must be coming.

Great continues, "I ran, calling for him. I searched in every nook and corner of that maze. I was in a panic. Someone working there finally realized something was wrong and went for help."

She stops talking for a long time. She's shaking and crying quietly. I look to Rhett and slowly wrap my arm around her back. She collapses into me. And even though I know how this story ends, I still hope for a way out of the tragic ending I know she's about to tell us.

"But we never found him. Ever. It's like he just disappeared into thin air. One minute he was there screaming, and the next, he was just… gone."

I feel tears running down my cheeks now and look up to see Rhett wiping away his own.

"My daughter has never forgiven me. And I don't blame her. I hate myself, too. I should have listened to her and kept him home with me that night. So, you see, it's my fault--the reason he's gone. They looked everywhere for him. If I weren't a God-fearing woman, I would have suspected ghosts or fairies snatched him up that night. But, as it stands, I have no real answer. Everyone joined the search-- the police, the community. Not a trace of Jimmy anywhere. Every day I waited for a phone call to tell me they had found him dead in the creek or that he'd wandered onto the interstate or frozen in a parking lot somewhere. I would have taken it. Anything. I was desperate for some sort of answer, but nothing ever came. I used to hike around these woods, searching for him, yelling his name. I swear I could hear his voice calling for me in the middle of the night. I'd get up and go look outside, but nothing was there. Sometimes, I still hear his voice at night and wonder if his ghost walks through my house. I know this sounds crazy, but sometimes I think that if we just knew what happened to him, then the ghostly whispers would finally stop."

Greta is a haunted woman. Haunted by the past, her guilt, her grief, and maybe even literally by her missing grandson. Silence fills the barn. It's dark outside now, casting the moment in eeriness.

"I thought you should know, Rhett, because you're the only child who was ever truly kind to my Jimmy. And your grandmother was one of the few who was kind to me. I don't want or expect any kindness from you, but… well, I don't think there is any reason for you to keep chasing this. He's gone. Forever. And digging this up again isn't going to do anything but cause pain for everyone who knew my boy." Her voice cracks on the last few words.

And I know at this moment that all of Rhett's past connections with Greta Clark have already led him to a decision. He's too good, too kind, to torture her further by pursuing this.

"Now you know why everyone hates me," Greta says.

"We don't hate you. Nor do we blame you." Rhett says into the heavy space between us. "But we do empathize with your pain. I'm sorry you've had to carry this for so long, and I'm sorry I stirred it back up for you again."

"No, no. I needed to tell you. I'm glad you showed up that day. It was the answer to a prayer, in a way. Thank you for listening to my story, my confession." She turns to look at me, eyes red and swollen from tears. "And I promise I won't interfere with the festival anymore. I know that it's not your fault or the festival's fault. It's mine."

"Is there someone we can call?" I ask her gently. "Someone who can sit with you this evening?"

"Oh no. That ship sailed years ago," she replies in gruff dismissal.

"Let us at least walk you home," Rhett says.

She nods, and together we walk her home through the now-dark field. When we finally get to her house, we walk her inside and make sure she's settled. We both write down our phone numbers, even though Rhett already gave her his card.

"Call us anytime," I say. "If you want to talk… or if you need anything."

I feel awkward. I don't know how to end this night after what she just told us. I want to wave a magic wand and fix the problem that will never be mended, go back in time, and bring her grandson back. I feel helpless and sort of cowardly for leaving her home alone.

"I think I need to rest for a while," Greta says as she leans back into her recliner and closes her eyes.

We nod and walk to the front door and then across the dark field, the moon glowing above us in silent sentry. The wind glances across our faces, whispering her secrets. It's eerie outside, and the thoughts of a small, ghostly boy wandering the woods in this field beneath the moon give me shivers. When we get to our cars, Rhett wraps an arm around my waist, and I reach up, wrapping my arms around his neck. We stand there for what could be a minute or an hour—holding each other, glad that the other is there.

Into the silence, I finally whisper, "Will you come over and sit with me for a while?" I feel his head nod into my shoulder.

"I'll follow behind you."

Chapter 24

RHETT

I pull in behind Lia's white hatchback and park in her driveway. When I open the truck door, I can already hear Tucker barking at us from his perch in the house's front window. Hand in hand, we walk into Lia's house. As the lights come on and I look around, I mentally check myself. Not a house, a home. I've been inside before, briefly, when I picked her up for our date. But this time, I revel in absorbing the space Lia lives in.

It smells like cinnamon and coffee with the musty hint of dog. Everything's a warm shade of brown—her cabinets, table, and chairs. Picture frames hold photos of Lia with Margie and a dark-haired woman who must be her mother. And there are piles of books everywhere. I see them stacked on her kitchen table, one on her kitchen counter. Peering into her living room, I see a cozy couch— also brown—and a recliner. Some bookshelves line a wall, and… yep, those are more books on her end table.

Tucker jumps up on me, tail wagging in greeting.

"Get down, Tuck," Lia chides. She looks at me, and I can see she's carrying the sadness from our talk with Greta. I am, too, if we're being honest.

"I think I need a glass of wine. Want one? Or I have beer if you like that?"

I nod. "A beer sounds good."

She pours a glass of white wine and pulls out a Great Raft beer, taking time to slide it into a koozie before handing it to me. She takes a deep sip of wine. "That was some heavy shit," she sighs, staring into the depths of her wine glass.

"Yeah. That was just really, really sad. I don't know what to do." I take a sip of beer and lean against her kitchen counter. She looks up at me, locking eyes. "Part of me wants to keep digging into this, help her find closure if I can. Another part of me thinks I should just let it go. Maybe the reason this sparked something in me wasn't so that I'd land some big story and get my reporter mojo back, but because some piece of me remembered them, remembered him." Things quiet between us as we both consider the situation.

Finally, Lia lets out a heavy sigh. "I need a mental break—from this case, from the festival work. Want to watch a movie? Take our mind off of everything?" I nod my head. She walks into her living room, nods to the couch, then digs through her Blu-ray collection.

"I thought everyone just streamed movies these days," I say, teasing her.

"Yes, but some movies, you need to be able to hold in your hands. To hug them on occasion," she says. "Now, close your eyes."

I follow her command, leaning back into the soft, deep couch. I smile at the thought of her hugging big piles of blu-rays. I hear her shuffle around by the TV and can tell she's dimmed the lights. Then I feel the couch dip as she sits next to me. I slide my hand over, blindly reaching for her.

"Can I open my eyes now?"

"No, just another minute." Her voice is light, excited.

And then I hear it, the words whisper into the dark room:

"I feel it in the earth. I smell it in the air. Much that once was is lost, for none who now live remember it."

"You didn't!" I laugh, opening my eyes just in time to see The Lord of the Rings logo pop up on the screen, the epic music filling the room. I look at Lia, and she's smiling at me, pleased with herself.

Reaching over, I wrap my arm around her shoulders, pulling her close. She melts into my side, resting her head on my shoulder.

"I thought we could both use a comfort movie tonight," she says.

I lean down, kiss the top of her head, and whisper, "Good choice, hobbit."

I don't know what we are to one another exactly, but this feels right. We lay like that for the entire movie, moving only to use the restroom or get another drink. Being with Lia like this, it's perfect. It feels like something I saw in a movie once, one of those with a happily ever after. The thought of having more evenings like this one, just the two of us together, watching a movie, holding each other. It's what I always thought marriage would be like. And I've been married, but it was never like this with Chels…

Chels.

I should probably talk to Lia about her soon. Tell her we got married. I wonder if she already knows? I should tell her we… but then I feel Lia's hand move to rub the inside of my thigh, and all of my thoughts come to an abrupt halt.

182

Chapter 25

AMELIA

Laying next to Rhett on my couch is intoxicating. I feel so relaxed, so comfortable, so cherished watching one of my favorite movies in his arms. And, yeah, maybe the two-ish full glasses of wine help, too. But it was never like this with Matt, with any of my past boyfriends. It was always about what they wanted or needed me to do for them. I let my hand slide to Rhett's leg, then to the inside of his thigh, fingers grazing across the rough denim. My mind slips to our afternoon in the corn maze, thoughts that I had pushed entirely to the side until this moment.

But now, with the warmth of the wine in my veins and the heat of his body soaking into me, I can't help but think about our stolen moment together, about what could have happened. I lightly trace circles on his thigh, memories of how his hands glided over me filling my thoughts and charging my desire. I look up at him, and he's staring down at me. His spicy, pine scent is heady, and I want to reach my face up and stroke my cheek against his close-cropped beard like a cat.

"You are so beautiful, you know that?" he says, voice gravelly. Then his eyes dip to my lips. I can't stop myself as I stretch up and meet his mouth with my own. Like before, I feel no shame, no embarrassment. Just a strong desire to touch Rhett. I long to feel him worship me with his lips and hands.

We kiss each other slowly, gently, taking the time to explore one another in a way we haven't in our few rushed, passionate encounters before. I rub my fingers through his trimmed beard, the prickling texture stoking my desire. Rhett reaches into my hair, guiding the kiss deeper until my tongue is completely intertwined with his. I ease into his lap until my legs straddle his hips.

I have dreamed of what he looks like under his button-up shirts and thin cotton tees. I can tell by how his clothes hug him and by what I've managed to feel that my dreams are likely on target with reality. I can't wait any longer. I pull away from our kiss and start unbuttoning his shirt with only the light of the still-glowing TV screen to guide me.

Rhett holds me tightly against him, his hands pressing my hips, but doesn't move to help. He lets me take my time as I make my way down the buttons of his shirt. And as I slowly pull them away, I see that the reality of Rhett Hebert is even better than I imagined. The strong muscles of his chest are lightly dusted with auburn hair. A tattoo of music notes wraps around his arm and bleeds onto his chest. Rhett stares at me, watching my reaction as I slowly run my hand across his chest. I give into the desire that I've dreamed of ever since the first time I noticed his tattoo peeking beneath his shirt sleeve. I trace the inked lines and music notes softly with my fingers. My hands drift lower, and, oh my gosh, he has *abs*. The abs of a man who spends a lot of time doing crunches.

He reaches for my shirt, and suddenly I feel self-conscious. I'm soft and curvy, where Rhett is all hard lines and firm body. I do my best to walk Tucker every day, but I also really love queso. And wine. When I freeze, Rhett halts, too.

"Lia, if this is too much, we can stop," he whispers.

"No, it's not that, it's just…" He reaches up and strokes my hair back from my cheek.

"What is it, hobbit?"

"Rhett, you're hot."

He bursts out laughing. "Um, thanks. I guess?"

"No, I mean it. You have muscles, and you like work out and… stuff." He's grinning at me.

"I fail to see the problem here."

"And I'm not. I mean, I'm kind of squishy and, erm, not exactly muscly."

"Lia? Seriously? You are easily the most beautiful woman I've ever met. You are gorgeous and sexy, and every single one of your curves drives me crazy… and I've only glimpsed them covered up." He frowns. "I want to see you. See all of you—if you'll let me."

He's so damn earnest that I know he means it. I muster my courage and firmly resolve to kick my self-consciousness to the curb. And then I fall into him, kissing him again, running my hands over his chest, across his abs. He reaches for the hem of my shirt, and this time when he tugs at its hem, I let him. He pulls my shirt completely off and stares, taking in my black bra before saying, "Yeah, this thing has to come off."

I laugh as he reaches around behind me and, just like before, manages to unhook it quickly. When it slides off, he stares at me, taking in my breasts, slowly reaching to touch them.

"Lia, you are so beautiful." Then he reaches down and takes one into his mouth, lightly licking. He pulls back and looks up at me. "Is this okay?" he asks. Always checking in with me.

"Yes." I gasp. "Definitely okay. More than okay."

He smiles and returns his lips to me, gently sucking, before moving to the other. And I am melting, turning into liquid under his mouth. I begin moving against him, and he responds in turn. He pulls away from my breasts and kisses me again, deeply, desperately.

He stands then, lifting me with him, and my legs wrap around his waist.

"Bedroom?" he pants.

And I point in the general direction. He carries me like some kind of beefed-up lumberjack to my room before dropping me on the bed and sinking on top of me. We are both shirtless now, and the skin-to-skin contact is driving us into a frenzy. I reach down for the button of his jeans, and he pulls back, looking me in the eyes.

"Lia, I don't want you to feel pressured to do anything you don't want to. You say the word, and it doesn't matter what we're doing. We stop. Immediately. Okay?"

And damn it, tears actually spring to my eyes at this. Rhett cares so much about what I want, about my consent. I've never been with a man like him. My heart aches with the way he touches me carefully, adoringly. The way he checks in with me constantly. I didn't know it could be like this, so hot, so good, so everything.

He unbuttons my shorts, pulling them off, inch by inch, and kissing his way down as he goes. I feel his lips press under my belly button, against my hip bone, down my thighs, against my knees, my shins, and even my ankle. And then my shorts are gone. He's back on top of me, hands roaming the dips and curves of my body.

I'm not nearly as graceful, trying to push his jeans down while he's on top of me. But he helps, and soon the only barriers between us are my cotton undies and his boxer briefs. When he rubs against me now, the friction is nearly unbearable.

"Lia," he whispers. "I, um, need to see if I have protection."

"It's okay," I say. "I mean, I'm clean and can't get pregnant. You?"

"Same. I mean, of course, I can't get pregnant, but... yeah. I'm clean."

I start laughing, and he does, too. This feels so comfortable, so right.

I feel his hand move down my body, just like this afternoon. But this time, there are no interruptions. He is purposeful with his hands, with my pleasure. His movements are slow and deliberate.

"Wait," I whisper, and Rhett stops, pulling back.

"Are you okay?" he says, panting.

"Yes. I just. Um." Hello, awkward inner ostrich. Please, for the love of all that is holy, go away.

"I want to make you feel good, too," I finally manage to get out.

"Oh Lia, trust me on this one," and his hand slides all the way down into my underwear. "You have no idea how much I've dreamed of this. How much I've wanted to touch you," he practically growls into my ear. I wrap my legs around his hips, reaching down in between us. I feel my way to the band of his underwear and manage to wiggle my fingers in, brushing him. But then he's pulling away from me... and taking my underwear with him.

My room is dark, with only the faint glow of the back porch light filtering through the window blinds, but it's enough. I know he can see me, see all of me. And so I reach up and push his underwear down too, exposing us to one another. Rhett leans back down, covering his body with mine. Our bodies touch in all the right places—chests, hips, arms, lips. I can feel him pressing into my hip bone as we lean into one another, seeking friction.

"Lia. I want to be inside you," he whispers into my mouth.

I lift my legs up and wrap them around him, lining us up perfectly. He pauses a moment before taking that final step of intimacy, searching my expression in the dark.

"You're killing me here," I say, and we both laugh. And then he eases in, taking care to make sure he doesn't hurt me. And damn. It's been a long time since I've had sex, but this is better than anything I've done before. He guides himself slowly in and out, easing us into the rhythm and feel of each other. He drops his forehead to mine as if in prayer.

"You undo me," he whispers. And then he's moving, and I'm moving with him, pleasure darting across the fields of my body. I let my hands roam his back, down to that beautiful behind I've been admiring in his jeans. Our rhythm aligns perfectly, and I feel the tension build to a crescendo. Then I'm soaring over the edge, pleasure racing through my body. I hear Rhett moan, and I know he has found his release, too.

We lay there for a moment afterward, breathing deeply, holding one another.

"Come here," I say, easing out from beneath him and crawling to get under the covers. He follows me, climbing in next to me. He lays on his back, and I roll over, laying my head on his chest, tucking in close. He encloses me in his arms, a pearl in a protective shell. Safeguarded, treasured. He holds me with ease and comfort like we've been together for years.

"You okay, hobbit?"

"Perfect," I reply. "You?"

"What's better than perfect? Infinity perfect? Because, yeah. I'm that."

I want to pause this moment, and preserve it. Make a snow globe out of it that I can shake and remember any time, any day. I don't want it to end. I want Rhett to stay with me. I want to be the person who can walk easily through life, grabbing joy by the horns. And why not? What's stopping me? So I muster my courage.

"Will you stay?" I ask Rhett a little nervously. "Just for tonight?"

"Hobbit, I dare you to try and kick me out of this bed." I feel him kiss the top of my head softly, and I know then, even in this short amount of time, that I'm falling for Rhett Hebert.

Chapter 26

RHETT

Two Days Until the Festival (Thursday)

Another busy workday and even more well-written articles in the bag, despite being utterly distracted all day long. I can't stop thinking about last night with Lia. It was like coming home to a crackling fire in the hearth: cozy, comfortable, and… hot. I never felt that sense of ease with Chels, not ever. Not even when we were teenagers screwing around in the backseat of my truck. Not even after years of marriage. Last night was next level. Years of wanting Lia, fantasizing about being together, and reality managed to be even better than the fantasy.

And I get to see her again in thirty minutes. My stomach is a frisbee, soaring across a field, bouncing along the breeze. Packing up my laptop, I text Jacob to let him know I'm headed out and will see him at band practice this evening. I wonder if Lia would like to come over and watch us, stay for dinner. I smile at the thought of her in my parents' house, joking around with my sister, having a glass of wine with mom, and patiently listening to dad's car stories.

It's probably too soon to meet the parents. I don't want to make her uncomfortable or push her into a relationship she's not ready for. That's okay, though. I've waited this long for her. I can wait a little longer for this, too.

WHEN I PARK AT THE FESTIVAL SITE, I immediately spot Lia and Beth together, building something out of... hay bales? I take a moment to watch her before she notices me. She's in her element, a born leader, though she'd probably argue with me if I tried to tell her that. And this festival is like nothing our city has ever seen. It's so damn professional. That Minden festival was a fifth-grade project compared to this.

Stepping out of my car, I walk across the field to Lia, sparing a glance at Greta Clark's house across the field. I make a mental note to ask mom to make a pound cake for her when I'm at their house for band practice tonight. My eyes find Lia again as I approach, so I see the moment she glances up and notices me. My heart jackhammers at her smile. Her smile for me.

"Hey there, Rhett," Beth says slyly when I approach.

"Beth. Doing alright there?" I reply. And then I feel Lia's arms reach around me, hugging me tightly. I close my eyes, drop a kiss on the top of her head, and breathe in her cinnamon scent, the same autumn smell that fills her house. Home. This is what home feels like, smells like. After all the pain of the past decade, I still can't believe I get to hold her, touch her.

"Alright, alright, you two. We have a lot of work to do," Beth says. "You can save all that for later."

Lia pulls away from me, still grinning.

"What can I do to help?" I ask.

"Selfie station. Feel like helping us stack hay bales?" Lia asks.

"Anything you need," I reply. And I mean it. I'd do anything for this woman.

"You should have brought this one in sooner, Lia. Alright, Rhett, here's what we need." Beth continues delegating tasks, and we build a hay bale pyramid.

I watch Lia hard at work, bending and lifting, hay flying around her. The site would be comical if my mind wasn't in the gutter. I sneak over to her when Beth is on the other side of the hay bale stack and pull her in for a kiss. I've missed touching her, and it hasn't even been twenty-four hours. I'm so wrapped up in our stolen kiss that I don't hear or notice anyone else walk up.

When I hear a throat clear, I blush, expecting to turn and see Margie there, ready to give us a lecture on getting back to work. Instead... I turn to see... *Chels? What the fuck?*

I feel an ice pick slam into my heart, its frigid fire radiating through my limbs and into my stomach. All the color and joy in my face drain away. I look at Lia, and she looks utterly bewildered. Our arms are still wrapped around one another. We're locked in place, as if our feet have become entrenched in the ground beneath us. I stare at the woman who has come to embody all the worst parts of my past. Burning shame hijacks my brain and locks my teeth together.

"What the actual hell is happening here?" Chels sneers at me. At us. And I hear it with that one question—all her venom, her resentment, her tirades of our past. And before I can throw up my mental boundaries against it, her voice slingshots me back into a thorny nest of feelings. Pain, shame, guilt, anger, feeling trapped, hated. I've got to get myself under control—to stop this, whatever this is.

Lia looks at me, her brow furrowing in confusion. Anxiety is hundreds of tiny ants digging into my shoulders, gnawing their way through to my stomach. I glance at Lia and pull away, watching as her expression melts from confusion to hurt. I try to tell her to hang on, that this is okay, but I know I have to calm Chels down first... and fast. I walk towards Chels, hands up like I'm attempting to calm a wild bobcat.

"What are you doing here, Chels?" I ask, no demand, of her. I channel all the coping mechanisms my therapist taught me. Stay calm. Be direct. Don't let her hijack the conversation and steer emotions.

"Really, that's what you're going to lead with? How pathetic, as usual," her derision slides down my back and into my gut like sludge, stinking and awful.

"I asked, what in the hell are you doing here?" I say again more firmly, determined to protect Lia from Chels' venom. I've stationed myself between them and brace to take the full force of her wrath.

Beth steps around the hay bails, walking to stand by Lia's side. She grips her friend's hand and the two of them watch us. It feels eerily like that day at the Chamber of Commerce when Matt showed up screaming at Lia.

"I followed you from work, Rhett. When you wouldn't return my texts, or my calls. I wanted to know why the hell you dropped off the face of the earth," she says, anger and indignation heating her cheeks. She's embarrassed. Chels has always gotten her way in everything. Everything but this, anyway.

"You have no right," I say firmly.

"Rhett, why is Chelsea McComb here?" Lia asks, false calm filling her voice.

Chels peers over my shoulder, locking Lia in her sights, and redirects her venom. Even before she says it, I see it coming like a head-on collision that I can't stop. "Why am I here?" Chels says incredulously. "I think the better question, you little slut, is why are you making out with my husband?"

Those words are a battering ram straight to my face. I feel the world spin around me, nausea filling my stomach. No, no, no. This is not how Lia was supposed to find out. I was going to tell her I was...

"What?" Lia says, deathly serious, her words a knife slicing through my heart.

"Oh, the bastard didn't tell you?" Chels asks with a mock laugh. "Yes, Rhett and I are married, have been for ... What? Six years now?"

Lia turns to me, hurt and horror radiating off her body in pulsing waves. "Rhett, is she telling the truth?" Her voice quivers, but with hurt or anger, I'm not sure.

"Go ahead, Rhett. Tell her. Am I telling the truth?" Chels taunts.

"It's not like that, Lia," I start to say, but she cuts me off.

"Are. You. Married. To. Chelsea?" Lia's quivering voice demands, each word a punch to the chest.

"Lia, listen," I try again.

"Is she telling the truth?" I hear her voice crack on the last word, and see tears in her eyes. Dammit. I want to grab all of this, stuff it into a box, and burn it. This is not what was supposed to happen.

"Answer her, Rhett," Chels sneers.

"Yes, but…"

"See." Chels cuts me off.

Lia's mouth drops open, tears rolling silently down her cheeks. I take a step towards her, but she steps back like I've struck her and stumbles into Beth, who wraps her arms around Lia.

"No, Lia, wait," I try desperately, but Chels cuts me off again.

"What? Did you actually think he cared about you? Some little nobody willing to spread her legs because some hot guy makes a pass at her? Yeah, unlikely." Chels says.

I stride to Lia then, desperate to stop this train wreck and make her understand.

She throws her hand up to stop me. "No," she says, halting my approach. We all wait to see what Lia will do. I'm so desperate to comfort her, to tell her that… God. Tell her I love her. I go to approach her again, but Beth chimes in now.

"I think it's time for you to go, Rhett," Lia says quietly, gaze filled with anger and disappointment.

"I need to explain," I try again, desperate.

"No, you need to leave," Beth says with calm, forceful certainty. "Now." She wraps her arm around Lia and says, "Come on, Lia, let's go to my place for a while, okay?" Then she looks back up at me, at Chels. "Both of you should leave. Go work out your shit somewhere else. You've done enough damage here."

And without another word, she spins Lia toward the barn, and they walk off. I see Lia's shoulders shudder, dousing the cautious joy I've begun to feel again. I should have known all of this happiness was too good to be true.

MY FURY AND DESPERATION SIMMER like oil in a pan as I watch Lia leave. I swirl and stare down at Chels, fury fueling me. "What the actual fuck, Chels?"

She flinches, but recovers quickly with a cruel, knowing smile.

She's furious and embarrassed, a recipe for complete disaster when it comes to Chels. She has never handled those emotions well. A born narcissist, she is incapable of accepting her own emotions and mistakes. Instead, she projects them onto everyone else, casting blame on every place and every person but herself. It's taken a lot of therapy for me to understand that, to learn how to build boundaries with the woman I let hijack my life, my happiness. A woman I once thought I loved.

"It's not my fault you decided to screw around while we're still married," she spits out. There it is, the blame and shame game. I name it, so it doesn't hold power over me.

"That is bullshit, and you know it. Our divorce will be final next week. And who the hell follows someone from work? Are you a stalker now?" Cold anger sizzles through my voice, wrapping itself around my words, so they land with steaming accuracy.

She pauses, re-evaluating me. She tries again. "Oh, I don't know, a woman who still hasn't had all her demands met," she practically spits at me.

"This, you ruining my life again, is about you not getting one hundred percent of the house that I bought? Hell, you're already living in it while I'm holed up in an apartment."

She just stares at me and raises one eyebrow, pulling out old tactics she used to push me around like before.

"You are insane and sadistic, you know it?" I say bitterly. "Nothing, not a damn thing, is sacred to you. Do you even know what happiness is? Or are you bound and determined to ruin the lives of every person around you?"

She flinches, frowning for a second, surprised to see me standing up to her like this, but then her cool mask returns.

"I told you that if you didn't give me the house, I would make your life miserable," she finally says. "It's the least you can do since you're leaving me."

"You know what, Chels? If that's honestly what it takes to make you go away. Then fine. Take the damn house. It's full of nothing but fighting, misery, and sorrow anyway."

"Perfect," she says with what I can tell is her attempt to muster contempt through anger and pain. "This is all your fault, you know. You could have saved our marriage, but you chose yourself over your wife's needs. You owe me a lot more than a tiny damn house. You should be thanking me that this is the only thing I'm holding to. I'll have my lawyer send you the contract tonight."

I'm seething. A decade of resentment is a hurricane writhing in my soul. But I also desperately want her to disappear from my life. I'm done. Just as I turn my back to her, she says, "Oh, and Rhett." I freeze but refuse to turn around, to even look at her spiteful face. "Try to back out of this deal again, and I have no problem calling the whole thing off. Staying married for as long as it takes to get my way in this certainly won't hurt me."

Her words stab me in the heart, just like she knew they would. A perfect bullseye of pain, right where my affection for Lia lies folded and protected.

Chapter 27

AMELIA

"I am such an idiot," I choke out as I sit on my couch next to Beth, sobbing. Again. Tucker slides his head into my lap. Beth rubs her hand in soothing circles across my shoulders.

"You're not, though," Beth says with the confidence she has about everything in life.

"I just don't understand. What is it about me that screams, 'Dear toxic, broken and married men, please come dump your baggage on me?'" Tuck looks at me with his one good eye, tilting his head as if processing my words.

"It's just weird," Beth says. "Rhett was the only man you've dated who seemed normal and healthy. I definitely didn't see a wife suddenly showing up—especially one like that. Yikes. She was definitely not Rhett's type."

"Well, obviously, she is *since they are married*. And they dated in high school. Oh God, they are high school sweethearts and *I am the other woman*." I feel sick at that realization.

"The whole situation was just weird," Beth repeats as if she's trying to puzzle through it and get to the bottom of something more. "I mean, Rhett was with you or at work *all the time*. You'd think if he were married, then he would, I don't know, not have that kind of time on his hands. And I see the way he looks at you, Lia. He can't fake that."

I just shake my head. "I'm cursed, Beth. I let myself trust Rhett and actually be happy with him. And look what happened. It came back to bite me in my perpetually unlucky ass."

My phone lights up, then. I look down and see a text from Rhett, and my stomach detonates, nausea and anxiety erupting like a geyser. I don't know whether to hurl my phone across the room or call him and pretend like today never happened. I open the text.

Rhett: I'm sorry. Can we please talk?

A wave of hurt rushes over me, drowning me. I turn my phone over, set it aside, and place a book over it. I refuse to look at it anymore. I grab a tissue to wipe my eyes and blow my nose.

Rhett's betrayal is eating me alive, and I am desperate to do anything to make the pain stop, even if it's just for a little while. "I think I should go to sleep. We have to be at the festival site at 7 a.m. tomorrow. There is still so much to do. Two more days until we open."

Beth looks at me with sympathy, not buying my attempt to change the subject. "Want me to stay the night? We can have a slumber party. I'll make mai tais."

"Thank you, Beth. But I think I need to be alone tonight. You've seen enough ugly crying from me for a lifetime. Plus, Tuck will keep me company. That's basically in every dog's job description." I pat his head again, offering him a wobbly smile. He licks my hand in sympathy.

I hear my phone buzz again… and again. Then it starts to ring. Unable to help myself, I knock the book aside to check… and see Rhett's number. I send it to voicemail. Beth looks at the phone and then at me. "Are you sure? I don't mind. Really. Dan is working late tonight."

"I'm sure. I just need some alone time."

We stand, and I wrap her in a hug. "Thank you, Beth, you're the best," I whisper to her.

"And you totally deserve me," she says. I squeeze her tighter.

THAT NIGHT I TOSS AND turn, the history of my past relationships playing like some bizarre fever dream inside my head, pausing to zoom in on all the terrible parts. Matt manipulating me. Chelsea sneering at me in the halls of our high school and making me feel like shit. Fast forwarding to her doing the same things again earlier today. I'm sweating and my sheets are clinging to me in a tangled mess. Growling, I throw them off, get up and storm into my kitchen to make a cup of tea—the kind that's supposed to help you sleep.

I grab my phone and see eleven missed messages: two from Beth, one from Aunt Margie, one from Jacob, and… seven from Rhett. For a minute, I panic, thinking something bad has happened. But as I open them, I realize Beth's and Aunt Margie's messages are just notes telling me how much they love me. I smile and realize that while my relationships with men tend to be complete disasters, at least I have Beth and Aunt Margie.

Next, I tap Jacob's message. He's requesting an interview tomorrow for a story on the festival's launch. Easy enough.

My thumb hovers over Rhett's name. The picture on his contact is one I snapped of him holding up that ridiculous caramel apple at the Minden fall festival. My heart gives a painful thump in my chest. Finally, like a bruise I need to press to make sure it still hurts, I open the texts.

I'm so sorry. Can we please talk?

Please, hear me out.

There are things you don't know.

I never meant to hurt you.

I'll buy you a lifetime supply of chocolate croissants and PSLs if we can just talk.

Please.

I'm sorry.

I put my phone down and sob. God, how many times was I lured back in by Matt with apologies? In my heart, I know Rhett is nothing like Matt, but the same feelings get stirred up. I can't do this again.

Instead, I grab my festival checklist sitting on the kitchen table. I need a distraction from Rhett, and there is really only one thing my attention should be on right now. Tomorrow is my last full day of prep work before the festival launches.

Chapter 28

RHETT

I miss the chord. *Again.*

"Rhett, what in the hell is up with you tonight?" My sister gripes, irritated that I am messing up every song with only two days left before we perform.

"Nothing. Just tired, okay? Let's do it again."

We do two more attempts before Katie throws her hands up and says, "This is impossible. Please go get some damn sleep and then come here tomorrow hyped up on Red Bull or coffee or a cocktail of both." Then she storms off, muttering curses under her breath. Jacob watches her leave, eyes lingering on the door after she leaves. Then he inhales deeply, sets his drumsticks down, and shakes his head.

"She's got a point, man. Where's your head tonight?"

But I don't have the heart to tell him what happened. If I say it out loud, if I acknowledge Chels showing up and Lia walking away crying, then it's real and final. My heart lurches painfully in my chest. "I told you, just tired. I'll get some sleep and be fine tomorrow."

I know Jacob doesn't believe me, but he's not going to push it, either. He packs up his things and waves as he leaves.

I walk into my parents' house to grab my keys, anxious to get out of here. But Mom is waiting on me, hands folded across her chest and a determined look on her face. And... I know I'm not getting out of this one. *Dammit.*

"Let's go sit on the front porch swing," Mom says, tucking her arm in mine. I follow her outside, and we sit next to one another, reenacting all the times we had a heart-to-heart when I was a kid. And now, just like then, we sit together for a couple of minutes, pushing the swing with our feet. The breeze runs through our hair and brushes our faces. I close my eyes and sink into the familiarity of the motion.

"Rhett, what is it? You have been so joyful these past two weeks. You were coming back to yourself. And tonight? It's like I imagined all of that."

"I don't know, Mom. This is really weird for me to talk to you about. I'm a grown man, not some little kid anymore."

"I know it. And I usually let you keep your own counsel. But I'm your mother, and I can't help but worry when I see you so out of it. If you don't want to talk about it, you don't have to. But Rhett, in matters of the heart, at least, I have some experience."

"How do you know it's a matter of the heart?"

She just lifts one eyebrow at me and stares like I'm an idiot. I chuckle. Some things never change.

"Fine. There's this girl," and now I really feel like a teenager, but I push on. "And she's perfect. I think you would love her." Mom gives me a closed-mouth smile, but doesn't interrupt.

"Things have been great. She gets me, and being around her makes me feel alive. But I really fu… I mean, um, messed things up." I hang my head, the shame of the day's events a boulder suspended on my shoulders. "And earlier today, Chels followed me when I left work. I didn't even notice her. And then she stormed up to me and told everyone within shouting distance that she and I are still married, even though--as you know--the divorce finalizes next week. And, of course, all of Lia's--that's the girl--all her friends, coworkers and family were there, too. It was a total clusterf… um, disaster." I'm too embarrassed to even look at my mom.

Finally, she says, "Rhett. Do you love this girl?"

I tilt my head to the side, looking at her. She always knows how to get straight to the heart of things, my mom. "I think I might."

She nods as if she knew this was exactly how I'd answer. "Yes, you should have told her about Chelsea. But Chelsea should not have done that. Total bitch move if you ask me."

I stare at my mother, slightly horrified. She never swears and this, more than anything, confirms how much she dislikes my soon-to-be ex-wife.

"I said what I said," she asserts. "And Rhett, you are such a *good, kind* person. You have so much love in your heart to share. If you love Lia, then apologize to her and fix it."

"I have tried to apologize to her, but she won't respond to my texts or calls."

"Texts. Are you serious right now?" She scolds. "Rhett, my boy, you have to try at least."

"I am trying!" I shout in frustration. Mom lifts one eyebrow again. I throw my hands up in the air in exasperation. "Fine, do you have a better idea?"

She smiles knowingly. "Rhett, you've always been the one with extraordinary ideas. Even when you were a child, you were a natural investigator, a problem solver. It's what makes you such a good journalist. So my advice to you is to apply that beautiful imagination of yours to find a solution."

Chapter 29

AMELIA

One Day Until the Festival (Friday)

"Those vendor signs need to go to the horse stalls, and those string lights go to the entry sign. Oh, wait, no, those go to the parking lot." I fly down my checklist, making sure everyone stays busy. It's the day before the festival, and I refuse to let my mind probe the fresh wound that is Rhett Hebert. Never have I been so grateful to have a fourteen-hour workday ahead of me. I pour myself into it, directing half the Junior League to set up stations and organize the children's craft center, and, oh my gosh, the goats are here.

"Lia," I hear Beth say cautiously. "Maybe you should take a short break. You've been going at it for hours now."

"No, I'm good, really," I insist. I know if I stop, even for a minute, all the pain of yesterday will break my carefully erected emotional dam. Once that floodgate opens, there will be no stopping it. And, right now, I don't have time for emotions. I see Aunt Margie and wave her over. "The goat man is here. Can you show him where the petting zoo area is?"

She eyes me up and down, noting the dark circles under my eyes and frenetic energy. She and Beth exchange a knowing look, but she simply says, "No problem," and walks off. When Aunt Margie has no quip back about goat duty, I know I must look really bad.

"Beth, the schools will be here with their decorated pumpkins for the scholarship contest in thirty minutes. Can you take charge of that and rally some of the Junior League ladies into making sure they all look okay?"

"Already on it, Lia," she says and hands me a water bottle. "Now, go sit down for ten minutes." As she walks off, I stand there dazed, my legs wobbling and my head swirling. She's right. I need to sit for a few minutes. I retreat to a corner and plop down in a folding chair, downing the water. The temperatures are finally dropping, but Louisiana humidity never goes away, and I am sweating like a sinner in church. My brain betrays me, and I think about how Rhett would make some lame joke about hobbits to make me laugh right now. But I shut it down, quickly and forcefully. Open cage, insert emotions, lock and throw away the key. I toss the empty water bottle into the nearby recycling bin and get back to work.

Checking my watch, I realize Jacob will be here for the story interview in fifteen minutes, so I step into the bathroom to freshen up. When I look in the mirror, I'm startled by the woman who looks back at me. I'm pale and disheveled. The combination of physical labor, stress, lack of sleep, and sadness makes me look like I could be one of the ghost decorations stationed around the festival site. I splash water over my face, smooth down my frizzy ponytail, and then pinch some color into my cheeks.

When I step out of the bathroom, I spot Jacob talking to Beth and slowly make my way over to them. Seeing Jacob, I can't help but think about Rhett, the two of them together in this barn a couple of weeks ago. And that knot of pain in my empty stomach winds tighter. I've felt nauseous ever since yesterday and briefly consider running straight back to the bathroom, but Jacob spots me and waves.

"Ready for that interview?" he says to me with his usual charm. I nod.

"Have someplace quiet we can go and chat so I can record?" he asks.

Besides the bathroom and the corn maze—which are both absolute no-gos—my car is the only quiet place I can think of. When

I suggest that, he nods, and we make our way over to my hatchback.

SLIDING INTO THE DRIVER SEAT, I crank up the air and aim it directly at my face, trying to revive myself for this. I'm suddenly totally and thoroughly exhausted.

"Are you… alright?" he asks. And I wonder if he has any idea what happened yesterday, but I'm not about to ask.

"Just tired. Long day." I can tell he wants to ask more but decides to stick to the interview script. I revive a little as I tell him about all the new things we have going on this year. It goes surprisingly well, and I relax a little, knowing I have managed to do something right. Jacob clicks off the recorder, then takes a breath like he wants to say something. My stomach starts jumping rope in anticipation.

"Lia, I know it isn't my place, but at band practice last night Rhett seemed, well, a lot like you do right now. Exhausted, sad."

He stares at me, but I don't answer. I just look down at my lap. My tears are burning embers that singe the back of my throat.

"Look, you should know that Rhett has come alive again these past few weeks after years of being a walking zombie. That started when he met you. And honestly, it makes me a little mad because I have been trying to wake him up for years, and then you show up, and bam!" He smiles at me a little, but I can't muster up one in return. I stare straight ahead, eyes tracing the stitching of my steering wheel. I don't want to cry in front of Jacob.

"I don't know what happened with you two, but I know you make him happy. Make him alive."

My anger boils over at that. I slam my hands into my steering wheel. "Jacob, Rhett is *married*. I don't care how happy we make each other. He is with someone else."

Jacob pales and looks down. So he did know. He shakes his head, brushing my comment off. "You don't understand."

"What don't I understand? That he's with that crazy bitch who made my high school years a living hell? That he hid that from me?" My voice cracks on my last word, and I try to douse the hurt threatening to erupt in a firestorm of tears.

"Lia, their divorce finalizes on Wednesday, and they have been separated for more than a year," Jacob says. "And Chels was awful to him. She bullied and controlled him, always made him feel like the worst person alive. She was even jealous of his conversations with his boss because she is a woman. His work has been crashing and burning as a result. I was scared he was going to lose his job. Hell, Rhett was ready to quit the job he loves and work at a hardware store. That's how bad it was. That is, he was. Until he met *you*."

"What?" I gasp quietly, his words knocking the wind out of me.

There are things you don't know.

I never meant to hurt you.

Those texts run through my head, and that ball of sorrow inside my heart somehow manages to grow larger, but not for me, for Rhett.

"Jacob, how can I trust him? He didn't even tell me about the marriage." I can't hold the tears back anymore, so I let them come. They trail silently down my cheeks as I stare at my pumpkin-shaped air freshener hanging from the rear view mirror.

"Awe, shit," he says when he sees me crying. "I am not good at this." He wipes his face with his hand.

"Lia, all I can tell you is that Rhett is a good person. One of the best I know, actually. And he would never intentionally hurt anyone. Everyone close to him can't stand his crazy ex-wife. She was awful to him. But you are good to him, good for him. Maybe you two should just talk about it?"

"I… I don't know," I say, reaching for the tissues stored in my dash console. Jacob just nods his head.

"Think about it. Trust me when I say it's not worth losing someone you care about over a misunderstanding." And with that, he climbs out of my car. But before he closes the door, he leans back down and says, "Oh, and we'll see you tomorrow. The Graveyard Gators will be ready to play at six. We'll be here for set up and sound tests at five."

As he walks away, all I can think is, "Oh shit. I'm going to see Rhett at the festival tomorrow."

Chapter 30

AMELIA

Festival Day

I'm awake when the sun rises. Even after a full day of very little sleep followed by physical labor, I still couldn't sleep last night. I am a mess between the festival launch today and everything with Rhett. *I'll sleep tonight*, I promise myself. I just need to get through this launch and Rhett's band playing—which I totally plan to hide in the barn for—and then I'll drink wine and sleep like the dead. My phone lights up.

Rhett: Good luck today, hobbit.

The text takes the wind out of my sails. *Why won't he just leave me alone?* I refuse to dwell on the message. Instead, I climb into the shower and crank up the temp as hot as I can stand, burning away the exhaustion and pain.

I go through the motions of making coffee. I feel Tuck nudge his nose against my leg. My good boy. He always knows when I need a little extra love. I kneel and rub his head. "It'll be okay, Tuck. We'll get through this together."

I hear a familiar horn in my driveway and look down at my watch. It's 8 a.m. on the dot. Stepping outside, I pull on my "I'm okay" mask and walk up to Aunt Margie, my ride for the day. She's worried about me and insists on giving me a lift. I don't feel like arguing, and honestly, it's kind of nice to have someone taking care of me when I'm so frazzled.

When I climb into the car, she hands me her flask. I look down at it, then at her. She shrugs. "Liquid courage. You'll need it today."

And for the first time in the past twenty-four hours, I smile a little. Instead of protesting, I uncork it and take one big swing before handing it back. She nods, tucks it back into her overalls, and backs out of the driveway. The sky is dark and raindrops dot the windshield as she drives us to the festival site. My stomach coils tighter.

"The rain will pass by ten. Don't worry." Aunt Margie has barely said anything to me this morning, but she knows when to push and when to let me simmer. And right now, she said exactly what I needed to hear. It may seem grim now, but don't worry. It will all be okay in the end. I stare at the churning gray sky, hoping she's right.

We're the first to arrive at the festival site. I look around, taking it all in. We've been working so hard this week, this month, hell, ever since I started making suggestions to Janet years ago. And this is the first moment I've taken the time to step back and admire our hard work. It's beautiful, festive, and oddly cozy. It's everything I've dreamed of since I took over as event manager. And I'm not sure if it's the exhaustion, Rhett, the joy of seeing it come together, or the swig of bourbon, but I feel a tear, then two quietly slip down my cheeks.

Aunt Margie reaches over and squeezes my hand. "You've done good, girl. You should be proud."

I LOOK DOWN AT MY WATCH. It's 11:30 a.m., thirty minutes until our official festival opening. Just like Aunt Margie promised, the rain has stopped, and the clouds have rolled out, leaving only wet grass that the sun is working to dry. The storm front brought a cool breeze with it, and I sigh at this small gift from Mother Nature.

Cars fill the parking lot. The mayor stands with Janet near the stage we assembled, ready to give the opening address. Jacob is among a handful of local reporters, photographers, and videographers mingling in front of the platform. I slide my gaze over the crowd, but I see no sign of the auburn waves I'm both scared and anxious to catch a glimpse of. Families are already lining up, ready to enjoy all the kid-friendly activities set up under nearby tents. The crowds are larger than last year's on opening day, and my soul runs a victory lap around the track of my heart.

Greta Clark has kept her word, and we've seen no signs or complaints from her since she visited us that night. I'm reminded again of how kind Rhett was to her that evening, of what came after. *Good luck today, hobbit.* My heart thuds like an over-soaked blanket stuck in an old dryer.

"Welcome to the Great Ruston Fall Festival," Janet announces from the stage. The sun glints off her ice blonde bob as all eyes turn to her. She spends the next few minutes dazzling the crowd with embellished explanations of all the improvements and additions to this year's festival. I feel Beth step up next to me then and squeeze my hand. *We did it,* I feel her say with that gesture. *We did,* my return squeeze says.

Then the mayor and Janet pick up a big pair of scissors and cut a giant orange ribbon, signaling the festival's grand opening. Everyone cheers and the crowd begins to drift through the craft tents along the field's parameter and the vendor booths inside the barn. The food trucks are open for business. I inhale, taking in the comforting scents of funnel cake and cheeseburgers. I watch as families laugh at the sight of the petting zoo. Joy surges through my chest. I close my eyes. *I can accomplish things. I can. None of it was easy, but, damn, we certainly made it look easy.* I open my eyes and turn to Beth.

"I'm going to go walk through the barn, make sure all the vendors have everything they need. Will you check in with the food trucks?"

Beth nods. "Let's do this."

THE DAY PASSES IN FLASHES of color and a constant barrage of text messages, phone calls, and yells across the vast festival space. I never stop moving—from fulfilling requests for more propane tanks for the food trucks to grabbing totes of craft supplies out of the storage trailer.

I even make a first aid run in response to a goat bite—*glad I made sure they had insurance*. Beth fulfills similar needs all day and we wave as we cross paths, our walkie-talkies blipping on and off like we're air traffic controllers—and I guess, in a way, we are.

I'm too busy to linger on thoughts of Rhett, pushing the pain of betrayal to the furthest reaches of my brain and locking them tightly in a mental cage built of tenacity and denial. I'm determined to ignore my exhausted legs and gnawing hunger pangs--mostly because I don't have time to take a break. Every time I walk into the barn, Aunt Margie runs out from behind her vendor booth–which, I distantly notice, is drawing an unusually large crowd. She shoves a water bottle in my hand, watches to make sure I down it, and then retreats to her station. I hop back up and start working again, anxious to make sure the first day goes off without a hitch. My whole festival team works together like a family of ants carrying our giant leaves and crawling through our festival ant hill. I'm proud of them, and even a little proud of myself.

Rolling another ice chest full of water bottles out to the corn maze team, I pass by lines of people waiting for icees, Natchitoches meat pies, and funnel cakes. I have to weave in and out of running children and teenagers staring down at their phone screens. This place is well and truly packed. Triumph rises through my chest, making me feel giddy and dizzy. At least, that's what I think it is. Though I'm not really sure when the last time I ate something was. I blink, shake my head and keep going, but the wooziness doesn't go away.

After I drop the water bottles off, I make my way back to the barn, taking slow deep breaths. The sun has begun to set, and I know Rhett and Jacob are likely at the stage setting up. I need to retreat into the air conditioning, to the little oasis I've created for myself in the barn loft, eat something and *hide*.

But as I near the barn, the dizziness suddenly becomes overwhelming. I feel the earth tilt beneath my feet, and my vision blurs. Distantly I hear someone say, "Lia," but it sounds like I'm underwater. Black dots fill my vision, and then everything goes dark.

Chapter 31

RHETT

Adrenaline pumps through my system in electric waves as we prepare to take the stage. Performing music in front of my family and friends was my first foray into overcoming the painful shyness that ruled my life for years. And this may be a small city festival, but it's been ages since I performed in front of any kind of audience. Old feelings of anticipation twist with nerves to form a double helix of stage jitters and have me moving ceaselessly. And then, of course, there's Lia. Scanning my surroundings, I hope to catch a glimpse of her dark waves and wry smile just once before we start playing.

I hope she's out there somewhere, or my special plan for the evening will look kind of dumb. But even as I search for her, my gaze keeps snagging on the sheer volume of people in attendance. My mouth is nothing but dust, and sand and I'm more grateful than ever that Katie is singing lead tonight.

"Alright, it's time, boys," I hear Katie say. She's exhilarated, channeling her inner diva. My sister has always stepped in to fill the space when my shyness made things awkward. And even though things aren't nearly as bad as they once were, it's nice to let her take the lead. We all walk up on the stage and take our places. The sun is beginning to set and stage lights shine in my eyes, making it impossible to see beyond what's immediately in front of us. Maybe that's a gift. As much as I'm dying to see Lia, I don't think I'll make it through the set if I see any sorrow or betrayal lingering in her eyes right now.

The speakers give an ear-piercing squeal before settling. Katie steps up to the microphone, all sunshine and smiles. "Hey y'all! We're the Graveyard Gators! Are you ready for some fun?" She calls out, stirring up the crowd. And they respond, cheering with excitement. And just as I hit the first chord on my guitar, I hear a yell. "Someone call EMS." We all pause, trying to see beyond the bright lights.

I know that voice–it's Margie. My gut tells me that something has happened to Lia. I don't stop to think. I lift my guitar strap off my shoulder, sit it down on the stage and take off running towards the commotion I see at the back of the crowd. I have to push through groups of people, but I refuse to stop. When I've finally made it through, I see Margie sitting on the ground, Lia's head in her lap–and Lia isn't moving.

Panic is an elephant atop my chest, stomping and flailing as I move toward them. I kneel next to Margie. Lia is white as death, and I can't stop myself from reaching for her pulse, and checking her breathing. *She's alive.* That's all I have time to think before EMS asks me to move, leaning down around her.

After an eternal minute, Lia's eyes flutter open. She looks dazed and surprised to be on the ground with so many people around her. Her gaze snags on mine and locks us both into place. I can't look away, and neither can she, it seems. She stares at me in confusion as the medics check her blood pressure and oxygen. Finally, one of them asks, "When's the last time you ate something, Miss?"

Lia looks at him, surprised he's there. "Um, I think I ate something, maybe last night?" He nods his head. "Exhaustion and hunger. You need rest and a meal. Do you have someone who can take you home?"

Margie nods. "Yes, I'm her aunt. I've got her."

"I'm not going home," Lia tells them. "I can't. This is opening night. I need to be here."

"Lia, honey, you have done enough for today. Let someone else handle it," Margie says, motherly affection and concern filling her voice.

She nods her head no, then seems to think better of it. "Just let me get oriented before getting in the car. I need a few minutes."

I step closer then, but I don't know what I'm going to say or do. Someone taps my shoulder then, and I look over to see Beth. She says quietly, "Rhett. Please go start the show. You, of all people, know how Lia is about falls and crowds. Do her a solid and get this attention off of her."

She's right. This is how I can help Lia right now. So I do the last thing I want to do in this moment. I turn and walk back to the stage. My family and best friend look at me as I climb back onto the platform. "Okay, man?" Jacob asks.

I nod. "Let's rock," I say with false confidence. I strike the first chord on my guitar, and the crowd turns to face us. Katie looks over her shoulder and smiles at me. Dad plays the opening chords to "Werewolves in London." And with the first few notes, the music eases into my soul, a soothing balm that coats my insides, forcing out everything else. It's like muscle memory the way it takes over. I let myself get lost in it, in the performance, the motions of my hands as they play the guitar.

It takes a couple of songs to get the crowd to shift from concerned to party mode, but Katie is a natural on stage. Before long, everyone is singing along to "YMCA." Kids are dancing and the hot apple cider is flowing.

About thirty minutes into our set, Katie turns and looks at me, lifting one eyebrow. She silently asks, *Are you ready?* When I nod, she turns back to face the thick crowd gathered in front of the stage. "Alright, everyone, if I can have your attention, please."

Her voice jolts me out of my music-induced reverie. I suddenly wonder if this is a very, *very* bad idea. I'm not even sure Lia is still here and… but as the stage lights dim a little, I see her. She's sitting in a folding chair, propped against the barn, the light from the doors lighting the side of her face. She's got something … a drink, food, in her lap–and she's watching us. Watching me.

Stepping up to the lead microphone and into the spotlight, I inhale slowly and strum my guitar. Then I lean into the mic and muster a smile, sliding on the lead singer persona I used to sink into every Thursday night in college at the local bar–the musician's mask I learned to use to hide my shyness. This Rhett, the one stepping to the front of the stage now, guitar in hand, knows a lead singer's confidence can win or lose a crowd. I stand a little taller, embody a little swagger, and crook a half smile. I channel all the years I spent practicing this stance, this confidence in front of a bathroom mirror. I remember all those hours of concerts I watched to see how lead guitarists win over a crowd. I push all that into the forefront of my mind, letting it take over, shoving my nerves firmly out the window—muscle memory.

"Thank y'all for coming out tonight and singing along with The Graveyard Gators!" I say, strumming another chord. My heart is a metronome in my chest, coaching me through the rhythm of the music. Everyone cheers, whistles, and hoots in response and that ticking ratchets up a notch.

Katie stands beside me, microphone in hand, ready to sing backup. She bumps her elbow into my ribs and whispers, "You've got this, big bro."

I nod and strum the guitar again, playing a few chords as I work up to the song I spent all last night practicing.

Chapter 32

AMELIA

Sitting with my back pressed to the outside of the barn in a shadow, I'm trying to make myself as small as possible and avoid people asking me if I'm okay. I know I should have probably gone home and rested, but I can't leave this festival, *my* festival, opening night… and I can't take my eyes off The Graveyard Gators, off of Rhett.

From here, I can watch him, and I'm just part of the crowd. I take him in, his long aquiline nose, a baseball hat pulled down over his tousled waves. As he strums the guitar, the tattoo on his bicep makes a brief appearance, reminding me of the night we spent watching *The Lord of the Rings*–and doing other things–together. Even filled with indignation, I can't take my eyes off him.

I'm still angry, still hurt, but underlying that tangle of emotions, I'm sad. If what Jacob said was true, then the growing relationship between Rhett and me may have been healing him just as much as it was healing me. And if that's true, well… But I don't want to think about those things right now. I just want to sit back and watch him. Watch them. Because damn, they really are good.

I thought Rhett was sexy before, but watching him in a worn Cowboy Mouth t-shirt, face locked in concentration and muscled forearms strumming the guitar. I swallow painfully. I can't ignore the fact that his performance is seriously turning me on. And from how other women and giggling teen girls are gathered around the stage dancing and staring, I know it's not just me who's noticed him.

Despite Rhett's rich baritone, he let me hear that day in the coffee shop, Katie continues to sing the lead. And talent must run in the Hebert family because her voice is the feminine mirror of Rhett's. She sings with a sultry rasp similar to Adele's.

I could sit and stare at them all night, but I know Aunt Margie will be back soon to check on me, and I can only delay her for so long. I close my eyes, listening to Katie finish singing Stevie Wonder's "Superstition." I'm glad I didn't push Rhett to stick to just the cheesy Halloween songs. Their set list is fun, and the crowd is singing along, too.

But when Katie steps away from the microphone and Rhett walks to center stage, my heart threatens to beat its way out of my chest and hurl itself into his waiting palms. I know I'm finally about to be treated to the sound of his voice, something I may have fantasized about many, many times since the coffee shop. I'm sitting at full attention now, and I swear Rhett looks right at me over the top of the crowd, but there's no way he can see me. *Right?*

Rhett strums the guitar for a few minutes, enjoying playing a solo. I swear I can practically see hearts in the eyes of women in front of him. Then he leans into the microphone, plays a chord on the guitar, and says, "Hey, everyone. I know I don't have quite my sister Katie's rock star diva energy. He extends an arm to his sister, and the crowd cheers and claps. "But I wanted to sing a song for y'all tonight."

Rhett lets out a husky chuckle and strums his guitar again. He looks down at it and fiddles with the tuning. "Well, I'm not being honest. I mean, I'm happy to sing for everyone here, but there's one person, in particular, I want to sing for. I'm not gonna name names because she would have my head for embarrassing her." He smiles to himself when he says this, and I think I might actually throw up from the nerves now polka dancing in my stomach. *No, it's not for me. It couldn't be.*

"You see, a little while back, this girl and I had a debate over the best kinds of Halloween songs. I still believe music from the great musicians will always trump kids' songs–sorry, kids," he says with a wink and hint of mischief, then strums his guitar again. Rhett radiates confidence and swagger… and I've never seen him like this before. My inner teenage girl is screaming.

"So anyway, enough of all that. This one's for you, hobbit."

He looks up and, even from this distance, our gazes connect. I'm hot and cold all over, but I don't move, not a single muscle. My ears are ringing, but jazzy music cuts in, and every part of my body is attuned entirely to Rhett.

And then he starts singing.

"Those fingers in my hair, that sly come hither stare, that strips my conscience bare, it's witchcraft. And I've got no defense for it. The heat is too intense for it. What good for common sense for it do? Cause it's witchcraft…"

It's official. Rhett can sing like Frank Sinatra… is singing Frank Sinatra…and he is singing to me, complete with that "sly come-hither stare." At that moment, I really understand why all those girls used to swoon when The Beatles took to the stage. I'm an overfull blender, spinning and on the verge of exploding. I'm thrilled and slightly embarrassed, even though no one knows he's singing to me. Okay, well, his band, Aunt Margie and Beth probably know. And please, God, don't let Chelsea be here. But he's doing this for me. And part of me wants to strut up to that stage, wrap my arms around his neck, lean down into the mic and say, "Mine."

When he finishes the song, the crowd goes wild, and he takes a little bow. Then he looks at me, stares at me. We lock gazes, and I'm utterly flustered. When Aunt Margie steps up beside me and asks me if I'm ready to go home, I finally break eye contact with Rhett and tell her yes. Because I know I can't talk to him tonight, not when he's supposed to be playing for another hour. Not when I'm mentally warring between slapping and kissing him.

I've already drawn enough attention to myself this evening with that embarrassing faint. I know talking to the hot guitar player who just sang a panty-dropping rendition of "Witchcraft" in front of a crowd of adoring women *will* draw attention.

I stand slowly. Aunt Margie clutches my arm like she fears I will hit the ground again. But with a belly full of plastic nacho cheese, chili, and a Sprite, I'm steady. She drives me home, and we resume our comfortable silence again. I stare out the passenger window at the full moon and wonder what might happen if I stop being a coward and talk to Rhett.

As I climb out of Aunt Margie's truck, I thank her for the ride. "That was some singing tonight," she says in return and stares at me knowingly.

"Yeah, it was."

"So, what are you going to do about it?"

"I… I don't know. I need to think about it."

She nods. "Just know, Lia, that none of us are perfect. We all make mistakes—sometimes really big ones. God knows I've made my share." She hangs her head, staring at her lap, then looks up at me. The moonlight reflects off her graying hair, and, for a moment, I see a younger version of Aunt Margie sitting in this truck. The same aunt who took mom and me in when things were at their very worst.

"But take it from me, sweetheart, holding onto pain and anger hurts the person who's still holding on to it the most, and you deserve better than that."

I'm not sure if she's talking about Matt or Rhett or both. So I just nod my head in acknowledgment and then turn to my house, Tucker greeting me at the door.

I strip off my clothes and crawl into bed, letting the exhaustion finally take me. But before I doze off, I pick up my phone one last time. And before I can talk myself out of it, I send a text.

Amelia: Tomorrow after your final set. Meet me at the rear barn doors.

Chapter 33

RHETT

The Next Day

Tomorrow after your final set. Meet me at the rear barn doors.

I keep reading Lia's text over and over. Part of me believes she just wants to tell me where to shove it and never call her again. But she could have done that via text message. She would have had every right to. My stupid heart is still hoping that this means she's at least giving me a chance to talk to her.

Thinking through last night, I smile, wondering what she thought of my performance. I wanted to make a big gesture but not embarrass her. I hope I did the right thing. She probably thinks I'm an idiot. At least today is Saturday, and I'm not assigned to any weekend news coverage. Though work has been a great distraction, my brain needs a break. So I pick up my phone and call my mom.

SEVERAL HOURS LATER, I'm leaving my parents' house, fresh pound cake tucked securely into my passenger seat. I'm headed to the festival site, to Greta Clark's house. I've been thinking about her since yesterday, wondering how she handled the loud noise outside her home, the memories she must be battling.

I trek across the field to her front porch, dodging the meandering cats that periodically dart across my path. Arriving at her front door, I knock gently, not even sure she's there. But after a moment, I hear footsteps, and the door creaks open. When she sees me, she opens the screen door and steps outside.

"Rhett."

That's all she says. I see grief lining her face.

"Hi, Ms. Clark. Care for a slice of pound cake?" I hold up the box. It seems I'm always offering this woman something–a chicken, a cake, a memory.

She stares at the white box in my hands, and then a smile–a genuine, real, honest-to-God smile–cracks her face, and she nods. "Come in. I'll make some tea."

I didn't know what to expect when I showed up, and I was worried our conversation would be awkward. She's quiet but kind, asking me questions about my life, and my work. She listens with intention, truly desiring to learn these things about me. An hour passes in the span of a moment. When I look down at my watch, I realize I need to get ready to perform tonight.

"I hope the noise isn't too bad," I say, nodding my head toward the festival site. She just shrugs.

"It is what it is, and it will all be over soon anyway."

We walk to the door together. "Rhett, thank you. For today. You are so like her, like your grandmother."

"I'm not sure if that's a good thing," I chuckle.

She barks a dry laugh. "Oh, it is. She may have been a showboat, but she had a good heart. So do you. I hope that girl you came here with last time takes good care of it. Please come back and see me... and bring more of that cake."

With a smile and a nod, I turn and walk back to the festival site.

THAT NIGHT, THE GRAVEYARD GATORS are on fire. We have fun on stage, and the crowd has fun with us. Kids dance around the stage. Parents and grandparents sing along to classics. I'm glad to have this time to burn off my anxious energy that's been building all day at the thought of meeting with Lia tonight. Our performance goes by in a blur, and before I know it, we're playing our last song for the evening. I look out over the crowd, hoping to spot that familiar ponytail. Maybe it's too dark, or maybe there are too many people, or hell, maybe she's not in the crowd at all. But disappointment sparks when I don't see her. I say a silent prayer that she hasn't bailed on me.

I pack up my guitar, carrying it with me in its case to the back side of the barn, our meeting spot. My nerves spark like lightning bugs across my stomach, skin, and hands. I search for her in the dark, and just as disappointment threatens to drown me, a light shines through a crack in the barn's back doors. Lia steps out and looks straight at me, as if she knew the exact spot I'd be waiting. I always thought "weak in the knees" was just some stupid saying, but right now, I think I might collapse right here in this dark field. She's here.

Gaze never leaving hers, I close the distance between us and set my guitar down. Lia's hands are shoved uncomfortably in the pockets of her denim shorts, and I can tell she feels awkward about seeing me. I do too, but I'm not going to waste this opportunity.

"You okay?" I finally say, fighting the urge to reach out and stroke her cheek.

She takes a deep breath, exhales, and looks at me. "Yeah. I'm alright. Can we go somewhere quiet to talk?" When I nod my head, she says, "Follow me."

I trail behind her as we enter the barn through the back doors. I catch glimpses of vendors making their final sales of the evening as we pass behind the old horse stalls and the equipment closet. Desire invades me as memories of our time together in that space hijack my brain. Lia keeps going though, and I follow her until we turn a corner to a tucked-away staircase. Without pause, she starts walking up them, so I follow behind her, holding my guitar case in front of me so it doesn't smack against the narrow walls.

When we reach the top, I look around at the barn loft in front of me. I've never noticed it up here, even though it looks out over the sprawling vendor fair below us. But it would be easy to miss. It's recessed and dark.

"I found the stairs when we cleared out the vendor stalls," Lia says. "No one comes up here. It's a nice retreat from the chaos when I need a few quiet minutes." She gestures to the back wall, angled where it meets the ceiling. There's a blanket spread on the floor and a couple of books stacked on its corner. Lia's retreat, indeed.

"If we sit towards the back, they can't see us from below. Just be careful. There's a gap between the loft floor and the wall." She sits on the blanket, and I join her, placing my guitar on the floor beside the blanket before sitting directly across from her, legs crossed. I look up at Lia. She's looking back at me, studying my face with those dark, beautiful eyes. The sound from below is muted this high up, and the musty smell of old hay is somehow comforting.

"I'm sorry," I say without any preamble.

She lifts one eyebrow and pulls her knees in close, tucking them into her body, resting her chin on them.

I push ahead, desperate to make her understand. "I should have told you about Chels. It's just… that part of my life? It's ugly and painful and almost over. I didn't want to drag all that pain and hurt into this happy thing you and I were building together. I know that's not an excuse, and it's unfair to you. I know I was an idiot. And I'm willing to answer any questions you might have and beg on my knees for forgiveness if you let me."

Lia's mouth opens, closes, and opens again. "Thank you. For your apology. But maybe I wasn't being entirely fair to you either, a bit of a hypocrite, even."

"Are you married?" I blurt out before I can stop myself, my heart thrumming painfully at the thought.

"Oh no, *noooo*," she says emphatically. "I just mean, you were there that day when Matt stormed up to me, screaming in front of everyone. And you didn't turn away from me. You stood with me. And I," her voice cracks. "I didn't do that for you when Chelsea showed up here doing the same damn thing. I know your heart, Rhett. I should have known that the whole scenario wasn't what it seemed." A flicker of hope kindles within me.

"But I'm just so used to being used and abandoned by men. First my dad, then later boyfriends. Especially Matt. My relationships with men never come easy. And in my heart, I've always thought this thing between you and me was too good to be true. Chelsea showed up that day, and it was what I was always kind of expected to happen. Like, I'm not allowed to be happy."

She folds her head back onto her knees with these words. I yearn to go to her, to comfort her, but I don't want her to flinch from my touch. Just the thought makes me feel like I'm flailing backward off a cliff. Finally she lifts her head, tears threatening to spill over, and continues. "And Rhett, you made... no, you *make* me so damn happy. And that scares me. Every time I find happiness, it turns out that it was all just some beautiful shell covering the ugliness beneath."

I make her happy. It's more than I could have hoped for. But then, something else she said caught my attention. "Wait a second. How do you know things with Chels weren't what they seemed?"

She grimaces slightly at my question. "Jacob came to interview me for a story on the festival opening, and afterward, he told me. About you and Chelsea, I mean." She looks sheepish when she says this, like she got caught with one hand in the cookie jar.

"What did he tell you exactly?" I ask cautiously.

"Just that it's over between you and Chelsea. It will be official next week, and that she wasn't good for you."

I start to speak, but she interrupts me. "He didn't go into detail or anything. I think the 'bro-code' kept him quiet on that. So... is it true?" She eyes me cautiously and maybe even a little hopefully.

I sigh, leaning back onto my palms, and look up at the barn ceiling. "I told you I'd be honest with you. I guess this is as good a place to start as any." My heart sinks as I drag up all the bad memories with Chels, sorting through where to begin.

"Chels... wasn't good for me, Lia. In the beginning, I thought she was. I mean, she was hot." Lia rolls her eyes when I say this. "And she was popular, and she liked me. And I needed to get over the puppy love that I harbored for… you." I look up at her, knowing my cheeks must be pink, but I push on.

"We started dating in high school, and we had fun together. But it was the kind of fun hormonal, horny teenagers have. Drinking together at parties, making out in the backseat of a car, you know what I mean." She flinches as if the thought of me with Chels causes her physical pain.

"And then all of a sudden high school was over. My friends all left town on athletic scholarships or to any university that would get them out of this small town. But I stayed, went to LA Tech, and so did Chels. I think we stayed together because we were the only ones left. I didn't realize it then, but in college, she started… I don't know if this is the right word, but *controlling* me more and more. If I went to a party and even glanced in the direction of another girl, she'd give me hell. Scream at me. Cry. Make me feel like a piece of shit. So, eventually, I just… stopped going." I trail off, lost in those ugly memories. But Lia grants me the same space I gave her. Finally, I take a deep breath and continue. "We moved in together, and I threw myself into my classwork and studying for my journalism degree. That's where I met Jacob, by the way, and thank God for it."

I run my hand through my hair, over my trimmed beard. "And then college was over, and Chels and I were still together, so marriage seemed like the next life step, you know? Looking back now, I realize how dumb that must sound. But we had been in it together for so long, and she was looking at rings and dresses, so…I asked her. She tried to push me into working for her dad's oil and gas business–she told me I'd make good money. But Jacob convinced me to take an entry-level position at the newspaper with him, to actually use my degree."

Lia's transfixed, but remains silent.

"Chels never forgave me for that. An entry-level reporter job doesn't bring in much money, especially at a small-town newspaper. Still, it's what I'd always wanted to do. It turns out Chels wanted to be a glorified housewife, and when she had to get a job so we could pay our bills…" I scoff. "Well, she did everything in her power to get me fired from my job, including trying to accuse me of having an affair with the editor-in-chief."

"You have got to be kidding me," Lia blurts out, the first words she's uttered since I started sharing my story.

I just shake my head, no. "Jacob testified against Chels' accusations to anyone who would listen. I thought I'd lose my job, though. No way my boss would want a liability working for her. But I didn't. Lauren saw the situation for what it was and doubled down, giving me amazing assignments and coaching me."

"But then, at the beginning of last year, Chels had a complete fucking meltdown and told me it was her or my job. She screamed at me, cried, and told me that I was the worst piece of shit husband. I believed her, but I also knew I still wanted my job: to write, investigate, learn, and grow. When I didn't leave my job, she left me. We've been separated for more than a year, and our divorce will be final next week. I think she's still trying to guilt me into begging for her forgiveness." I look up and straight into Lia's eyes. "But I've finally had a taste of what an adult relationship should be." She blushes and looks away.

"It's over between Chels and me. Really over. And that's the truth," I say, willing Lia to hear the sincerity in my words. "And two days ago, that bullshit with her showing up and following me? She's willing to do anything to control me, to get as much money out of me in this divorce as possible. She thinks I owe it to her because of my career choice. In her jaded mind, she believes I ruined her happiness, and she will stop at nothing to do the same to me." My voice shakes on those last words, and their weight settles between us like a rock floating down into the murky depths of a river.

Lia doesn't say anything for a moment, covering her mouth and shaking her head. "Rhett, I…"

Darkness washes everything as the barn lights cut out.

JESSICA BOOTH

Chapter 34

AMELIA

"What the hell?" Rhett exhales into the now dark space that's crept into every corner of the barn.

I tap the flashlight button on my phone, and his face is washed in bluish light.

"Everyone is closing up for the evening. They must not realize we're still here," I respond. "But don't worry."

I use my phone flashlight to navigate over to a box of supplies I've kept in my little retreat space. Digging through it, I pull out a flashlight and a couple of candles. As I light them, their warm glow washes over us, and the flickering light and shadows dance across Rhett's handsome face. I'm a happy audience of one to the way the light licks his face, how the shadows chase each other through his hair. My eyes flick to his, and I see him staring back. I clear my throat, look away and walk back to the blanket, where he's still sitting. I hesitate, then sit next to him. I pull my knees up against my chest and fold my arms around them again, creating a protective turtle shell against the outside world. Our shoulders bump. Together we look out into the vast darkness in front of us, only the slight glow of the twinkle lights around the barn's ceiling lighting the chasm below us.

At any other time, the low light, the candles, the twinkle lights would be romantic. But Rhett has just bared his pain to me. He's vulnerable and likely wondering if I'm going to kick him out of my life.

"Rhett." He's leaning back on his hands; legs stretched out in front of him. He turns to look at me, pressing his shoulder into mine. He traces my features with his eyes, his gaze snagging on my mouth. I swallow, imagine meeting his beautiful, full lips with my own, drinking him in, making love to him in the candlelight…

I ruthlessly cut off those thoughts, immersing myself in our shared pain. "I'm sorry that happened to you with Chelsea. Thank you for telling me your story, and for trusting me with it."

He places his hand over mine, which rests on my folded knees. He squeezes gently. I inhale his spicy, pine scent and let it calm my nerves.

"You deserve to know the truth. I'm sorry I hurt you," he whispers, leaning into the shrinking space between us tentatively, questioningly. "And Lia, you make me happy, too. So happy. You have no idea."

His soft exhales tickle my lips as he holds the small space between us. Letting me decide, always giving me a choice. I force myself to hold still, to check in with myself. I've cocooned my heart in a protective film since Matt, determined not to let another man inflict further damage on its delicate scraps. I was slowly peeling those layers back for Rhett, and when Chels showed up, they reflexively snapped back. *Is this what I want? Is he who I want?*

I close my eyes, remembering all the ways he's sought to build me up. The way he ensures that I have a voice. How he teases me but never wants to hurt me. Even now, he's bared his pain to save me from my own. And there it is. There's my answer.

I close the lingering gap between us and slowly touch my lips to his. Our kiss is soft, tentative, and questioning. It's a gentle bandaid over the pain that's been festering in both our hearts. Then I feel Rhett's hand cup my face, thumb lightly tracing my jawline. I lean into that touch, letting him hold me. All the anxiety, betrayal, and confusion I've felt over the past two days slowly begins to ebb away, falling like dandelion seeds to the ground. I let my heart's protective layers peel back again, and life begins to pump back through its valves.

I reach, letting my hands roam over him, feeling his arms and chest through his plaid button-up. I soak him in through my fingertips. His hands respond in kind, roaming over my body, worshiping me with feather-light grazes. I know that tonight he wants me to guide us. To tell him what's okay. So I push further into him and deepen our kiss, aching to fill the gulf that divided us over the past two days.

He meets me touch for touch, kiss for kiss. He drops his hand from my face and rises on his knees to tilt my head back, kissing me more deeply. I rise to meet him, both of us on our knees, clutching at the other as if we're going to drift away into the shadows surrounding us. Up here, in a dark barn with only a small candle-lit circle, it's as if we are on another planet. One where no one else exists. All is quiet except for our sighs and heavy breaths. I lose myself in Rhett.

I let my hand slide down, reaching for the button of his pants. I adjust my leg, accidentally knocking over a stack of old boxes next to us. They clatter loudly to the floor, and a hurricane of screeching and howling comes rocketing toward us from behind the boxes. I scream in terror. Rhett shouts and jumps backward as a dark shape flies at us.

And then everything slows down. The whole world seems to enter slow motion. I can see what's happening but can't stop it. Rhett pulls his hands up as a shield to avoid being hit in the face by a panicked, black, hissing cat straight from the bowels of hell. He loses his balance and topples backward into the gap between the loft floor and the barn wall.

No no no no no. I lurch forward, scrambling to catch him, but he's already gone.

"RHETT!" I screech in panic. My heart is racing as I lean over the edge and look down into the dark well. "RHETT! *Oh shit, oh shit, oh shit.* Answer me. Rhett!"

"I'm okay." I hear him say over my pounding heart. "I'm okay." A noose that I didn't realize had tightened around my stomach slowly loosened. I grab the flashlight, then shine it down into the space. I can see him, probably eight feet below us. He's covered in dirt and spiderwebs, but he's alive.

"Are you hurt?" I yell down, chocking on sobs.

"My arm," he gasps. "Fuck. I think I broke it."

"Can you stand?"

"I think so," he groans, pain tinging his voice.

"No, wait, don't. You're not supposed to move with these kinds of injuries, right? I'm calling 911."

I toss a flashlight down to Rhett and reach for my phone. He manages to grab it when it lands next to him. As we wait for emergency help to arrive, I stare down at him, wishing I could rewind time and prevent this from happening. His brow is knitted, his teeth grinding as he breathes through pain.

"Thank God this hole didn't go all the way down to the floor," he grunts. I nod, out of words.

He shines the flashlight around the space. "I wonder if there's anything I can use to stand on and climb out of here."

The flashlight lands on pieces of trash that have probably been there for decades.

"Nothing… Wait. What the hell?"

He leans up, crying out in pain.

"No, Rhett, just stay where you are. Don't move." But he ignores me, slowly pulling himself off the pile of rotted cardboard that broke his fall. I say a quick prayer thanking whoever decided to dispose of the old boxes down here ages ago. He limps forward, looking straight ahead, but I can't see what he sees.

"Rhett! You shouldn't move. What if the floor gives out, what if.."

"Holy shit."

"What is it?" Panic pushes my voice into a squeak.

"Lia, you are not going to believe what's down here."

A chill runs over my whole body, and I start shaking as I hear Rhett say, "There are bones down here, Lia. *Human* bones."

I FINALLY SEE THE FLASH of ambulance lights and run outside to meet the paramedics and lead them to Rhett. When they shine their lights down into the space, his face is blanched, but whether in pain, shock, or both, I can't tell. Lowering a harness down into the small space, the EMS crew pulls him out. While they check his vitals, he tells them about his gruesome discovery.

It's jarring to watch them strap him to a board and carry him to the ambulance. But I'm not leaving his side, not now, not after everything. As they're loading him into the ambulance–despite Rhett insisting it's not necessary–the police arrive. I tell them about Rhett's discovery in the barn walls and point them in the right direction. But I have to let them handle that on their own. I clamber into my car to follow Rhett to the hospital.

The whole drive, my heart is pounding as the adrenaline crashes through my body. I keep replaying the sight of Rhett tumbling over the edge of the barn loft, my nausea increasing with every mental replay. I focus on the flashing ambulance lights in front of me, letting their lights sear a path into my brain, hoping that staring at them will numb my emotions and help calm my breathing.

I SIT WITH RHETT IN THE ER ROOM. Monitors beep in a steady rhythm. An arm cuff inflates, beeps, and deflates, counting out Rhett's blood pressure, and measuring his oxygen levels. Telling us that he's alive, he's here.

Both of us are grimy, covered in the dust and muck of the barn loft, and God knows what else that lurked in the walls of that old barn. We're quiet, our adrenaline crashing and burning into a smoldering heap. I sit perched on the side of the hospital bed, holding his uninjured hand, stroking my thumb over the lines of his raised veins, reassuring myself over and over again. He's here. He's alive. A nurse walks in to check on Rhett, letting us know the doctor will be in soon.

When a medical technician shows up to wheel Rhett off to get x-rays, I curl up in one of the sterile chairs in the room, hugging my knees. I focus on taking slow breaths, the astringent smell of the hospital infiltrating my senses. I wish the antiseptic could wash the pain from my mind. The past forty-eight hours have left me exhausted, a tumbleweed bouncing idly across a long desert plain.

When they finally wheel Rhett back in, I stand and search his face. He gives me one of those half-smiles, dimple popping up, then grimaces when he accidentally bumps his injured arm into the bed railing.

"Hanging in there?" I ask. He nods, reaching his good hand back out for mine. I move to him and sit on the edge of his bed, delicately wrapping my fingers around his.

I'm sitting like that, holding Rhett's hand in mine, stroking back his hair from his face with my other, when his parents arrive. I know this is his mom as soon as I see her auburn hair, the color a perfect match to her son's. There are tears in her eyes. She rushes up to him wanting to wrap him in her arms but is scared to touch him, to hurt him.

"It's okay, Mom," Rhett rasps. He lets go of my hand, reaching up with his uninjured arm to grasp hers. "Just a broken arm and a few bumps and bruises. I'll live. And you have my knight in shining armor, Lia here, to thank for it."

His Mom looks at me, and I blush deeply. "Oh no, it's my fault we were up there. It's all my fault."

"Don't be ridiculous," Rhett says. "It's that damn cat's fault."

"What were you doing in a barn loft after the festival closed?" His Mom asks.

"Just talking. And, Mom, I'm an adult. Please don't treat me like I'm a teenager."

"Then don't act like one," his Mom says with a hint of irritation. But that only lasts a second before her face folds with worry. She finally reaches down to hug him, wrapping Rhett tightly in her arms.

"Ow, Mom. Careful." But she doesn't let up. Still hugging him, she reaches across him and grasps my hand, squeezing it in gratitude.

RHETT IS RELEASED TO GO HOME with a cast and pain medication a few hours later. His parents drive him back to his apartment, and I follow them in my car. Anxiety takes the driver's seat of my thoughts, and I wonder if this is too much. Am I overstepping? After all, I'm not family. Hell, I'm not even really Rhett's girlfriend. We've only just begun to heal this thing between us. But I know I won't be able to sleep tonight unless I know he's settled and okay. So when they park, I get out of my car and follow the three of them inside.

I'll just hug him, tell him I'm glad he's alright and go. I was there when it happened, so that's not weird, right? Maybe he wants space, or just wants to be with family right now though.

I hesitate just inside his apartment door, more than halfway convinced I should turn and leave. Rhett and his family have already gone in, but I'm locked between the outside and inside worlds, frozen on the precipice of indecision. When Rhett turns to me, confusion clouds his features, and I ease a foot further out the door, prepared to run back to my car.

"Lia?" His voice interrupts my escape plan. "Aren't you coming in?" he asks.

I'm so shaken up by the night's events that my hands are trembling. I'm depleted and know my thoughts aren't processing correctly. So I say and do nothing.

"We'll let the two of you talk," Rhett's mom finally says into the awkward silence I've created. She walks up to her son and kisses him on the cheek. When they approach the door to leave, I'm finally forced to move, so I step into the apartment hallway. I awkwardly press into the wall to get out of their way. But Rhett's mom pauses in front of me on her way out and studies me. Finally, she pulls me into a brief hug. It should be weird and uncomfortable. But it's... not. I reach around her for a quick hug. Then we pull away from each other, and they leave, closing the door behind them.

I hover for a minute, unsure what to say. "Rhett, I'm so sorry we went up to the barn loft. I should've been more careful," I stammer, not looking at him. I can hear the tremor in my voice.

"Lia, that was not your fault. It was that stupid cat's fault. I mean, did you see that thing? It was like a bat out of hell coming straight for my face."

I look up at him. "That was pretty terrifying," I admit. "You're taking this surprisingly well."

"I'm not, though. Not really." He starts to reach for me, then scrubs his hair with his good hand, unsure of what I want.

I take a cautious step towards him and, as if the light just turned green, he closes the distance between us. He presses his nose into the top of my head.

"Stay," he whispers.

"What?" I whisper.

"Stay." He reaches out with his good hand and tucks a strand of hair behind my ear. "Please."

I nod my head, a bit dazed. With my hand in his, he guides me to his bedroom.

"I am covered in dirt and bones of roughly a hundred dead rodents and one million cockroach carcasses," he says, frowning down at himself. I grimace, knowing he's right. He sighs, then tries to pull his shirt over his head, but his temporary cast makes it nearly impossible. I go to him and help him get it off. Then he unbuttons and pulls off his jeans, letting them fall to the ground where he stands. And I know he must be exhausted when he does this because the rest of his apartment is clean and organized. He drags his navy bed covers back and crawls in, sighing as he leans back on his pillow.

Then he looks up at me where I stand, staring at him like a dazed idiot. He pats the bed next to him, inviting me in. I know I probably should feel shy or embarrassed, but this feels normal somehow-- like this is how things are supposed to be with Rhett. So I kick my shoes off and strip off my jeans and t-shirt. Wearing only my panties and camisole, I climb into bed next to him and snuggle in deep next to his side. He sighs, and even though I know pain killers are racing through his body, I still smile when I hear him say, "This is where you belong, Lia."

He's right. Laying in bed with him, his good arm wrapped around my shoulders, the warmth of his body cradling mine – it feels like home.

Chapter 35

RHETT

Cinnamon and... dirt?

Those are the first things I smell as I wake, but I keep my eyes closed, enjoying the warmth around me.... And then the pain hits. First, my arm throbs like a second heartbeat, and then a dull ache creeps across my back and down my legs. As I shift to try and alleviate the discomfort, I feel something stirring next to me, and I freeze.

Slowly the events from the night before trickle back in. And Lia is, oh, *she's in my bed*, and I'm curled behind her, around her. Her ass is pressed into me. I groan. I stop moving, lay my head down on my pillow, and bury my nose in her hair, breathing in her cinnamony scent. I'm aching to trace her curves, let my hand drift over her body, but my arm draped across her waist is bandaged and pulsing with pain. She moves a little then, pressing her body closer into mine, causing desire to temporarily overpower the pain. I nuzzle into her neck and drag my nose down the side of her throat and press a kiss to her pulse point.

"You're supposed to be recovering," she mumbles, eyes still closed.

I smile and do it again, letting my lips linger, then nip her neck lightly. "It's hard to be a good patient when I wake up with a beautiful woman in my arms."

She turns slowly, rolling to face me, and tucks her head under my chin. "You okay?" she mumbles into my neck.

I kiss her forehead. "I'm okay. You?" She nods into my chest and then pulls back and looks into my eyes. Her hair is sleep-tangled, and creases from the bedsheets line her face. She looks a little disoriented. The combination of it all is… sort of adorable.

"You scared me last night," she whispers, her words bringing me back to reality. "I thought you were dead for a minute, that I had lost you, and I panicked." I can hear the tears in her voice and I brush the fingertips of my bandaged arm down her back.

"It's alright, hobbit, I'm here. We're here, together." She leans up and presses a soft kiss to my lips. But when I try to deepen the kiss, she pulls back and covers her mouth shyly.

"Morning breath," she whispers. I huff a laugh

"I have some extra toothbrushes in the top cabinet," I tell her as she rolls out of my bed and makes her way into my bathroom. And the sight of Lia climbing out of my bed with mussed hair and wearing only a camisole feels like a fever dream - so much so that I wonder what painkillers they gave me for a minute. But when she pauses on her way to the bathroom and smiles at me over her shoulder as her camisole strap falls, I know that every detail of this is very, very real.

When Lia emerges from the bathroom, she's carrying my toothbrush, a travel-sized tube of toothpaste, and a cup. She sits down next to me in bed and gestures for me to sit up and take them. "I'm still capable of walking, you know," I say with a smile as I brush my teeth in bed. But I like that she's caring for me.

"It's okay. I don't mind. It's the least I can do after dragging you up to the barn loft with me," she says and takes the cup and toothbrush back to the bathroom. When she returns, I'm sitting up, my legs hanging over the side of the bed. I'm waiting for her.

"Need some help standing?" she asks.

Ignoring her question, I lean forward and snag her around the waist with my good arm, pulling her between my thighs. Lia leans down and kisses me then, pressing a soft kiss to my mouth. But as she tries to pull away, I urge her closer. I reach for her mouth again and kiss her deeply, our tongues tangling. There's a hot and cold sensation as the minty toothpaste mixes with the heat of our mouths pressed to one another. Still standing over me, Lia reaches down and runs her hands through my hair, fingernails tracing patterns on my scalp. It feels amazing. I lift my uninjured arm up, stroking her breast through her camisole, teasing her.

"Rhett," she gasps. "You need to rest today."

"I'm fine. Barely feel anything," I murmur as my mouth replaces where my hand was, breathing hot air onto her breast through her camisole. I move my hand to her back, sliding it down into her panties, giving her ass a squeeze. When my phone rings, Lia pulls back and rests her forehead on mine.

"You should probably get that," she says.

"It can go to voicemail," I say and try to kiss her again.

"What if it's your parents? They were so worried last night. You have to get it."

Sighing, I pull back and reach for my phone. I look at the screen and see that it's Jacob calling.

"Hello?"

"Glad to hear you're alive," he says.

"Yeah, yeah, I'm fine."

"Heard you decided to do a little exploring in the walls of a barn last night."

"Something like that."

"Seriously, Rhett. You okay, man? I heard it was a nasty fall."

"And who did you hear that from?"

"Janice, my story contact at the police office." I sigh. "She also told me something else. She said you stumbled upon some bones when you took your little plunge… *human* bones."

In the midst of the police rescue, hospital stay, and waking up next to Lia, that fact had temporarily slipped my mind.

"Rhett? You still there?" he asks.

"Yeah, I'm here."

"Are you sitting down?"

"Yeah, I'm still in bed like a good little patient." I wink at Lia when I say this. She rolls her eyes.

"Okay good, because, Rhett, you're never gonna believe this. They ran DNA testing on the remains overnight. Those bones you found belong to that missing boy Jimmy Roberts."

LIA AND I SPEND OUR DAY debating what to do with the information. They've closed the festival for the day so the police can explore the scene. I know she's worried about the festival's future after such a strange and gruesome discovery on the grounds. And I know she's also concerned about me—how I'm processing the news and my physical recovery.

I'm still in shock over the information. I want to talk to Greta, but I don't want her to think I'm showing up as a reporter ready to cash in on her pain. I *do* want to interview her though, and the guilt of that weighs heavily on me. After all, *this* is the big story I was chasing. But Greta is more than just an interview now. She's a connection to my past, to my grandmother. And, hell, I care about her being alone when she finally learns what happened to her grandson.

Lia convinces me to stay home and recover, though I am chomping at the bit to do something, *anything*. So I drag my laptop into bed and start typing, giving myself over to writing.I get lost in telling Jimmy's story the way I used to when I was at the top of my game as a reporter. I know this is just a draft, so I write it all. I mention the old newspaper clippings, the chat with Greta, and her later confession of what happened that evening. It's shifting into more of a feature piece, but I don't want to stop, so I let the words flow through me and onto the page.

Lia has been with me in my apartment all day, even though I've insisted it's okay to leave and tend to festival business. She's worried about me, checking on me constantly until she finally drags a chair into the room and sets up shop next to me on her laptop. While she fields press questions about the police investigation at the festival site, I write. She pauses every once in a while to check on me and make us lunch – grilled cheese sandwiches and tomato soup – which she informs me is the ultimate comfort food. Our day flies by in companionable silence. We work together, check on each other, and touch one another as we walk by. It's comfortable despite the stress we're both facing right now.

When I finally finish my article, I ask Lia if she'll look at it. She squeezes in beside me in bed and pulls my computer into her lap. I slide my arm around her back, reading along with her. I'm tempted to pull the laptop back and tweak things as she reads, but I force myself to stay silent, letting her read all of it. When she finishes reading, she tilts the screen down and looks at me, tears in her eyes.

"Rhett, this is amazing."

"Yeah?" I ask. She nods.

"But I think we should tell Greta about it," she says.

"Yeah, I think you're right. Think we could squeeze in a visit this evening? I know I should be resting, but I've been a good patient today," I say with a smile.

"C'mon. Let's get dressed," Lia says.

I attach the article to an email and send it straight to Lauren, my editor-in-chief, then close my laptop and get dressed.

WE PARK IN GRETA'S DRIVEWAY just as the sun is beginning to set. As we walk up the creaking front porch steps, she opens the door like she was waiting for us. There are tears in her eyes and, without a word, she walks up to me and wraps her arms around my waist, sobbing. I hesitate in surprise for only a moment, then reach down and wrap my uninjured arm around her small frame, holding this tired old woman and letting her cry out twenty years of pain. Lia places her hand on Greta's shoulder, rubbing slowly, and then the old woman's arm shoots out and pulls Lia into the embrace.

The three of us stand there for a while, a cobbled-together family holding each other up. Finally, Greta looks up. "Come in. Please."

She asks us to sit at the kitchen table while she makes coffee. I look at Lia anxiously, knowing I have to tell Greta about the story, worried I will make her grief worse. After placing coffee mugs in front of us, she joins us at the table. Her eyes are puffy, but the corners of her mouth are tilted up.

"I can't believe it," she rasps into the silence. "After all this time… I thought I'd never know what had happened to him. Rhett, the police said you found him. You did it."

Guilt is hammering at me now. "I don't deserve the credit. I mean, I found him, but it was a complete accident." I hold my bandaged arm up as evidence.

"No, you found him," she insists, wrapping her hands around her coffee mug. "From the moment you started looking into this, your lives, our lives were connected. You were drawn to him. I know it."

I want to protest but don't have the heart to try to douse her small ember of happiness right now. "There's something else I need to tell you," I say. My heart is running a million miles an hour now. "I wrote a story about him for the paper."

Silence fills the room.

"When… when will it print?" she asks hesitantly, but not with anger.

"I'm waiting to hear back from my editor, and we still need to fact-check some things with the police, but I wouldn't be surprised if it runs tomorrow or Tuesday."

"Thank you for telling me," she says resolutely.

"And Ms. Clark, Greta, you should know that you are in the story. It was the only way to make all the puzzle pieces fit together. I don't want you to be surprised when you see it. I…" swallowing, I try again. "I don't want it to upset you. I'll email my editor tonight if you don't want us to run it."

Her head snaps up then. "Rhett, I'd never ask you to stop the story. The newspaper is going to run something. They won't ignore a decades-long cold case suddenly solved. But. My boy, *you* know the whole story. And you'll get it right. That's all I ask for—the truth."

My heart snags at the way she says, "my boy," like she's welcomed me into her small family of two. I look at Lia, maybe three.

AS WE GET BACK INTO MY TRUCK, my phone rings. It's Lauren, The Boss. I answer and don't even have a chance to say hello.

"Will Greta Clark confirm this story?" she asks, wasting no time.

"Yes," I say.

"Good. I've got our junior reporters fact-checking everything with our police contacts now. I'm running this on the front page tomorrow morning if all this checks out. Keep your phone on you in case I need you to make any changes."

"Yes, ma'am."

"And Rhett? Damn good job." Her phone disconnects.

I look at Lia. She's smiling at me with unshed tears in her eyes. "You did it, Rhett."

"Come back to my place and celebrate?" I ask her.

"How about mine? Aunt Margie's been taking care of Tucker, but I think he misses me."

Chapter 36

AMELIA

As we pull up to my house, I know something has changed between Rhett and me. Despite our short amount of time together, the events of the past thirty-six hours have drawn us closer. Tucker greets Rhett with the enthusiasm of an old friend when we walk up to my front door. Rhett leans down and pats my one-eyed dog, greeting him with soothing puppy talk that makes Tucker's whole body wag. My heart gives a little thump, and the tears that have been threatening to spill since last night well up again. Rhett fits here, in my home with my rescue dog and me.

We order takeout and eat chicken lo mein out of cardboard containers as our conversation wanders from the events of the past two days to our favorite foods, and places we've traveled, carefully avoiding the painful moments, and smiling at the happy ones. When we finish eating and cleaning up, I help Rhett wrap a trash bag around his arm so he can take a shower.

"You're wrapping me up like your own personal Christmas present," he laughs as I place the final piece of duct tape on my makeshift water guard.

While he's in the shower, I toss his clothes in the washing machine, knowing full well that I have nothing in my house that will fit Rhett. And I am not mad at myself about that decision when he emerges from my bathroom wearing nothing but a towel slung low over his hips and a black trash bag taped around his arm. Water is still dripping off his damp hair and down his muscled chest. I sit back and take him in, studying how his tattoo fits the contours of his shoulder muscles. This man has pulled all my heart's protective layers away and pushed himself firmly into me, entangling our souls into a hopeless, happy mess.

"See something you like?" he asks, mouth quirking as I continue to stare at him half naked and dripping on my carpet.

"Oh, definitely," I reply breathlessly.

He's grinning widely now. "Lia? Where are my clothes?"

"They stunk, so I washed them," I say unapologetically.

"What, exactly, am I supposed to wear then?" he says, lifting a teasing eyebrow.

"I like what you're wearing now," I say, smirking as my gaze drifts down his body... "But I do have some more trash bags if you'd like me to make you an entire suit."

He looks down at his wrapped arm and then back to me with a half-grin that shows off that dimple. I can't stop staring at this beautiful man in front of me, especially as he prowls toward me, hunger in his eyes. He leans down to where I'm sitting on the edge of my bed and whispers in my ear. "I think I'm at an unfair disadvantage. I'm in nothing but a towel. You still have all your clothes on."

My belly clenches with those words, and I am two seconds away from ripping that towel off of him when he says, "I think it's only fair that you dress in a towel, too." He kisses me chastely on the cheek.

"That sounds fair, I guess," I say huskily. "I'll just go take a shower then."

"I'll be waiting," he says.

I practically sprint to the bathroom, but once I'm in the shower, I take my time scrubbing every surface of my body, washing my hair, and letting my stress wash down the drain with the water. When I finally emerge, I'm wrapped in a towel matching Rhett's own. Rhett is laid back in my bed, towel still wrapped around his hips. But when he looks at me, the heat that's been slowly simmering in his eyes flares to life.

"Come here," he says, and I practically run to him. He sits up, moves to the edge of the bed, and pulls me in between his thighs, recreating our moment from this morning… sans underwear. "You smell so good. I think I could eat you." My whole body lights up with anticipation.

"Hmmm, could you now?" I whisper back.

His only response is to pull me down to him and lick the column of my throat where a drop of water is running down from my still wet hair. I melt into him completely, letting my body fall into his. "What about your injuries?" I manage to protest half-heartedly.

"Trust me, Lia," they aren't going to be a problem, then he pulls me on top of him, kissing me. We let ourselves get lost in our desire. He manages to get my towel off, and my naked back is exposed to the room, goosebumps rippling across my skin. His uninjured hand slides over me, running up and down my back, down to my bottom, where he squeezes. He rolls me over onto my back, pulling the towel completely away, and kisses his way down my body. I run my fingers through his hair, and my body ignites with anticipation as he continues to make his way downward. He pauses, just below my belly button, looking up to grin at me.

"Rhett," I groan. "Please." He laughs into my skin, nuzzling his nose into my stomach.

"I love hearing you beg for me," he says before descending on me, placing his tongue exactly where I want him to. My hips buck, but he holds me down with his good arm, enjoying the taste of me, taking his time, exploring what gives me pleasure. And then the pressure is suddenly too much. I'm cascading over the edge. When the waves of pleasure subside, he climbs back on top of me. His towel is gone now, and I feel how much he wants me.

"I was right," he whispers into my ear. "You taste amazing." And then he's kissing me passionately, desperately, and I lift my hips, welcoming him into my body. He makes love to me like a man starved. I kiss him back with the same desperation until my desire has completely reignited. And then neither of us can hold back anymore, and we're both falling over the edge together.

He stays on top of me, letting his forehead drop to my own. But as the haze of pleasure starts to dull, I see Rhett wince in pain. "My arm," he groans and rolls off of me.

Guilt surges through me. "You okay? Can I get you anything?"

But he just pulls me into his side. "Just you. You're all I need, Lia." And we drift into sleep like that, nestled in each other's arms.

RHETT'S PHONE RINGS EARLY the next morning. I look at the clock - it's 7 a.m. He glances at the screen and sees Jacob's name. "Hello?" he says groggily and puts the phone on speaker.

"Your story is blowing up, man. I think you better get to the festival site. Call Lia and bring her with you."

"Is everything okay?" Rhett asks.

"Yes. I think so. You're not going to believe what's happening. Get your ass down here."

Lia's phone starts ringing then, too. "It's Janet," she whispers.

"Wait, why is there another phone ringing in your house at seven in the morning?" Jacob asks. And then, "Oh, wait. Don't answer that. Just bring Lia with you." He hangs up.

"Hello?" I answer. "Lia, people are showing up in droves at the festival site. You need to get down there. Now."

"I'll be there in twenty," I say and hang up.

Rhett and I stare at each other in confusion. "Well, good thing I remembered to put your clothes in the dryer when I got up to use the bathroom last night," I say and shrug. "Otherwise, you'd be strutting out there naked, and we'd have another PR crisis on our hands."

A loud laugh rips out of him, and he presses a kiss to my lips. I wish we could lounge in bed all day together, but we both know we'll have to delay that for a while.

WHEN WE ARRIVE AT THE FESTIVAL site, I'm shocked. It's not even

8 a.m., and the parking lot is packed. We climb out of the truck and make our way to the crowd gathered around the barn. There are bouquets—hundreds of them—lying against the barn. People stand around holding candles, heads downcast. This is a memorial, I realize, for Jimmy Roberts. I recognize faces in the crowd: Aunt Margie's friends, Junior League members, and people I went to high school with. My gaze snags on Aunt Margie as she spies us and makes her way to where we're standing.

The sun is newly risen, casting a warm glow over those who have arrived to keep vigil. Rhett holds my hand as we stand together, bearing witness to this–acknowledging the life of Jimmy Roberts. As the sun rises, some people leave, but more arrive to take their places. And in it all, I'm struck by just how much of a community we really are, especially when we all have something we can unite around.

My phone buzzes and I walk away from the crowds to answer. "Hello?"

"How are we going to clear them out of there when the festival opens at two today?" Janet barks into the phone.

"Well, I'm here now, and I don't think making people leave is the right approach," I say, boldly asserting my opinion in a way that neither of us is used to.

"No one will want to *celebrate* when there's practically a *funeral* happening there right now," she says exasperated.

"Janet, I need you to trust me on this one. I haven't let you down yet. I'm reading the room, and trust me when I tell you that kicking people out right now will cause a riot. We'll open at two as planned, but I am not making people leave."

Rhett looks at me with pride shining in his eyes. He gives me an encouraging thumbs up.

After a beat, Janet replies, "Fine then. Whatever happens is on you," and hangs up.

"Well, isn't she just a ray of sunshine?" he says under his breath.

"You have no idea," I reply.

"Up for some coffee?" Rhett asks.

I groan. "That sounds amazing, but I really shouldn't leave because the media could show up any time."

"No problem. I'll run and get some breakfast for us and come back."

Rhett returns thirty minutes later with two pumpkin spice lattes and a bag of chocolate croissants. We sit in his truck together, eating the delicious flaky goodness, drinking our coffee, and watching the unplanned memorial unfold.

When the news vans inevitably show up, I do the interviews and lean into the moment. I tell reporters that we are grateful to see our community united, that we welcome people making the pilgrimage to our site to honor Jimmy Roberts, that, yes, we will still be open at 2 p.m., and, yes, visitors are still welcome to honor the found boy. We will have a dedicated space for them.

WHEN WE OFFICIALLY OPEN at two, I am in awe. Yes, visitors are still arriving to leave flowers, but in some sort of unspoken agreement, the entire community has shown up to support the festival. As the day carries on, we hit a record number of attendees. Our craft tent volunteers have to go for a supply run as busy children paint pumpkins and make Halloween picture frames. Painted faces roam the corn maze and the owl specialist from the nature center in Shreveport has a huge crowd.

The day passes in a whirl, just like it did opening day. I'm so caught up in making sure everything is running correctly that it takes me by surprise when I notice the day fading away to dusk. As the sun sets, I smile to see the jack o'lanterns light up around the field's perimeter. Classrooms, Girl Scout troops, church leagues, and everyone in between has submitted carved pumpkins for the festival contest. A cool breeze drifts across the field, and I smile for a moment, caught up in the perfect autumnness of it all.

All we're missing is... "I've got something for you, Lia!" Aunt Margie's beautiful, loud, Southern drawl calls from across the field. She walks up to us holding... no. She didn't. She holds up a monogrammed pumpkin tank top with pride. "Here you go, darling. Now put this one on, and let's go have some fun."

I duck into Rhett's truck and change quickly, laughing as I see that in addition to my monogrammed initials over the front left pocket, the back says, "Just here for the boos," with a big wine glass and a ghost next to the words. When I step out of the truck, I do a little twirl for Rhett and Aunt Margie. They both grin and clap for me, though Rhett's grin is a bit feral, like the sight of me in a tank top might inspire him to pull me back into that equipment closet.

"Don't get any ideas," I whisper to him and grab my flannel button-up, draping it over my shoulders like a light jacket. He grabs my hand, and we walk into the crowd. The Graveyard Gators aren't playing tonight, so he's able to enjoy the evening with me.

We walk hand in hand and stop to enjoy every moment. Rhett pauses to play a festival game, using his good arm to fire off ping pong balls at targets. He wins a stuffed jack o'lantern, which he promptly hands over to me like a prized diamond. I insist on walking the corn maze, even though I've walked through it a million times. After all, it's different at night. Rhett smiles and bumps my hip with his when we walk past the nook where we had our little tryst. I laugh, then lean in and press my lips to his. When I pull away, I see his smile taking up his whole face.

When we finally make it out of the maze, we see the rows of carved pumpkins lit up against the night sky. Their fiery insides call revelers to examine them. We walk slowly, examining them all.

"Wow, the Methodist church ladies really pulled out all the stops," he says, admiring the twenty or so pumpkins with various detailed flowers carved into each. We smile at the submissions. I'm particularly fond of the ones that are, apparently, an adaptation of famous painters' works. They were submitted lovingly by the local art guild.

"Who knew Minecraft pumpkins would be the big thing this year?" Rhett asks, nodding to the school submissions.

As we reach the end of the pumpkins, I see someone kneeling, adding more to the end of the row. It's dark, so I can't make out the details of the person's face. But as we get closer, I realize that it's Greta Clark. I feel the weight of her presence and pain fall like an anvil on my chest and pin me in place. Rhett pauses too, as he realizes who stands before us.

She looks up, surprised, but the rage that usually simmers just under her surface is nowhere in sight. Greta waves timidly when she recognizes us. We finally move together, slowly making our way to where she stands. And to my surprise, Greta is smiling a bit bashfully.

"Hi, Ms. Clark. So good to see you out here tonight," Rhett says, voice filled with warm Southern charm.

"Greta, please. And yes, it's a nice evening. I thought I'd take in the nice weather and look at the pumpkins," she says, still a bit awkward. I look down and notice a couple of pumpkins at the end of the row, one with a grasshopper carved into it and another that simply says, "JR."

When she notices me staring at the pumpkins, Greta says, "They're for Jimmy. I think… I think he would have liked them."

Rhett nods. "I think you're right," he says. "They're perfect."

Her eyes crinkle. "Wonderful. Well, I think I'm going to turn in for the evening. It's been an emotional day."

"Can we walk you home?" Rhett asks.

"No. I think I'd like some quiet for a while," she responds.

When she turns to walk home, Rhett reaches for my hand. We're suspended in the moment, pumpkins glowing beside us, the darkened woods a short distance away. We watch Greta slowly meander back to her house after finally gaining some closure on the ghost of her grandson. In silent agreement, we turn together and make our way back toward the hustle and bustle of the festival site.

"I need to go home and let Tucker out. He's been inside a long time," I say quietly to him.

"Mind if I go with you?" Rhett asks.

"I was hoping you'd say that."

Chapter 37

RHETT

One Week Later: Halloween

Sitting in my office cubicle, I soak in the quiet, interrupted periodically by the few other reporters finishing up weekend stories. It's Sunday and Halloween, so everyone with kids cleared out a long time ago or has the weekend off. Today is the fall festival's final day, and Lia has been onsite for hours prepping for the final events: costume and pie eating contests, trunk-or-treating, and the ghoul ball.

I'll see her in an hour when I head out to meet up with The Graveyard Gators for our final night of playing together—though we've already had a couple of requests to play at weddings—so maybe this is only the beginning. My arm is in a real cast now, so Katie has offered to play guitar tonight while I step into the lead singer position. I thought she'd be disappointed with the change in roles, but she's having too much fun teasing me about the crowd of older women who have been regularly positioning themselves right in front of me on the stage every time we play.

I'm still trying to put a dent in my ever-growing inbox. Writing that story on Jimmy Roberts was like kicking over a community anthill. Suddenly everyone is an expert, claiming they knew him, his parents, and Greta. A pile of letters from readers sits on my desk.

Jacob and I have made a game of guessing if a letter is kind or mean based on the handwriting outside the envelope. Turns out it's a skill that I'm quite good at, with about an eighty percent accuracy rate.

And the response to the story has been overwhelming. I've received letters and emails of gratitude for a case solved at last. Others rail against the police department's failures. Some—written by people who obviously have too much time on their hands—are filled with conspiracy theories and say that Greta harmed her grandson and hid the body. Most of them are letters of relief, sharing stories of how they feared for their own children when Jimmy went missing.

Scrolling through the hundreds of emails, my eyes inexplicably snag on one. The subject line reads: "Thank you for finding our boy." My eyes slide to the left, searching for the sender, and there it is, Jennifer Roberts.

I click open the email, my eyes jumping across the lines of text.

Mr. Hebert:

I know you are busy and may never read this, but there are words swirling around in my head, keeping me up at night. I had to say them to someone, to you.

I guess I should tell you who I am. I'm Jennifer Roberts, Jimmy's mother. After everything happened with Jimmy, when he went missing, and I knew he was never coming back, I left town. I couldn't live around people gossiping about my son and whispering every time I walked into a room. I couldn't look at my mother, Greta. Though I guess you already know that since she was featured so prominently in your story.

An old friend called me when she saw the story you wrote in The Ruston Daily Leader. She sent it to me. It's difficult to describe what I'm feeling. I'm devastated and sad and angry and guilty and… I spent all night after that phone call imagining what my boy went through as he lay trapped and dying. And then I couldn't stop thinking about my mother, how awful I've been to her since it happened. The guilt of that and the pure relief I felt at finally having an answer…

That's not what I set out to tell you. Let me try again. Thank you. Thank you for caring about Jimmy and my mother. Thank you for telling his story and not blaming me, my mom, the community. Maybe it's the time that's passed or the way you told the story, but I finally feel, like after two decades of being trapped underwater, that I can breathe again.

I don't know how to fix what happened with my mom. But, if you stay in touch with her if you even read this, would you consider sharing it with her? I know this whole thing is a long shot, but maybe this is the sign I needed from the universe, from God, to try.

So I'm casting my bottle into the ocean.

Sincerely and gratefully,

Jennifer Roberts

I read through the email a couple more times, heart in my throat, noticing Jennifer's email signature at the bottom—it has her phone number listed. I wonder if showing this to Greta will hurt her, but then that's not really my place to decide. I hit the print button, grab the paper off the printer, fold the sheet in half, and then walk out to my truck.

THE FESTIVAL PARKING LOT is completely packed. I search for an empty space, noticing that people have even parked in the surrounding field. *Lia did it. She saved this festival.* Once I finally find a space in the field, I park and hope my truck won't get stuck.

I look across the field to Greta's house, the printed email tucked in the rear pocket of my jeans branding me. Tonight will be hard enough, I think. After all, it's the anniversary of the day Jimmy went missing. So I grab my guitar, rescued from the barn loft by the police, turn from her house, and walk towards the festival. No way I'm going to find Lia in all this chaos, so I unlock my phone and send her a text.

Rhett: Hey, hobbit. Meet me by the stage?

No immediate response, but I'm not surprised. She must be running around like a tornado bouncing from one location to the next. Thinking of her frizzy ponytail swinging while she instructs the pumpkin carving contest judges on the rules makes me smile. I tuck my phone in my pocket and make my way to the stage.

I take a minute to look around when I step up on the raised platform to set my guitar down. The sun has just begun to set, casting an orange glow over everything. The corn stalks ripple in the wind, and I hear laughs and screams as people make their way through the maze. Kids run past dressed as their favorite princesses and superheroes, with the occasional witch and ghost stomping by. The smell of crackling wood is on the wind, and I see that fire pits for s'mores have been set up for the evening. Already the jack o'lanterns have been lit, and their fiery grins light the field's perimeter.

I'm so caught up in it all that I'm taken completely by surprise when hands cover my eyes.

"Guess who?"

I spin around and pause.

"Do you like it?" Lia says, giving me a little spin so I can admire her costume. She's wearing a belted vest, skirt, and a cape. Her hair is down and in ringlets. It takes me a second, but then it clicks.

"Are you a…?"

"Hobbit? Yep." She says with a laugh.

I burst out laughing and wrap my good arm around her, kissing her temple.

"It's perfect, Lia. You're perfect," I say into her ear as I nuzzle her neck.

"Almost perfect," she says with mischief, then she leans down and grabs a tote bag I hadn't noticed before. Opening it, she pulls out a shirt, vest, belt, cape, and cropped pants. "For you," she declares. "I can't very well be the lone hobbit tonight."

"You can not be serious."

"Oh, I am so serious, my dear Samwise."

"You want me to stand up on this stage, with lights shining on me in *that*? I'll wear the vest and shirt, but you can keep your cropped pants."

She laughs, the sound of it swirling around me and tucking itself into my heart.

"What if I promised you I'd make it up to you later?" she asks with a wink.

"Well, when you put it that way…" I bend down and give her a lingering kiss, her ringlets tickling my cheeks. She pulls back, shoving the bag into my waiting arm.

"And don't worry, I have costumes for the rest of The Graveyard Gators, too. Now go change."

BY THE TIME I GET BACK, the rest of the band has shown up, and I realize that even though I'm wearing these embarrassing pants, I could have had it much worse. Dad is wearing a long white beard and wizard's hat but seems quite proud of his ensemble. Jacob also sports a beard, but his is long and brown… with braids.

"This is badass," he says, donning a Viking helmet. "This dwarf costume will make me look like ZZ Topp up here."

And Katie is quite pleased with her costume. She's wearing a long white gown, and… yep, those are elf ears. She grins at me. "Nice pants, bro."

"Why is it that *my sister* gets to dress as an elf queen while I am dressed like I'm getting ready to cross a creek?" I ask Lia indignantly.

Just be glad I didn't make you wear the wig," she says, stifling a laugh. And with her carefree laugh and rosy cheeks, she really does look like she just stepped out of Middle Earth.

Lia leaves to check on some things, and we do our warm-up. I can't remember the last time I've felt like this, so real, so alive, so happy. We've saved up all of our Halloween songs for tonight, and I can't wait to see Lia's face when she hears us play all her cheesy favorites.

DESPITE OUR CHANGE IN BAND roles for the evening, we are in perfect sync as we play for the next couple of hours. Children dance around the stage as we crank out "Thriller," "Witch Doctor," and "Purple People Eater." Around us, we watch as couples laugh, children chow down on candy, and visitors admire the carved pumpkins. Lia makes her way to the stage and signals to me that she needs to make an announcement.

Walking onto the stage, Lia grabs the microphone.

"It's time to announce the winners of our pumpkin-carving and costume contests!" The crowd cheers and then falls silent.

"But before I share the winners, I have a few quick things to say. First, thank you to everyone who came out tonight and those who have made it a point to support the festival this week. Your attendance and enthusiasm mean our fall festival hit record numbers this year, ensuring it will be here next year, and hopefully many more to come."

Polite clapping and a couple of whistles fire off in response.

"And a special thank you to The Graveyard Gators, our band this evening!" More whistles and cheers, louder this time. Katie takes a little bow, and we follow suit.

"And finally, I know this has been a difficult week for our community. We can't ignore the discovery that happened a week ago, finally solving the case of Jimmy Roberts."

The crowd falls silent and somber.

"I know this discovery opened old wounds and, hopefully, helped close others. But we are a community, and the way all of you showed up..." she chokes on a sob, and takes a deep breath. I step beside her, unable to help myself. I rub my hand on her lower back, trying to comfort Lia as she wrestles with her emotions. "The way you all showed up to memorialize Jimmy Roberts shows what this city's heart looks like. No matter our differences and disagreements, no matter how much time has passed, we are a community, and we are here for one another."

Claps ripple out across the crowd in solidarity.

"With that in mind, we've renamed our costume award. From this day forward, the annual costume contest winner will receive the

Jimmy Roberts award, complete with a donation made to The National Center for Missing and Exploited Children in their honor." The crowd claps in approval. "So, without further ado, this year's winners are…"

As Lia calls out the winning names, a little girl dressed in shimmering white from head to toe, complete with a curled rainbow wig and unicorn horn, approaches the stage. Next is a gruesome zombie. The kid plays it up, dragging his leg behind him and making groaning noises, inspiring the crowd to laugh. And this year's winner is… Justin Flennigan. A mom pulls a wagon to the stage. They have converted the whole thing into a Batmobile. Inside is a tiny toddler Batman, who proudly belts out "Na na na na na na BATMAN!" all the way to the stage.

As the crowd erupts in applause, I slide my arm around Lia's lower back and hug her.

AFTER WE'VE FINISHED PLAYING for the evening, Dad, Mom, Jacob, Katie, Beth, Dan, Margie, Lia, and I sit around one of the picnic tables, pints in hand. Beth is dressed as a fairy, perfect and prim rainbow wings sprouting from her back. Her husband wears a gnome costume, fitting in perfectly with all the other bearded and costumed men at our table.

I notice that Jacob has made a point to sit next to Katie, taking every opportunity to touch her, wrap his arm around her shoulder, and tease her. And Katie doesn't seem to mind. In fact, that's the most welcoming I've ever seen her around any man. My big brother instincts tell me to step in and say something, but Lia knows what I'm thinking and reaches under the table to squeeze my thigh before whispering, "Leave them alone. Jacob's a good guy."

I let it go, taking another swig of beer.

"Well, look what the cat dragged in," I hear Margie mumble under her breath. It takes me a minute to realize what she's talking about. I look around and notice Greta walking slowly up to our table. She looks like she's trying to decide whether she should approach or turn and run. She has something in her hands. Before she can bolt, I stand up and walk over to her.

"Won't you join us?" I ask.

She shakes her head. "No. I just wanted to bring this to you to thank you. For everything." She hands over a box. I open it up and peer in. A perfectly baked pumpkin pie is tucked inside. I take a deep breath, inhaling nutmeg and cinnamon– smells that remind me of Lia.

"You didn't have to do that."

"I've managed to find my autumn spirit again. Unlucky for you, though. You're the only person who's nice to me, so you have to eat everything I cook from now on."

I realize that she's actually making a joke and crack a warm smile at her. That's when I remember the email… which is in my jeans, not these ridiculous hobbit pants. I motion for Lia to join us.

"Will you two wait here for just a few minutes?" When they nod, I dart off to my bag by the stage and riffle through my clothes until I find the note. I say a silent prayer that this is the right thing to do, then jog back over to them.

Handing Greta the note, I tell her, "This is for you."

She looks confused and starts to open it. I place my hand over hers. "Not here. You'll want privacy." She nods, reaches out, and gives us both a hug, then turns and walks back to her house.

When we return to the table, everyone is staring at us. "Well, what was that about?" Margie asks, eyeballing the box I place in the center of the table.

"I think I've made a friend."

"Well, considering she handed that box to you instead of throwing it at your face, I reckon you have," Margie retorts.

We ease back into our comfortable conversation. Lia and Katie are fast friends. Beth jumps right in with them. I shudder to think of the trouble those three will get up to together, but seeing the woman I care about getting along so well with my sister—as well as my mom and dad— it's like a final puzzle piece sliding into place. I never knew it could be like this, not really.

My divorce from Chels finalized on Wednesday, and even though none of us bring it up, I know everyone at the table is quietly celebrating the end of a bad era in my life.

Margie and Dad have a long conversation about tools and repairing things around the house, and Mom glances at me periodically with a warm smile. This is what she's always wanted for me, that smile says. This comfort, this happiness, this joy.

I feel Lia's hand wrap around mine as she leans in and whispers, "Can we sneak away for a few minutes?"

"We'll be back in a few," I say to our merry table as I follow Lia's lead, hand still in hers.

"Don't do anything I wouldn't do!" Jacob laughs as he shouts.

Lia rolls her eyes and tugs me along. We make our way to the edge of the festival, where the jack o'lanterns are lined up, the faux candles the only real source of dim, warm light out this far.

"It's been a busy week. I just needed a few quiet moments alone with you," she says as she leans into my shoulder.

I wrap my arm around her shoulders. "Look at that," I say as we gaze out at the twinkling lights around the festival. "You made it all happen."

"I couldn't have done it without you," she says.

"Oh yes, you could have, and *you did*," I say. "I think the only thing I managed to do was nearly wreck the whole thing by falling into a barn wall."

"Nonsense," she whispers. "These past several years, I wondered why things seemed to come easy to everyone but me. I agonized over what I did to encourage such bad men into my life. I beat myself up for struggling to meet my goals and succeed in my career. I thought that if only I had done this or that differently, my life wouldn't have been so messed up. I thought that if I had moved or changed jobs, I would have been happy. But the reality is that none of those things would have made a difference. I needed them all to get where I am now." She waves her hand towards the lively festival in the distance.

"And all of those failed relationships? They showed me what a gift I have in you, Rhett." She looks into my eyes then, and I stare back into hers, drinking her in. "You're the pumpkin spice to my latte," she says with a smile.

"Yeah, you're alright yourself," I say back to her.

She wraps her arms around my waist, holding me tight. We stand there together, looking out at the festival's twinkling lights. A fall breeze kicks up suddenly, whipping our hair around our faces. Dried leaves tumble across our feet. I smile as I brush her curls away from her eyes and behind her ear.

"It's a full moon," she says, resting her head on my shoulder and gazing upward. "And you know what they say about full moons."

"They turn people into werewolves?" She rolls her eyes and smiles.

"No, you goof. They say if a couple shares a kiss under a full moon, their relationship is destined for happiness."

"I think I can live with that," I say, then lean down and kiss her. She stretches up on her tiptoes and kisses me back slowly, sweetly. And above us, the full moon shines down, giving us her blessing.

Epilogue

AMELIA

Ten Months Later

Rhett's leg is tapping anxiously under the tablecloth. Sliding my hand over his thigh soothingly, I lean in, offering the only comfort I can at this moment. "You look really hot in a tux, you know," I whisper. That earns me his signature dimpled half-smile.

"You look pretty sexy yourself. You should wear a tiny little dress more often." His leg stops its nervous rhythm under the table as he wraps an arm around my lower back and presses a kiss to my temple. "Only two more categories. I just want to know one way or another so I can finally stop thinking about it," he says.

"Even if you don't win, I'm still getting you a badge that says 'Winner of the Sexiest Reporter in Louisiana' button," I say.

"Only in Louisiana?" he lifts an eyebrow.

The audience around us claps politely as the winners are announced for Newspaper Photo of the Year. Picking up a spoon, I reach out and scoop up a bite of my dessert: bananas foster. The flambeed bananas and rum have completely melted the ice cream by now, but I can't stop sampling the delicious soup it's turned into.

"Feature Story of the Year," the emcee announces. "The nominees are…"

I stare at Rhett's tense face, noting the slight crinkle lines around his eyes, his mouth drawn tight with anxiousness, and trimmed auburn beard setting off his green eyes. It's a face I've come to love over the past eleven months, a person I've come to love.

"Third place: 'Possums and Potions: How One Vet Developed a Life-Saving Tonic for Local Wildlife.'"

"Seriously?" I whisper incredulously to Rhett.

He quirks an eyebrow and his leg starts tapping again. "Hazardous research."

"More hazardous than having a gumbo pot chucked at your head?"

"Shhh."

"Second place: 'Cancer Won't Win: A five-year-old's Journey to Bring World Peace.'"

"What the hell? I'll never win against that," he says, shoulders sinking.

"And the winner of Louisiana's Feature Story of the Year goes to…. 'Lost and Found: Old Barn Answers a Decades-Long Cold Case' by Rhett Hebert.'"

I squeal and erupt into a standing ovation, as does our entire banquet table—including Rhett's parents, Jacob, Katie, Lauren, Aunt Margie, and Greta Clark. I go to give Rhett a celebratory hug, then realize he's still sitting down, staring at the table in shock. Laughing, I reach down and wrap my arms around him. "Better stand up, hot stuff. Your fans want to hear from you."

He looks at me, still in shock, and finally stands, slowly navigating around the round banquet tables to the podium at the front of the room. The emcee motions to the microphone, handing Rhett a small award. He stands there for a moment, staring at the mic, then looks up, taking in the room. Finally, he focuses on our table, on me.

"I'm speechless," he says, and the room lets out a quiet chuckle. "Thank you for honoring this important story, one that helped bring closure to a community, to a family. I know this is when I should tell you how honored I am—and I am—but you should know this wouldn't have been possible without two very important, courageous women. Lia, you are my rock, my encouragement, my strength. This story would have never happened if I hadn't met you when I did. And Greta," Rhett chokes up, pauses, then looks up again. But when he speaks, his voice is thick with emotion. "Greta, I am so sorry you lost your grandson. Thank you for trusting me with your story."

The room erupts in applause. I wrap my arms around Greta's small frame, embracing her. Over the past ten months, she has become like family to Rhett and me. I look at her, and we both have tears running down our cheeks. I know we're proud of Rhett, but she's also still mourning her grandson. This, at least, is a way to show that his life was noticed. That people still care.

THE AWARDS BANQUET, we head to Greta's house for a post-party. We're all tired, but when Greta told us that she had purchased some bottles of champagne to celebrate Rhett's nomination, we couldn't tell her no. When we pull up in her driveway, the lights are already on inside, the warm glow inviting us in from the dark field around us–a field that we are already starting to transform for this year's fall festival.

We all pile inside, stepping around cats as we go.

"I've prepared something special," a feminine voice calls from the kitchen. I inhale deeply, and before I even see it, I know pumpkin spice is the flavor of the evening. When we step into the kitchen, I smile at the woman standing there. Holding a pumpkin pie and a bouquet of floating congratulatory balloons is Jennifer, Jimmy's mom.

After Rhett gave Greta the email printout, she decided she had wasted enough of her life in secluded mourning. She called her daughter, and they spoke for the first time in over two decades. It's been slow and painful, but Jen makes the trip to visit her mother every couple of months now. I can see from their shared smiles that they are beginning to heal together.

"And I brought a surprise, too!" a loud Southern drawl bellows from the front door. Aunt Margie walks in, Greta's large pot in her hands, filled to the brim with her signature chicken and sausage gumbo recipe. "Figured it was time I returned this sucker to you."

That's been another surprise–how well Aunt Margie and Greta

get along now. They spend weekends at each other's houses, working in the garden, cooking, and griping about the latest person to get on their nerves. It was scary when those two were at odds but even more terrifying now that they're a united front.

"I hope you made a video of that gumbo for your YouTube page before we dig in," I tell Aunt Margie. It turns out that Aunt Margie has a knack for mixing up delicious recipes. That combined with her rather interesting personality has made her somewhat of a social media sensation. Her booth last year drew crowds from all over the Ark-La-Tex and inspired Lauren, Rhett's editor, to personally write a story on her, boosting her followers to nearly 50,000.

Rhett's parents walk in then, hugging us before greeting the others. His mom immediately springs into action, pulling out plates and a pie server. I look out the front door and see Katie and Jacob lingering for a moment. We have a bet on when they're finally going to stop flirting and make it official, but neither of us wants to push them. Another car pulls up, and then Beth and Dan are running up to the house, arms full of party hats, glow necklaces, and pretty much anything you could possibly need for a celebration. So much for a quick glass of champagne before going to bed.

Greta makes the rounds, handing everyone a glass brimming with bubbly. I look up at Rhett; he is taking it all in, beaming at everyone around us. My heart swells with pride and love at my handsome, intelligent boyfriend. He turns to look at me, his gaze heating as it darts to my lips. I bump him with my hip and whisper, "We'll celebrate later." He lets out a low chuckle.

Someone taps the side of a glass with a spoon, and I realize it's Rhett's dad. "Thank you all for joining us here this evening. We are so proud of Rhett, but more importantly, we are grateful to Greta and Jen for letting us all embrace their family and tell Jimmy's story. Let's toast to his memory and to all the people who now know and share his story."

A collective "Cheers!" rings out as we all sip from our cups.

Then Rhett speaks up. "I second that, Dad. Thank you all for your support and love. I've known more love in the past ten months than I have in my entire life–no offense, Mom and Dad." Everyone laughs good-humoredly.

"Here here!" Jacob calls out.

"There's really only one thing left to do to solidify this family," Rhett says as he turns to his dad and hands him his champagne glass to hold. Rhett turns back to me, holds both of my hands, then sinks down to one knee. I gasp audibly as he reaches into his pocket and pulls out a black velvet box.

"Lia Murphy, love of my life, my best friend and favorite hobbit, would you do me the great honor of marrying me?"

I can barely see Rhett through the tears now filling my eyes, and then I fall to the ground with him, wrapping my arms around his neck. I don't even look at the ring he's offered up because I'm too busy saying "Yes" over and over. And then I'm kissing him, not even caring that we have a huge audience in front of us.

Everyone is clapping and cheering. Arms wrap around us, and lips find our cheeks as everyone we love most celebrates our engagement. Rhett finally manages to slip the ring on my finger, and I stare at it in wonder, not quite believing this is real.

"I love you, Lia," he whispers into my ear. "And I can't wait to spend the rest of my life drinking pumpkin spice lattes and going to fall festivals with you."

Acknowledgments

Seeing my book formatted and in print is one of the most surreal experiences of my life. It is a lifelong dream realized and one I could not have done without the support of many amazing people.

First and foremost, my husband, Mark. Thank you for taking the kids out to run errands when I needed quiet writing time or when little eyes kept trying to peer over my shoulder while I was writing those scenes.

Thank you to my oldest daughter who, despite declaring me a "cringey Millenial," offered to design stickers for my book launch.

To my early readers, especially Jodi, Susan, MC, Mindi, Stephanie, and Lucy. Your feedback on everything from what a man would actually say to the appropriate (or in this case inappropriate) use of the word "magma," was extremely helpful.

Kristin Avila, my editor, thank you for giving me multiple crash courses on everything from the publishing industry and character wounds to reading through my novel as many times as I have. *AMMIA* truly would not be the book it is today without your experience and insight.

To my Mama, who took me to Ruston, Louisiana, more times than I can count. Thank you for allowing me to spend so much of my childhood in a small, Southern town with my inspiring grandparents. And I'm so grateful that you read my book when it was still rough and didn't balk at what you found in its pages. Your support means everything to me.

Celia, my writing bestie and biggest cheerleader. What would I do without you? You have always been the first to tell me you'll help in whatever way I need you and offer up new ideas to help me spread the word about this book. Thank you, my friend.

Sierra at Bookery Cincy, your support for my book baby has been humbling and inspiring. Thank you for helping amplify my little book to a much larger stage and offering a place to sell it in a brick and mortar store. Independent bookstores have my heart, and yours has the biggest piece of it.

To the bookstagram community. Wow, just wow. Thank you to every person who has liked, commented, supported, shared, DMed, my posts about this book. I continue to be amazed at the positivity and beauty of an online community inspired by books. You're the best people in the world. A special thanks to Cincygrammers and the Hey It's Carly-Rae Team. You ladies are some of my most favorite people in the entire world. Your support and belief in me has sustained me more than you will ever know.

And finally to all the romance authors out there who helped me realize that wanting to write those happily ever afters is a thing of beauty, and we always need more beauty in the world.

About the Author

Jessica is a lifelong reader and writer. She earned a bachelor's degree in communications and professional writing before making a career in journalism and editing. Jessica has always dreamt of writing a book, and her love for novels spurred her into becoming an avid bookstagrammer. She loves books that make people happy. Although she grew up in North Louisiana, Jessica now resides in Southwestern Ohio with her husband, pack of rowdy children, and a couple of hounds. They love to spend their time together visiting indie bookstories, or outside digging up worms and transforming piles of sticks into castles.

Follow Jessica on Instagram at:
https://www.instagram.com/readbelievelove

www.ingramcontent.com/pod-product-compliance
Lightning Source LLC
Chambersburg PA
CBHW061234310726
48971CB00007B/2057